I Love You, I Hate You

Elizabeth Davis is a full-time nerd whose interests include cold weather, rainy days, coffee, Minnesota Public Radio, and rom coms where characters' homes vastly outstrip the income they would get from their jobs. Born and raised in suburban Milwaukee, she now lives in Minneapolis with her husband and two children.

You can find her at **elizabethdavisromance.com**, and on Twitter **@E_Davis_Romance** and Instagram **@elizabethdavisromance**.

I Love You, I Hate You

ELIZABETH DAVIS

First published in 2021
by HEADLINE ETERNAL
An imprint of HEADLINE PUBLISHING GROUP

1

Cataloguing in Publication Data is available from the British Library

ISBN 978 1 4722 8330 6

Typeset in 11/14 pt Minion Pro by Jouve (UK), Milton Keynes

Printed and bound in Great Britain by Clays Ltd, Elcograf S.p.A

Headline's policy is to use papers that are natural, renewable and recyclable
products and made from wood grown in well-managed forests and other
controlled sources. The logging and manufacturing processes are expected to
conform to the environmental regulations of the country of origin.

HEADLINE PUBLISHING GROUP
An Hachette UK Company
Carmelite House
50 Victoria Embankment
London EC4Y 0DZ

www.headlineeternal.com
www.headline.co.uk
www.hachette.co.uk

For Mom

Prologue

Two Years Ago

Victoria Clemenceaux had never been more ready in her life. She had some pre-court jitters, but those were to be expected for her first appearance. But you didn't get a job like this at twenty-six by being timid and downplaying your abilities. Plus, the case was easy. Victoria might have been a little uneasy when it came to Smorgasbord's ridiculously exploitative employment practices, but they didn't pay her to care about that. They paid her to win, and that was exactly what she was going to do.

Victoria braced herself and pushed open the heavy courtroom doors. The clerk was already calling her case, so she hurried to the front, eyes snagging on a man about her age with striking blue eyes and red-blonde hair that was just a bit too long to be professional. He grinned at her, friendly and relaxed, and she wanted to smile back. She had spent so long in law school building up her walls, brick by brick, keeping everyone else out. It was easier to not let anyone in, to keep away anyone who could make her feel vulnerable.

And yet, with a single grin, this guy had her reconsidering.

She wasn't here to ogle, though, so Victoria tore her eyes away and swept past him to step up to the defendant's table before the judge.

She had been guessing her opponent would be the square-jawed, grey-haired man three rows back—he looked like roughly three-quarters of her coworkers—but suddenly Courtroom Hottie stood and hustled to the plaintiff's side. Victoria stiffened, and when he looked over at her again, she kept her eyes firmly on her paperwork. She couldn't afford to be distracted, not now. His handsomeness and appealing smile were utterly irrelevant to the job at hand and she ignored him until he looked away. She had worked too hard and come too far to let one good-looking guy distract her.

She took a second to smooth down the dove-grey suit she was wearing, picking off a tiny thread she'd missed last night. Her eyes had been blurring by the time she finished tailoring it, but it was worth it. Victoria would bet good money no one in the courtroom would be able to tell it only cost $60 off the clearance rack. She straightened, ready.

"Your client is claiming breach of contract, Mr. Pohl?" the judge began.

The name stuck out, oddly familiar. For a second she couldn't figure out why but when she did, Victoria's eyes widened. She should have recognized him earlier from Cassie's Facebook photos, but those must be a few years old. His hair was longer now, and he definitely wasn't wearing a suit in any of those. Of all the people to take a Hail Mary case against one of the state's biggest employers, she hadn't guessed it would be the son of one of the richest families in the Upper Midwest. While a part of her might find that admirable, a bigger part of her was really fucking annoyed. Owen Pohl had grown up in the lap of luxury and gone to an Ivy League law school before starting his own firm, while Victoria had bounced around from crappy apartment to crappy apartment with her mom, barely scraping together enough money and scholarships to attend the University of Minnesota. She had loans the size of a mortgage she'd be paying off until retirement and had to take the highest paying job she could find, conscience be damned, and meanwhile this guy had a trust fund. Of course he was smiling and relaxed going into battle against a major corporation—it didn't matter to him if he won or lost. His job wasn't on the line.

"Yes, your honor." Owen flashed his grin at the judge and was rewarded with the glimmer of a smile. Victoria narrowed her eyes, knowing exactly what game he was playing and not buying it for a second. Guys like him coasted by without ever putting in the work while people like Victoria had to fight tooth and nail for every little scrap.

"And Ms. Clemenceaux, I assume Smorgasbord would like to start with mediation?"

"As is required by their contracts, yes," Victoria said without looking at him.

Owen cleared his throat. "Actually, I'm moving that since Smorgasbord was in breach of contract, the mediation clause is void. I'd like to proceed straight to litigation."

Victoria blinked. It was a big swing, proposing this right off the bat. While Owen might think the combination of his daddy's money and his laid-back charm entitled him to skip a few steps, Victoria hadn't graduated at the top of her class for nothing. She scoffed audibly and rolled her eyes. "If you'd read the statute, you'd see that if the plaintiff wishes to avoid mediation they are required to appeal to the board of directors first," she said, finally looking at him. He attempted a smile, probably hoping to disarm her, but she shot him a cold look and it withered on the vine. She allowed herself a small moment of pleasure at getting one up on him, and then got back to business. “Have you bothered to tell your clients that?”

“Right, because the company that wrote the contract gets to decide if it’s in violation of it? That’s garbage and you know it.” He was way out of line, but that was exactly what she wanted. An opponent who was mad was an opponent who was not thinking clearly.

She made sure she looked affronted. “That’s the law, counselor.”

“The law your company wrote,” he retorted.

“It’s still the law,” she said icily. He was glaring at her now, all the merriment gone from his eyes. In its place was pure loathing.

“It’s still bullshit, is what it is,” he snapped.

“That’s enough,” the judge interjected. “Ms. Clemenceaux is right, counselor. You can’t skip mediation without first appealing to their board. Would you like to petition them, or go straight to mediation?”

Before Owen could answer, Victoria dropped the hammer. “If I may, your honor, if you look at the statute’s third subsection and the following appendix, you’ll see that attempting to circumvent mediation at all prior to the petition being filed with the board is grounds for dismissal entirely. Since my opposing counsel didn’t bother to do his homework, I move that the case be dismissed.” She looked at him, stone-faced except for her eyes. She couldn’t keep those from dancing.

Owen curled his hands into fists. “Your honor—”

The judge shook her head. “I’m sorry, counselor, she’s right. Case dismissed without prejudice. You may refile once you’ve completed the outlined terms in the correct order.”

Owen’s face went ashen. She’d won. And even quicker than she thought. She smirked at Owen as she swanned past, floating on the high that came with doing her job well. He gathered his things and hurried after her, anger making him clumsy. "What the hell was that?" he hissed when they hit the hallway.

She stopped, eyebrows lifted. "You know, the generally accepted way of greeting someone is 'hello' followed by introducing yourself," she said coolly. "I'm Victoria, by the way. And you are?" She was just being a dick now, but she couldn't help it. It felt good to put a rich kid in his place.

"Owen," he said through his teeth. "And I repeat, *what the hell was that*?" he growled.

She smirked at him again and turned on her heel. "That was you losing. Get used to it."

Eighteen Months Ago

Direct Messages: Nora @Noraephronwasagenius

@Lukethebarnyardcat

Okay, awkward question: would you want to meet sometime? Or even just exchange numbers? It feels weird to talk to you nearly every day for the last six months but only through DMs

@Noraephronwasagenius

Awkward answer: no to both, but not for any of the reasons you're going to think.

I just don't think I can be this honest and open with someone who knows me. It's not that I don't want to, it's that I'm worried if we meet we'll lose what we have. Anonymity is what makes it work for me, you know? I don't think I could tell you half this shit if I knew I had to look you in the eye one day. If that's too weird and you just want to dip out from this entire friendship-through-the-DMs-thing, I completely get that. But if you're willing to stay anonymous, I swear I will never lie to you.

@Lukethebarnyardcat

I see your point. It's unconventional, but then again so is our whole friendship. If anonymity is what you need, then that's what you'll get from me

Chapter One

Present Day

Victoria dropped her head back against the wall and Owen's lips found her collarbone. Of all the decisions she had made in her life, this one was either the worst or the best. Years of enmity, all undone by one searing kiss. One of his hands spanned her waist and the other laced with hers. He pinned her hand above her head, his knee pressed tightly between her thighs. She kept making soft, needy noises she would find embarrassing if she was capable of coherent thought, but right now she was too far gone to care.

For the last two years, Victoria had loathed every single thing about Owen Pohl. His stupid red hair, his stupid self-satisfied grin, his stupid habit of leaning back in his chair while she made her arguments, looking for all the world like he was relaxing on a park bench instead of sitting in front of a goddamn judge. He was too casual, too laid-back, too insouciant for their profession, always on the edge of being too disheveled for an attorney, and everything about him said *privileged*. She hated him, even as tonight threatened to turn everything upside down. He was easily the most obnoxious person in her life, but she also might explode if he didn't kiss her right fucking *now.*

His gaze bored into her and he tugged his tie loose. Victoria swallowed hard, the silence suddenly too heavy for her to process. "You chickening out on me?" she challenged, lifting her chin.

His eyes darkened and the smirk deepened. Her stomach coiled; he threaded his fingers through her hair and gripped it just hard enough to sting. "Only if you are, Vee," he growled. She surged forward to kiss him because kissing was easier than seeing him look at her like that. Besides, if they were kissing he couldn't call her *Vee* in that tone of voice again, because that was dangerous.

Because holy *shit* did she like the way it sounded. Normally, if Owen bothered to address her at all, he called her *Your Majesty,* or perhaps *Queen Victoria* if he was feeling like taking his life into his hands. In court it was always *opposing counsel* or *Ms. Clemenceaux*, but tonight was the first time he'd called her anything even resembling her first name and Victoria wasn't about to let herself think about how much she enjoyed it. She sternly reminded herself this was just another way of working out their aggression like they did in the courtroom, just with a martini and a half in her system and two old-fashioneds in his.

Owen withdrew his hand from her bare skin and she actually whimpered, which only served to make him grin in almost predatory triumph. Apparently, hooking up with Owen was just like fighting him in court; a battle of wills with no surrender. He moved and she matched him beat for beat, both of them unwilling to give a single inch as they stripped each other bare. Before she had a second to catch her breath Owen spun her and jerked her against him, arm secured around her waist to keep her pinned, her back against his chest.

Four hours ago, if someone had told Victoria she would be nearly incoherent with want, on the verge of begging Owen for *more, deeper, more* as he delicately traced her folds with his fingertips, she would have laughed in their face, but now she was putty in his unfortunately competent hands. She twisted her head and met him in a messy kiss, more teeth and tongue than anything else, and he urged her onto the mattress, watching her with a soft smile that did something strange to her heart.

Owen had a nice smile when he wasn't mocking her. It was bright and almost boyish, the sort of smile that clichéd writers claimed could light up a room. He cupped her face delicately, thumb sweeping back and forth along her cheekbone, and she rolled them over so she could press their lips together.

Victoria was very rarely ever without words. Being a litigator meant being quick on her feet, and she was quickest with Owen sitting across from her. But now her gift failed her, every snarky retort withering away when she looked into his eyes. She had never seen him like this, sincere and open and hovering on the edge of vulnerable. And then he was inside her, fingers flexing on her thighs as she lowered herself onto him.

It was good. Too good, actually, for what this was supposed to be, and she forced herself to ignore the way her heart softened as she looked down at him. She snapped her hips, driving them both inexorably towards their peak. His gaze was heavy on her skin as she touched herself, his cock filling her so perfectly it didn't take long before she was coming, falling apart with a sharp keen that had him groaning. The pleasure rolled through her, each crest sparked by the way he moved inside her, deeper and deeper, and then he was pulsing, coming with a harsh sigh that she felt in her bones.

She stilled, his hands resting on her waist, and let her dark hair fall forward. Owen reached up and brushed it back, his palm curving around her cheek tenderly, and Victoria recognized that The Moment had come. She had gotten very good at noticing when a case balanced on a knife's edge, when one wrong move could make the difference between victory and defeat, when a judge was poised to throw a case out or hand her a massive win. She knew how to turn those moments to her advantage, which was how she was already in-house counsel for a major corporation before her twenty-ninth birthday. Recognizing The Moment and seizing it in her favor was her specialty. And here was, unmistakably, A Moment.

She could lean down and kiss him, like she wanted to, which would lead to her lying down next to him, letting his arm draw her closer as she rested her cheek above his pounding heart. She would probably drift off, lulled by her orgasm and the reassuring thump of his heartbeat, and wake up tomorrow morning tangled in Owen Pohl's arms, not nearly hungover enough to blame it on the alcohol. There would be an awkward goodbye and he would probably text her to make sure she got home okay, because despite her disdain for him he seemed like the type who tried to at least seem like he cared.

Or she could leave now and maintain some semblance of dignity. They had a status quo established, and leaving would preserve that balance. And because Victoria always chose dignity above whatever soft noises her heart kept making, she straightened. Owen slid out of her and the part of her that whispered *don't leave* felt a slight sense of loss, but the rest of her—the part that kept her shit together—told her she was making the right choice.

Victoria sat on the edge of his bed and found her bra while he threw away the condom. Owen smoothed his hand down her spine and rolled to his side. "Stay," he said in a sex-roughened voice that had her almost considering listening to him.

But the thought of waking up next to him and seeing the annoyed expression on his face when he wasn't addled from coming stiffened her resolve. She had withstood enough of his barbs in the courtroom to know exactly how it would go, and beneath her polished exterior she was far more delicate than he assumed. "Ha, right," she said sarcastically.

She risked a glance over her shoulder and watched his face shutter. She almost felt bad, but then he barked out a laugh. "Sorry for assuming you would do anything so plebeian as cuddle after sex, Your Majesty," he said in that tone that got under her skin.

"Screw you." She found her underwear and stepped into them, shimmying them up her hips.

"Just did, but give me fifteen minutes and I can service you again."

Victoria bunched her hands in her dress to keep from punching him and tugged it on. She should have walked out of the bar the second he offered to buy her a drink, but she had been feeling rather maudlin after a case ended with yet another result that was clearly biased in her company's favor. But even being maudlin into too many martinis was better than this. She smoothed her skirt down as best she could and stepped into her heels, all while Owen lay on his back, hands tucked behind his head.

"You're not even going to walk me out, are you?" she snarled, even though it was giving him far too easy of an opening. But fighting with Owen came as naturally as breathing, and for a second there she was worried they were slipping into something softer.

"Pretty sure you know where the door is. Don't let the cat out when you leave," he said, bored with her already. He reached for his phone and blue light lit up his face. The asshole was already on social media, like she hadn't just seen his O face.

She stood in his doorway and considered unveiling a torrent of insults that would reduce him to cinders, but that would mean prolonging this interaction and she had already let down far too much of her guard with him. Instead she stalked out of his bedroom and down the stairs to his back door, where her purse was tossed on top of a jumble of boots, bags of cat litter, and an old bicycle tire. *What a fucking mess*, she thought, angrily tapping at her ride-share app. Fortunately, a car was only two minutes away, so she went outside to wait, grateful for the warm summer air.

Victoria wrapped her arms around herself and paced back and forth in front of Owen's 1930s bungalow, refusing to look up at the dormer and see if his light was still on. She kept her phone clutched in her fingers, desperately checking the progress of her driver, and perched momentarily on the retaining wall lining his sidewalk. But then she was up and pacing again, back and forth in front of his walk like the Energizer Bunny until her ride pulled up.

Safely ensconced in the cool backseat she opened up her Twitter app. She would have seen an alert from Luke if he'd DMed her, but she had been running on pure adrenaline and alcohol for the last few hours and could have overlooked it.

But no, no new messages waiting for her. She wrinkled her nose, because Luke almost always messaged her in the evening. It was silly to be disappointed, especially given what she'd just been up to, but her heart sank all the same. She looked forward to their nightly chats, their anonymity allowing her to be more honest with him than she had ever been with anyone. Plus, a message from Luke would be a welcome distraction from the way Owen's scent was lingering on her skin, musky and male and far more appealing than she cared to admit. The car rumbled onto the freeway, the Minneapolis skyline bright in front of her, and her phone *pinged* with a new Twitter notification.

A familiar bolt of excitement shot through her and she opened it immediately.

@Lukethebarnyardcat
Do you ever have a day that's going really, really well—impossibly well—and then it all goes to shit? Because I just did

Sometimes, it was eerie how well they understood each other. And sometimes they would have days like this—mirrors of each other, twisted only slightly in reflection.

@Noraephronwasagenius
Yes, actually. Although today started shitty, got unexpectedly better, and then went straight to hell.

@Lukethebarnyardcat
Fuck, I'm sorry
At least we had shitty days together?

Victoria couldn't help it. She smiled to herself. Whenever Luke messaged, her day got a little bit brighter. She settled back more comfortably and started to type.

Owen twisted the handle on his shower and water hissed out, splashing cold against the tile before warming up. He was about to step in when his phone rattled against the counter with a reply from Nora.

@Noraephronwasagenius
What is it about the universe? Is it conspiring against us?

@Lukethebarnyardcat
I think it is, yeah
Thank god we have each other, right?

He stepped into the scalding hot water and closed his eyes. Today had not gone the way he thought it would. He was supposed to meet a potential client for drinks at Whistle and Plum, only to get an email canceling just as the bartender handed over his old-fashioned. He should have gone home, but when he spotted the one and only Victoria Clemenceaux, looking glum halfway through her martini, he changed his mind.

Yes, it was petty of him, but he liked riling her up. She had such a picture-perfect facade, from her iron-straight dark hair—hair that he now very inconveniently knew was softer than silk—to her perfectly manicured nails. Nothing ever ruffled Victoria; not objections to her line of questioning, not reprimands from judges, not a sudden squall on a hot summer day. Nothing, it turned out, except for him. He discovered his talent for getting under her skin early on, and he had kept on antagonizing her partly because he liked her fire and partly because, deep down, Owen was sort of a dick.

He should have walked away tonight but instead he found himself leaning against the bar next to Victoria, goading her into snapping back at him and then eventually buying her a second drink, because he never did know when to cut his losses. And somehow they went from snarling at each other at the bar to trading heated kisses in the dingy hallway to the bathroom, and from there it was short work to call a car and stumble into his bed.

He initially figured he could handle it, but the moment he saw Victoria sprawled out on his pillow, eyes hazy and lips swollen from his kisses, he realized he was in way over his head. There was something powerful about seeing the implacable Victoria at the absolute limit of her control, and it made his heart do things it rarely bothered to do.

But of course he would be cursed to only get a glimpse of her like that, and of *course* he would be foolish enough to think it marked a shift in their relationship. Of course he would be the dumb, sentimental type who thought the Ice Queen would want to spend the night with him, rather than fuck him and leave. He'd covered as best he could, but the moment his front door slammed shut he forced himself out of bed to shower, because otherwise he'd just lie in bed, breathing in her lingering scent and feeling shitty about himself.

At least he had Nora. He wasn't sure what he had with Nora, exactly, since all he knew was a nickname and a general location, but he was damn sure it was more real than whatever had just happened with Victoria. Nora was warm and funny, and while she shared a certain sharpness with Victoria, Nora's wit was leavened by a humor and kindness that was utterly foreign to Victoria. Plus, Nora had alluded to growing up poor with a single mom—*picture a less genteel Gilmore Girls*, she said once—and Victoria clearly came from money. Victoria's clothes were frequently nicer and better tailored than Ashley's, and Owen's stepmother didn't exactly pinch pennies. Between that and an in-house position at Smorgasbord, one of the largest mid-range grocery chains in the United States, straight out of law school, which was a job you only got if you knew exactly the right people, he could tell Victoria grew up at least as rich as he had, if not more so.

Owen let the hot water beat down on his shoulder blades to erase the memory of Victoria's teeth and nails on his skin. He reached for the shampoo and hesitated, and then cursed himself for being so stupidly mushy as to not want to wash her away completely. This was Victoria Fucking Clemenceaux he was dealing with here, not someone he actually *liked*. She was cold and robotic and sure, maybe there were a few more things he wanted to do with her, but those were all sex things, not romantic things.

Part of him wondered if he should gently broach the idea of meeting with Nora again, even though she had soundly shut him down the one and only time he tried. He wondered if Nora was worried he wouldn't think she was attractive and considered telling her he didn't give a shit what she looked like, but then realized it very well might be the other way around: she was worried *he* wasn't attractive. Or maybe she wasn't who she said she was at all, and he'd gone and fallen in love with a cisgender man, which wasn't really a dealbreaker for him so much as something he'd like to know about himself if it was a possibility. A simple selfie-exchange could fix all of that, but that would be breaking her anonymity rule, so he had to be content with simply knowing that somewhere out there, there was a woman named Nora who knew him better than he knew himself.

He'd just never actually *met* her.

Direct Messages: Luke @Lukethebarnyardcat

@Noraephronwasagenius
Have we done most embarrassing moments yet? I feel like we have, but I also feel like I would remember mocking yours, and I don't.

@Lukethebarnyardcat
My most embarrassing moment is probably in college when I got drunk and tried to prove to a pretty girl that I was a hockey superstar. I am not, and it turns out I'm actually very bad at skating while drunk. Long story short I now have a cap on one of my front teeth

@Noraephronwasagenius
OMG
Did you cry? I might have cried.

@Lukethebarnyardcat
NO
Okay maybe a little

Chapter Two

One of the many good things about Victoria's job, aside from the salary, was she didn't have to see Owen Pohl very often. He was a nuisance, to be sure, but unless one of his numerous lawsuits made it through layers and layers of red tape, she rarely had to deal with him head on. It would be even easier if she didn't secretly agree with him, but that was irrelevant. Her job was to defend Smorgasbord Corporation from lawsuits, full stop, regardless of her personal opinions. Smorgasbord was an enormous company, having cornered the market on not-super-cheap-but-also-not-expensive groceries in the United States, and they paid her handsomely to make sure no lawsuit filed against them made it to litigation. Smorgasbord was proud of its completely undeserved reputation as a socially conscious company. No, she wasn't making a difference in the world, but Victoria hadn't gone into law for anything so idealistic as that. She went into law because she needed the money.

She had grown up semi-nomadic, her childhood spent floating from small Minnesotan town to small Minnesotan town while her mother worked whatever job she could find. Kimmy had a habit of falling behind on the rent, less because she was irresponsible and more because being poor was fucking hard. Sometimes her job was standing on the line at a meatpacking plant or working as cashier at Smorgasbord, and sometimes it was cleaning scummy motels just off the interstate. As a result, Victoria spent her early years in a series of crappy apartments, run-down duplexes, and the occasional trailer park where the winters weren't just cold, they were downright brutal.

It wasn't that Kimmy was a bad mother. In fact, Victoria thought back on some of their worst housing situations almost fondly, because her life had always been filled with more than enough love, if not enough money. But Kimmy had Victoria when she was in high school and with only a GED there weren't a whole lot of employment options, especially out on the prairies. Kimmy Clemmons always wanted more for her daughter—so much so that she gave her a new, fancier-sounding last name in hopes that she would rise above their working class status—and Victoria busted her ass to get good grades at each of the three high schools she attended. She worked herself to the bone studying for four years in undergrad and then another three in law school, taking out more loans than one human should ever have to face repaying. The best day of Victoria's life was graduating from the University of Minnesota's law school, and her mother's beaming face out in the crowd made it all worth it. Every pricked thumb from patching the torn clothing Kimmy found for her at a thrift store, every late night studying, every box of Kraft Macaroni and Cheese with hot dogs because they couldn't afford anything better; all of it was worth it if it meant making her mom smile like that.

Landing the gig at Smorgasbord was pretty damn good, too. Victoria was now making enough to pay her loans, make rent on her apartment downtown, and have money left over to make sure her mom never had to leave town ahead of an eviction notice ever again. She dreamed of one day buying the home Kimmy always promised her—a yellow house with a blue door and a white porch, complete with swing—but for now, she contented herself with monthly contributions to a savings account in her mother's name. Victoria had a few splurges that she allowed herself, like one pair of expensive shoes every six months and an appointment at a fancy salon every eight weeks for her hair and eyebrows, but frugal habits died hard. She still tended to buy her clothes from consignment stores and tailor them herself, and her only pricey indulgence in makeup was a $50 lipstick palette. And even that came with seven different shades, so in the end it was still a good deal. Few of her law school classmates had understood her strict budgeting—stinginess, most of them called it, or being just plain cheap—but Victoria didn't give a shit. She had worked hard to get where she was, and even harder to make sure she looked like she belonged.

Victoria wasn't ashamed of her mother or her childhood, but she knew how rich people operated. If they suspected you weren't one of them, you'd be boxed out forever. You had to fit in with them, and she was good at that. Very few of her high school classmates had ever figured out just how poor she was, thanks to her sewing skills and steadfast refusal to be close enough to anyone to have them over. It made things a little lonely, and Kimmy had always tried to push her into making real friends, but by the time she was fourteen Victoria had her armor and walls securely welded shut, and that was that. The only place she let her guard down was online, where she could be safely, utterly anonymous. That was where she found her friends, and where she let herself truly *be.*

Victoria walked down the long hallway of the twenty-seventh floor of Smorgasbord Corporate and had her office keys out when Gerald rounded the corner in front of her. A thin, spare man with a greying mustache, her boss was a decent enough guy, if somewhat prone to avoiding his kids and wife by working too much overtime. Decent enough, but still shitty. "New addition to the big one," he announced. "Details in your inbox. It's our favorite pain in the ass again."

Victoria grimaced sympathetically, but her stomach turned inside out. It had been a week since her ill-considered, martini-fueled fuckup, and she'd been hoping she would get more of a break from Owen. *Maybe I can bury him in paperwork*, she thought, but once she had her computer on and scanned the details she knew she wasn't going to be so lucky.

Owen was, for all his faults—and she could list them for days—a highly competent attorney. He didn't pick just any cases; he picked the cases that would most damage Smorgasbord's faux-progressive image with devastating accuracy. Smorgasbord's employment contracts for retail employees were legal in the strictest sense of the word, but they were, to put it mildly, exploitative. The law was on Victoria's side because Smorgasbord spared no expense hiring lobbyists to make sure it was, but more often than not Owen could lay claim to being on the side of moral righteousness.

Unfortunately for Victoria, this was yet another one of those cases. He was allied with a local worker's rights organization and he had clearly done his homework before stepping in as lead counsel last week. This meant she was almost guaranteed to see him again, and probably sooner than she'd like. She sighed and rubbed her eyes in exhaustion.

Owen had never worked for anything in his life and she hated him for it. Rumor had it he had a giant trust fund that came through when he turned twenty-five, and she'd bet good money he never spent six hours after school smelling like fries and scrubbing down a burger grill. He could afford to take on these minor, long-shot cases against a behemoth like Smorgasbord because money literally didn't matter to him. He didn't have loans to pay or a family to support, either. If it wasn't for the fact that she resented that he could do whatever he wanted just by virtue of being born into the right family, she would almost admire his commitment to altruism.

But for now, there wasn't much for her to do about it other than get to work. Victoria settled into the familiar routine of her workday. She had a meeting in a few weeks where she was going to pitch allying with Reproductive Justice for a Uterus-Havers 5k sponsorship. It would be a big lift to get anyone at such a conservative corporation on board. But she wanted to try, at least, if only for her own conscience. She read files, typed briefs, prepped her presentation for the 5k, and slurped coffee until it comprised 80 percent of her body mass before taking a long lunch out on the plaza, soaking in the sunshine.

Lunch was the highlight of her day for many reasons, and not just because it was when she and Luke stole a few minutes to chat. She wasn't sure what he did, but she suspected it was legal-adjacent. Politics maybe, or lobbying. Sometimes he sounded just like a lawyer, but there was a lyricism to his words that law school tended to beat out of you. Whatever he did, she suspected he was very good at it, because he was so clever he'd made her break her one hard-and-fast internet rule: no dudes.

Victoria had made that rule after far too many Twitter interactions that ended in death threats, rape threats, dick pics in her DMs, or all of the above. She had a mildly popular Twitter account, largely because she had the skin of an elephant and a habit of picking fights with smug jackasses, which was oddly enough a one-way ticket to Twitter popularity as well as a good way of working off some latent aggression. She had made plenty of friends online, bonding over dumb memes and thought-provoking articles at the same time. But all of them were women, because her interactions with men were almost universally negative. So when @Lukethebarnyardcat showed up in her mentions one day, wading into a cesspool of grossness to tell off some Gamergate bros, she had been surprised and pleased to see him taking up the mantle. She couldn't even remember exactly what that fight was about; a thread of hers had gone viral, which attracted the usual mix of white supremacists, misogynists, and obnoxious men who simply had to correct her on something pedantic, and then there he was, hilariously taking each of them down a peg. He never once tried to white knight her and get her to thank him for helping her out, he just quietly joined in to tag team them into submission. She monitored his account for a solid two weeks after that to make sure he wasn't a creep, but mostly he seemed like a liberal politics junkie who was entirely too fond of his cat. His Twitter profile picture and header were even both pictures of his cat looking grumpy in ridiculous costumes, one as Santa and the other as a jedi. Once he'd passed her Creep Test she followed him, breaking her No Cis-Dudes Except Lin Manuel Miranda rule for the first and only time since she instituted it.

They chatted more after that, but only publicly. She would reply to his tweets and he to hers, and one night, after two glasses of wine and the discovery that he hated *Westworld* as much as she did, she did the unthinkable: she DMed him.

Within weeks, they were talking every day. First just in the evenings after work, and then eventually on their lunch breaks too. She was careful to guard her identity—he called her Nora, and she let him believe she lived in Chicago, which she often hinted at publicly to further protect herself from creeps—and by the time she trusted him enough to tell him the truth, she found she didn't want to.

The anonymity of their DMs let her tell him things she barely even told herself. She had thought about seeing if he wanted to meet, to find out if they had the same chemistry in person, but she was scared they wouldn't click and she'd lose her best emotional outlet. So, anonymous they remained, even if part of her wondered if more might be possible.

Luke, Owen's cat and the reason for his Twitter name, leapt into his lap and meowed plaintively for attention. "Shush, Rogue Leader," he said fondly. He couldn't remember the last time he had used his cat's actual name, preferring to use a vast array of *Star Wars*-based nicknames instead. It drove his father nuts, but that was just icing on the cake. He scratched his head absently and clicked over from his email to his browser. He had to meet a client later today, but one of the advantages of running his own firm meant he could set his own schedule for the most part. It also meant the freedom to check Twitter at exactly 12:35, which was usually when Nora started her lunch break. And right on schedule, her daily message popped into his inbox.

@Noraephronwasagenius
What is it about midwestern summers that compels us to be outside as much as humanly possible? Is it just fear of winter, or something deeper?

@Lukethebarnyardcat
It's the chronic vitamin D deficiencies, I'm pretty sure
How's work today?

@Noraephronwasagenius
Same as always, although I found out I'm going to be dealing with Nemesis again.

@Lukethebarnyardcat
Just say the word and I'll make him disappear

The ellipsis indicating an imminent reply hovered and he bit back a smile. He straightened the stack of files next to his computer while he waited, but it was generally a lost cause. His house could charitably be called cluttered, but more accurately should be considered a disaster zone. He had food for Luke stacked near the door, along with the bike he kept meaning to fix and boots left out from the last time it snowed, which was a solid four months ago at this point. Books and papers littered every elevated flat surface, and Luke's multitude of toys were scattered all over the ground. Growing up, there had always been a housekeeper to tidy things for him, and when he moved out he'd never quite gotten the hang of picking up after himself and instead just got used to the mess. It was the one place where Victoria's sneers about him being a spoiled little rich boy were entirely too accurate.

He glanced at his computer, waiting eagerly for Nora's reply. He suspected Nemesis was intimidated by her competence, because Nora was nothing if not adroit. He'd admired her coolness under fire from afar for months on Twitter before engaging with her. She was witty and composed and capable of delivering devastating eviscerations to those who tried to tear her down. Her first DM to him had sent a spike of adrenaline skittering through him. *Westworld isn't nearly as smart as it thinks it is.* That was all she said, but with those ten words, he tripped into something strangely intimate and tender. Over the course of their friendship he had come to see her side of things: the anonymity of their relationship made it possible for him to be vulnerable with her in a way he never was with anyone else.

A new message appeared, and he stopped pretending to tidy up.

@Noraephronwasagenius

What about you? You were working on a project with the Ice Princess soon, weren't you?

Ice Princess was his nickname for Victoria. He thought about going with *Queen Victoria* initially, but some instinct made him hold off, if only because that felt vaguely unfair to Victoria to use her real name. There weren't too many striking brunettes in their late twenties named Victoria in general, and within the midwestern legal community there were even fewer. Just on the off chance Nora knew people in Minnesota, he erred on the side of caution and had gone with something that still applied to Victoria, Queen of the Heartless Robots, but somewhat preserved her anonymity.

@Lukethebarnyardcat

Not really working with her. More like against her. But yeah, that's going to be sooner than I'd like

Victoria would have received notice this morning that he was joining the case, taking over for a firm that wanted to drop the nonprofit after two years of drawn out mediation. He was asking for a new deposition of the hiring manager for one of the complainants, which would mean sitting down across a table from the Ice Princess herself just as soon as it was scheduled.

To be perfectly frank, Owen was just the tiniest bit aroused and terrified of that possibility. He'd never forget the first time they'd gone toe to toe. When Victoria swanned through the doors like royalty, he couldn't help but notice her. Everyone did, of course—between her height and long dark hair and movie star good looks, she tended to turn heads wherever she went—but for Owen that day, time stopped. There was no hint of the woman he'd had in his bed the other night; just cool, ruthless efficiency in a perfectly tailored outfit.

He could have fallen for Victoria right then, but the moment proceedings began that went out the window. That had been the end of that, at least until last week when he let his dick do the thinking.

@Noraephronwasagenius
Are you going to be okay with that? I know last time she really got under your skin.

@Lukethebarnyardcat
I'll be fine. Spoiled rich kids just bug me like none other

@Noraephronwasagenius
You're not one of them, if that's what you're worried about.

Nora always knew what to say. Owen hated rich kids because for a long time, he *was* one of them. He didn't have to care about anyone or anything, and his dad's money fixed any mistake he made. Hell, he had only started Pohl Law Office because it would piss his dad off, and it wasn't until after he started working that he realized just how tilted the scales of justice really were. Now he was committed to righting whatever wrongs he could, and took on the sort of cases that other lawyers passed on because they were hopeless. He had the privilege of not worrying too much about money, and this was how he was going to use it.

He only wished Victoria Clemenceaux felt the same.

Direct Messages: Nora @Noraephronwasagenius

@Lukethebarnyardcat
Okay, your turn. Most embarrassing moment: go

@Noraephronwasagenius
Straight up thought Martha's Vineyard was a winery owned by Martha Stewart.

@Lukethebarnyardcat
That's not embarrassing, that's ADORABLE

@Noraephronwasagenius
If I tell you I was 25 when I learned it's actually an island off of Cape Cod is that more or less adorable?

And that I found out when I mentioned that I assumed Martha's Vineyard had really good brownies because Martha Stewart has really good brownies and a whole bunch of rich kids looked at me like I was a moron.

A friend had to pull me aside to explain what it was.

@Lukethebarnyardcat
. . . maybe a little less adorable
But that's still pretty damn cute

Chapter Three

Despite the slim generational gap between Victoria and Kimmy, her mother never quite understood how "hanging out with friends on Twitter" could feel the same as going out and meeting people for drinks. But Victoria was closer to her Twitter friends—even not counting Luke—than she was with anyone from work or law school. Cassie could usually be counted on to text her if she was getting a big group of law school people together for something, but Victoria tended to beg out of those. She always felt a little fake around her law school friends, and she hated standing on the edges of a circle of friendship. She knew she came across as cold, but really it was simply that she had a hard time opening up to people face to face.

Online, she had no such reservations. Her girl squad knew her name wasn't really Nora but they let her remain vaguely anonymous even as the rest of them had no such reservations about their identities. Like with Luke, they knew her better than anyone who hadn't given birth to her. What's more, they were a bunch of open-minded, fiercely feminist wise-asses who never failed to leave her in stitches. Victoria adored them all, even if they had never met in person, and she saw nothing wrong or strange about spending a Saturday night tweeting with them, no matter her mother's opinion.

Nora @Noraephronwasagenius

Being a woman in a male dominated profession means never having to say "I don't understand" because there will always be a man willing to explain your job to you.

Keith Smith @redorblueyouchoose0928

Maybe they're just trying to be helpful, did you ever think of that?

Victoria rolled her eyes and immediately quote-tweeted him, because if there was one inevitability of Twitter, it was a white dude presuming a woman was either stupid or a bitch. Plus, she'd tweeted that largely because she felt like picking a fight. It was that or think about Owen, and fighting with randoms on Twitter seemed like a safer prospect.

Nora @Noraephronwasagenius

Oh wow no my eyes have been opened. Any other mysteries of the universe you want to share, oh wise one?

Kara Hates Nazis @Neverthelesskararesisted

Question for @redorblueyouchoose0928: do you hear yourself

Kara Hates Nazis @Neverthelesskararesisted

Like really, truly hear yourself. Is this a choice you are consciously making, or are you just on mansplain autopilot

The moment Kara jumped in, Victoria knew they were off to the races. Maybe baiting idiotic men into fights on Twitter wasn't the most kind-hearted way of spending the night, but it was a fun pastime for her. She never went looking for fights specifically, just laid the trap and waited for their inevitable idiocy to lead her victims into it. It helped her vent her spleen at the world, if nothing else. And she had strict rules about who she would fight with: no punching down, no fighting with someone who was clearly a child, and when someone with more experience on a topic challenged her opinion, stop and think before responding. That way, she could fight morons and not feel guilty, and usually her girl squad joined in on the fun.

@Redorblueyouchoose0928
Your bitches

Reiko @Keanuisadreamboat
*You're

Reiko @Keanuisadreamboat
Unless you're signing a formal letter, and then yes, we are truly Your Bitches

Your Bitch @Noraephronwasagenius
Thank you, Keith. I've been needing a new Twitter name

In response, @Redorblueyouchoose0928 blocked them all. That was preferable to the ones who would get angry and create new accounts to harass her, but Victoria had learned her lesson on open DMs about 1,000 followers ago, so their options were limited. Men who were genuine, decent, and willing to listen to women were so few and far between online, which was how

Luke had caught her eye in the first place. The rest of the girls approved of him too, and retweets of Cat-Luke were one of the most common features of her timeline.

Victoria opened up the group chat and scrolled back through the last few messages, mostly sent while she was at work. Kara was a writer and struggling with a stubborn character and Reiko was in a lull between meeting her clients, so most of the messages were Reiko helping Kara bounce ideas back and forth. Victoria loved knowing women from so many different professions and so many different backgrounds. Reiko, for instance, knew the court system intimately but in a very different context than Victoria, since her job as a social worker meant she was always in and out of a courtroom. Maddy was the fourth leg of their little crew, but she was deep into her psychology graduate program and staring down the barrel of a committee meeting on her progress next week, so she was probably going to be radio silent for a while.

Victoria made sure she was caught up with everything they'd discussed while she was at work before starting to type.

@Noraephronwasagenius

So you know how I sorta hatefucked my nemesis the other day, right?

@Neverthelesskararesisted

YES

But there was an APPALLING lack of details.

Like how and why and how and WHY.

@Noraephronwasagenius

Look, it just sorta happened but that is not the problem here.

The problem is, now he's sort of . . . filing a lawsuit against my company.

@MadisonHughes95
Breaking my self-imposed hiatus to say I SECOND WHAT KARA SAID WE NEED SOME DETAILS BEFORE YOU GO ANY FURTHER
I am so hard up these days I will even take m/f sex details if that's all that's on offer

@Noraephronwasagenius
Struck out with the Lady Scientist?

@MadisonHughes95
More like didn't even get up to bat, because her wife came to an event and WHO IS MARRIED WITHOUT EVER EVEN MENTIONING IT ONCE IN CONVERSATION THAT IS SOMETHING YOU SHOULD ALWAYS CASUALLY DROP IN CASE THERE ARE SOME GAYS WITH CRUSHES AROUND

@Neverthelesskararesisted
Didn't you talk to her like . . . once for two seconds.

@MadisonHughes95
IRRELEVANT
Also we are losing the plot here, which is: NORA GOT LAID BY A DUDE SHE HATES AND SHE WON'T TELL US DETAILS WHICH MEANS IT WAS REALLY REALLY GOOD

@Noraephronwasagenius
What is with you and your capslock today?

@MadisonHughes95
GRAD SCHOOL IS HARD AND STRESSFUL AND I'LL YELL IF I WANT

@Neverthelesskararesisted
Don't think you're getting away with changing the subject there, Nora.

@Noraephronwasagenius
FINE the sex was great and it turns out he really, really knows how to use his tongue and not just in the courtroom.
HAPPY?

@MadisonHughes95
Honestly, almost never
But yes, happy for you
Glad you found a straight dude who knows his way around a vagina as it's my understanding that is a rare treat for y'all

@Neverthelesskararesisted
That is so sad and accurate.
Also: he's suing you?

@Noraephronwasagenius
Not me, my company. But I'm going to be in charge of the case, which means a lot of face time with him.

@Neverthelesskararesisted
Is the problem an ethical one or just like, you're not sure you can see him all the time and not sit on his face again?

@MadisonHughes95
What Kara said

@Noraephronwasagenius
I don't know. It just feels vaguely unethical? Even though there are a lot of lawyers who have hooked up and then gone head to head.

Yes, Maddy that was another dirty joke go ahead and laugh.

@MadisonHughes95
HAHAHAHAHAHA I cannot believe I have taught you to make dirty jokes

I'm so proud I could cry

Also this really sounds like there's no problem here unless you WANT it to be a problem

@Neverthelesskararesisted
(What Maddy said)

@Keanuisadreamboat
I know I'm coming into this a little late but 1) YAY FOR GOOD SEX YOU DESERVE IT and 2) yeah I'm not seeing the problem.

Unless the real problem is Luke?????

@Noraephronwasagenius

Luke and I are just . . . whatever, it's not going to be an in-person thing and I KNOW how you guys feel about that, but we have an arrangement that works.

@MadisonHughes95

I maintain that an arrangement like that that doesn't include some form of internet sex, either text based or facetime based, is pointless

@Keanuisadreamboat

No one asked, Maddy.

@Noraephronwasagenius

(Thanks, Reiko)

And I don't know if the problem is Luke, because Luke is just . . . Luke, for me. This guy is another issue.

@Neverthelesskararesisted

But what IS the issue there?

@Noraephronwasagenius

Fine. I might want to bang him again but idk if I CAN, what with the whole "he is suing my company" thing.

@Keanuisadreamboat

So bang him, but like, ethically. Meaning: don't talk about work, keep your papers locked up and your laptop password protected, and just don't tell anyone.

To be fair idk exactly how ethical that is, but damn girl, you've earned this.

@Neverthelesskararesisted
I second that. And didn't you say you have to like, REALLY try to get disbarred? So you're fine. Get laid, enjoy it, and leave a good Yelp review.

@Noraephronwasagenius
What sort of Yelp is there for sex?

@Neverthelesskararesisted
It's an app I'm going to make, just as soon as I learn how to make apps.

Victoria shook her head, still chuckling. She had found these women slowly, over the course of a few years on Twitter, but they were like family to her. The talk in the group chat turned back to Maddy's upcoming exams (she wasn't ready and was melting down) and whether or not Reiko should move in with her boyfriend of three years (he was a keeper, they were all unanimous on that, but she was just a little terrified of the permanence.) If the chat thought she should stress less about the chances of hooking up with Owen again, she would take their advice to heart. She found a Hallmark movie on TV and put it on for background noise while she laughed and talked with her friends. Onscreen, a blandly pretty white woman found out her job was sending her to her hometown for completely contrived reasons, while her high-school boyfriend—also blandly pretty, also white, but a baker instead of a vaguely defined businesswoman—wrestled with getting his orders out on time. It was the perfect, low-stress movie to watch while she bantered with her friends. Her mother might not understand it, but this was Victoria's life and she was happy with it.

Direct Messages: Nora @Noraephronwasagenius

@Lukethebarnyardcat

How pathetic is it to get into your career just to piss off your dad?

And in the interest of full disclosure, roughly 30% of everything I do is just to make someone mad. Or at least annoy them. Idk why. Does this mean I need therapy?

@Noraephronwasagenius

Honestly? I'm the same way. And I think we could all use some therapy, tbh.

Chapter Four

Victoria climbed out of her car and smoothed down her skirt. She was a solid half hour early, largely because she found she could slightly throw off her opponent's game if there appeared to be a ticking clock. She could amuse herself just fine in whatever drab conference room he shunted her into, but Owen would be feeling the pressure of the deposition bearing down on him all the while. It was petty, perhaps. But effective.

Besides, she was annoyed and looking to leave the office, thanks to the higher-ups roundly rejecting her request that they help sponsor Reproductive Justice's Uterus-Havers 5k. *Just a bit too liberal; wouldn't want to upset the red state customers* had been their response after only a couple of weeks of deliberation, and no amount of *people in red states deserve access to health care too* could change their minds. Sometimes she hated working for Smorgasbord, but then she would get her paycheck and remember why it was worth it.

The deposition was on the fifth floor of a nondescript building out in the suburbs, and the structure slung dark and imposing across her line of vision. Heat radiated off the asphalt parking lot in shimmering waves. A sign indicated the building housed a dentist office, a packaging company, two independent law firms, and a consulting company with a garishly pink logo. Apparently Owen Pohl could not be bothered with anything so uptight as an actual office, preferring to rent conference room space from one of the firms as needed. The thrifty side of her that had grown up counting every single penny might have admired that, but this was *Owen Pohl* she was talking about there. He got no credit for anything, ever.

Except for perhaps the ability to give her knee-shaking orgasms, but that was utterly irrelevant at the moment.

The elevator doors had *out of order* signs taped on both of them and Victoria sighed. Five flights in three-inch heels was not her idea of fun, but at least she'd given herself plenty of extra time. She could duck into the bathroom and pat away any sweat and still have time to be obnoxiously punctual.

The stairwell door clanged shut behind her. The hallways had been the standard office park beige, but the stairs were industrial grey. Harsh fluorescent light made her squint, and an AC unit hummed in the background. Victoria hiked up her skirt to her thighs to make this marginally easier on herself and started up. Her footsteps echoed and somewhere several floors up, another door opened. Steps thundered down towards her and she smoothed down her skirt and made sure to tuck back the lock of hair that tended to slip out of her bun before she came face to face with anyone.

He had his head ducked down as he barreled towards her and if it were anyone else, she probably would have stepped aside. But one glimpse of that chin-length red hair and she decided not to bother, forcing Owen to draw up short and nearly lose his balance one step away from crashing straight into her.

It was remarkable, really, how quickly Owen's face could go from handsome and pleasant to curdled with annoyance. "Deposition isn't for another half hour, you know," he said. His stubble was longer than the last time she saw him but it did nothing to hide the sharp line of his jaw.

Victoria drew herself up to her full height on the landing, acutely aware that this was the first time they had met since the night they were in his bedroom. This close she could breathe him in, the scent-memory doing something completely absurd to her stomach. "I was unaware there was a law banning me from arriving early," she said evenly, even though blood was roaring in her ears so loudly she could barely think. Owen had that effect on her, and even more so when he looked at her like that, like he was remembering the exact same scenes that were flashing behind her eyelids right now.

"You're trying to throw me off," he said, narrowing his eyes. "You think because you're going to be sitting in the conference room, ready and prepared, I'll feel pressured." He stepped toward her and she took an unconscious step back, more than a little surprised he'd twigged to her game so quickly. Her back bumped the grey cement wall and the chill of the bricks drove home just how heated she suddenly was. Owen licked his lips, looking her up and down predatorily. "Nice try."

She lifted her chin and looked down her nose at him. "Oh?" she said, but much to her chagrin, he didn't back away. She felt the warmth radiating from his skin, saw the way her presence was raising goosebumps on his arms. She dropped her voice to a low, sultry purr. "If it's not working, then why are you panting?"

Owen's lips curved into a smirk and his eyes darkened. He leaned forward, his lips almost grazing hers. He skimmed his nose over to her jaw and his lips went to the shell of her ear, his breath hot. He didn't speak, but his breath stirred a few loose tendrils of her hair and she curled her hands into fists to keep from touching his face. *This is not happening. This is not happening. This is a hallucination or a dream, and in a minute, I will wake up in bed, annoyed and horny. You don't want to kiss him, that's unprofessional and unethical. Don't kiss him. Don't. Do. Not, Kiss. Him.*

His hand dropped to the hem of her skirt, playing with the fabric, his fingertips sparking against the thin skin on her thigh. *Dammit, definitely not a dream. But still, no kissing*, her brain admonished. Her lungs lost the ability to work and her mouth went dry. Owen inched the fabric up and against her better judgement she let her knee fall open. He found the top of her stockings and traced the edge so lightly she whimpered. This was not in her game plan, at all, ever, and she tried desperately to get her liquid limbs to move. But they stubbornly refused, too eager to feel his fingers skate higher and seek out the dampness between her thighs. His thumb tucked into the hollow of her hip, so close to where she needed him and yet so far. The rest of his hand spanned the inside of her thigh and she considered rolling her hips in search of the friction she needed. Her underwear was nearly ruined and her self-control right along with them.

Owen's other hand came up to cup her cheek and he dragged his eyes up from her mouth. "Seems like I'm not the only one out of breath," he growled and abruptly stepped back.

It was like being doused with cold water. Owen grinned at her and resumed his race down the stairs, leaving her swallowing hard with the somewhat embarrassing urge to rub her thighs together to relieve the ache between them. The door slammed at the bottom of the steps and she collapsed back against the cinderblock, stunned.

This was not at all what she planned to have happen. She was supposed to unsettle him, not the other way around. Her body vibrated with the memory of his presence, but she had to get ahold of herself, and fast.

Her underwear was uncomfortably damp but there wasn't anything she could do about that right now. She dug through her bag and found a blotting sheet to control the light sweat prickling her forehead, and determinedly finished her climb. She stopped in the ladies' room to check her makeup before she went to the conference room. She was breathing heavily at first, but by the time she sat down and pulled out her list of questions, she had stopped thinking about the way Owen's lips would feel on her neck.

Mostly.

Unbelievable. The woman was a goddamn robot. Owen couldn't believe his eyes when he saw her sitting primly at the conference table, not a hair out of place. There was maybe a slight flush to her cheeks, but he unfortunately knew from personal experience it was nowhere near the deep, enticing pink she got when Victoria was really worked up.

He, on the other hand, had needed a solid five minutes' breathing deeply and glaring at himself in the men's room mirror to get himself under control. He didn't know what had come over him, but the desire to see her flustered and turned on had overridden literally every rational thought in his brain. He wondered if Victoria understood just how close he was to losing control with her, or if this was all just a stupid game to her.

He really wished she didn't have that effect on him, and he sincerely, devoutly wished he hadn't picked her up in the bar that night. It would be so much easier to ignore his body's reaction to her if he didn't know exactly what it felt like to be inside her. He could still feel the texture of her nipples on his tongue and hear the way she moaned in his ear, but those were massively inappropriate things to be thinking about his opposing counsel, even if he happened to know that her flinty grey eyes could go soft and hazy if he kissed her long enough.

But nothing—and he meant nothing—could shake Victoria. It was like he was a complete stranger when he walked in, client at his side, and throughout the deposition she gave no hint she had ever even met him before, much less that they had come close to tearing each other's clothes off less than thirty minutes ago.

Owen did his best to focus, and the deposition went well enough. His client was well-prepared and they had an airtight case, because Smorgasbord was clearly violating their own contracts with their required off-the-books overtime for managers. Owen was damn good at his job and he refused to let the way Victoria clicked her pen with her perfectly manicured fingernails drive him to distraction, remembering how she dug them into his back when he kissed her just under her jaw.

On second thought, maybe he was just a goddamn disaster. He shouldn't have risen to her bait in the stairwell, and he certainly shouldn't have brought them so close to the edge. She wasn't just someone he ran across sometimes anymore, she was the opposing counsel on the biggest case of his career.

Victoria lifted a perfectly arched brow at him. "Unless you have anything else, I think we're done here," she said in that icy, throaty voice of hers.

"We can be finished for now," he agreed. There was a flurry of papers as the court recorder stood up and Victoria began gathering her things. Owen pulled his phone out of his pocket—it was almost time for his lunch date with Nora—and set it on the table, turning to Amina to answer a question she had about their next step in the process. Victoria set her bag on the table near his phone and said something to him, but he pretended not to hear her and she swanned out without another word.

It wasn't until he'd walked Amina out to her car, Victoria already roaring out of the parking lot, that he looked down at the phone in his hand. He frowned at the lockscreen. His was of his half-sisters, grinning with ice cream cones at the State Fair, and this was a nondescript standard wallpaper option. For half a second he wondered if his phone had restarted, but then he flipped it over and looked at the case. He definitely didn't have a rose-gold outline of a bee on the back of his, which meant that, somehow, he and Victoria had swapped phones.

Sighing angrily, he walked back up to the conference room and opened his laptop.

Direct Messages: Luke @Lukethebarnyardcat

@Noraephronwasagenius
My best childhood memory is probably singing in the kitchen with my mom while she made me macaroni and cheese and hot dogs.

@Lukethebarnyardcat
Wait did she make you macaroni and cheese sometimes and then hot dogs other times or did you eat that TOGETHER

@Noraephronwasagenius
Shut up you heathen it's delicious.

Chapter Five

From: Owen.Pohl@gmail.com
To: Victoria.Clemenceaux@Smorgasbord.com
You have my phone

Victoria read the email twice to be sure she wasn't hallucinating, and then dug her own phone out. She hit the home button and was startled to see two sticky-faced little girls—nieces, she assumed, since as far as she knew he didn't have kids—with blonde hair and familiar jawlines pulling faces for the camera. The case was not her gold bumblebee but a black insignia she recognized as belonging to the Rebel Alliance in *Star Wars*. Owen must have left his phone next to hers while they were packing up and she'd been trying so hard to *not* think about the moment in the stairwell she hadn't so much as glanced at the phone she grabbed. There went her plans of messaging Luke—she would never use company property for something that personal—and she felt strangely naked without her phone. Plus, Owen's phone being vaguely nerdy reminded her of Luke and that only served to annoy her further, because how *dare* Owen be anything like Luke.

From: Victoria.Clemenceaux@Smorgasbord.com
To: Owen.Pohl@gmail.com
Then come get it. Office 2721. I'll leave your name at security for a guest pass.

She was agitated the rest of the day, even though the deposition had gone as well as could be expected. Smorgasbord was in a grey area with their manager policy, which Victoria was aware of firsthand thanks to all the long shifts her mother had pulled there over the years. Owen had a better case than Smorgasbord cared to admit, in her opinion, but she wasn't getting paid for her opinion. There was just enough wiggle room she might be able to pull this one off. She didn't like it when things were this precarious, however, and it got under her skin.

Owen didn't respond with an ETA, annoying her further. And he'd probably done so specifically to bother her, which made it worse. The hours ticked by and he still hadn't shown. His phone buzzed with a text and instinct made her pick it up. She instantly wished she hadn't.

Ashley
When are you coming over? Haven't seen you in way too long.

Great. Of course. He's got someone else. It wasn't that she cared, or that Victoria even expected he had any feelings for her aside from lust and hatred, but to see blatant proof of another woman bugged her more than she thought possible.

He didn't even have a last name for Ashley, which meant one of several things: she was a long-term girlfriend, rendering last names superfluous, or she was a random hookup and he didn't know her last name. A sister was a possibility too, but limited though Victoria's experiences were with siblings, the text seemed too *nice* to be from a sister. A long-term girlfriend was obviously the worst option, but the more she thought about it, the less likely that seemed. There had been zero sign of another woman's presence in his house, and if he did have a girlfriend, bringing a not-so-drunken hookup back to his own place—after Victoria had offered hers—would be an unnecessary risk, and he didn't seem like the careless type. Obnoxious and self-satisfied and irritating and entirely too sure of himself and a dozen other synonyms for those qualities, yes, but careless? Not really. That left another random hookup, which was the less crappy option, but somehow made her feel worse.

It meant she was just one of several. Which, okay, that was hardly against the rules, of which they had none anyway, but it pissed her off. She wondered if Ashley knew he was seeing other people, and for half a second she considered texting back herself to find out. Instead, she sat down at her computer and called up his email.

From: Victoria.Clemenceaux@Smorgasbord.com
To: Owen.Pohl@gmail.com
By the way, Ashley misses you and wants to know when you're coming over. Make sure you don't disappoint her.

Victoria hit send with far more force than necessary and stood up, only to immediately sit back down and hit *refresh*. Nothing.

Well, of course there was nothing. He'd barely had time to read it, much less respond. She stood up and told herself she needed to go for a walk and get a goddamn grip, but then her inbox showed a new message and she sank back down into her chair.

From: Owen.Pohl@gmail.com
To: Victoria.Clemenceaux@Smorgasbord.com
Noted

Noted. *Noted?* What the fuck kind of response was that? She paced back and forth behind her desk, relieved that the glass facing the hallway was thickly frosted enough to keep her movements private. She wanted to vent to the group chat, but without her phone she couldn't. She considered simply driving to Owen's house and throwing the phone at his stupid face, but that risked missing him on his way to Smorgasbord. She once again considered responding to Ashley just so the poor woman knew where she stood with him, but Victoria was loath to hurt another woman even if doing so would stick it to Owen and his stupid face. Ugh, everything about him was so frustrating it made her want to scream.

Especially because she couldn't forget the way his breath fanned across her neck in the stairwell. It was borderline malpractice—or at the very least an ill-advised proposition—to have sex with her opposing counsel, no matter what the girls said. He got under her skin, and she hated it. It made her feel weak and exposed, and even worse, she *liked* it. If he'd kissed her this afternoon she would have kissed him back, absolutely no doubt about it. She would have clawed open his shirt and fucked him right there, because whatever there was between them—aside from unadulterated hatred—was powerful beyond belief.

It wasn't that Victoria was a stranger to chemistry. She'd had boyfriends and flings in the past, and she still thought very fondly of a summer hookup after her 2L year with an intern who'd ended up in Milwaukee after graduation. But nothing compared to the force of nature that was what she had with Owen. It was propulsive, explosive, and incredibly distracting.

Throughout the deposition she'd fixated on his lips, remembering what they felt like on her skin. When his eyes sparked with righteous anger she remembered how softly he'd looked at her after they both came, like she was something precious to him.

She had just managed to pull herself out of a very dangerous reminiscence spiral when there were two sharp raps at her door. It was almost seven, the sun sinking behind the horizon and painting the sky outside her window pink and gold. She slipped her high heels back on under her desk before standing, touching her hair to make sure it was securely in place. "Come in," she called, certain she knew who was on the other side.

She was right. Owen opened her door, already rolling his eyes. "It's not enough that I have to come fetch things from you, Your Highness?" he snarled. "You couldn't just leave it at security?"

"I was busy," she said with a shrug. *And maybe I wanted to see how far I could push things*, a traitorous voice in her brain whispered. She took a moment to smooth out her skirt because she knew it would bug him, and picked up his phone. "This is yours. Don't forget to respond to Ashley," she added archly. "And I'm just curious, how many of us do you have in rotation?"

"Don't," he gritted out.

"Oooh, have I found a sore spot?"

His eyes flashed. "Don't," he said again, a muscle in his jaw ticking.

Victoria wasn't quite sure what he meant by that, whether it meant he didn't have anyone else or he simply didn't want to talk about her, but either way her mouth went a little dry at the way he was looking at her.

"Tell me," he said with a dangerous glint in his eye, "are you like this on purpose?"

"Like what?" she asked primly. He plucked the phone from her hand, his fingers brushing against hers, and electric sparks raced unbidden up her nerve endings, crackling through her skin.

"Cold. Robotic. Inhuman."

"Just because I don't melt at your pathetic attempts at charm doesn't make me cold. It makes me a functional human with a brain," she said haughtily.

He snorted. "You might have a brain but you're sure as hell heartless. You'd have to be, working here."

"Smorgasbord's philanthropy—"

"Smorgasbord's entire business model depends on keeping your employees in poverty and you know it," he snapped.

"Save it for the courtroom, counselor," she said evenly. Nothing bothered him more than seeing her unruffled so she made sure to keep her words clipped even if her heartbeat picked up several paces when he stepped towards her.

"How can you?" he said, voice almost strangled. "What you have—and you work *here*?"

"Better than a dilettante who only chooses cases where he can play the savior," she said nastily. She held out her hand and he slapped her phone into it angrily. Victoria stalked past him to the door and gestured wordlessly out into the deserted halls. "Well? Was there something else?"

"You'd like that, wouldn't you?" he sneered, once more standing toe to toe with her. Victoria lifted her chin and arched a brow. Owen smirked at her, his blue-green eyes dropping to her lips.

And just like that, they were kissing. They crashed into each other and she blindly slammed her door shut, grateful that the rest of her coworkers had already left for the evening. Like in the stairwell, Owen quickly pinned her against the door, and she hated how much she liked that feeling. His teeth nipped at her lower lip, just this side of harsh, and her nipples tightened in response.

This time, when his hand found the hem of her skirt, he didn't torture her. He slid his palm up her thigh to the place where her stockings met bare skin, and the moans they made into each other's mouths were identical. She tunneled her fingers into his hair and drew his head down, first to just under her jaw and then to her collarbone, his kisses a potent mixture of teeth and tongue. His hand worked busily under her skirt, palming her ass and teasing the lacy edge of her stockings, and she jerked his tie loose. His coat fell to the floor with a soft rustle and he nearly ripped her blouse open trying to undo the buttons one-handed.

Owen gave up when her bra was visible, nudging it down just enough to reveal her breasts. And then his mouth was on her again; hot, wet suction that made her stuff her fist into her mouth to muffle the noises she desperately needed to make. Owen's hand under her skirt skated up to trace the seam of her panties. He straightened, her nipples now exposed to the cool air, and nuzzled against her jaw. "What color are they today?" he growled.

"Why don't you see for yourself?" she gasped, because his fingers were touching her lightly *everywhere* except for where she wanted to be touched.

His hand slid down her inner thigh to her stockings again and he pinned her wrists above her head with his other hand. "I've been thinking about these fucking thigh-highs all damn day," he said in that same rough, needy voice. "Did you wear them on purpose to wreck my concentration?"

Obviously, as "nearly getting fingered in a stairwell" hadn't been on her to-do list, she hadn't. "Been thinking about me, have you?" she said, and captured his lower lip between her teeth.

"All fucking day. Couldn't stop thinking about what they'd look like against your skin."

"There's nothing stopping you from finding out now."

His dark grin sent shivers down her spine. For the space of a heartbeat they looked into each other's eyes, heat rising between them. He nipped at her lips, his touch like a brand on her skin, and waited for her nod before he moved.

Her office phone rang, shattering the tension between them.

Owen seemed to come back to his senses first, shaking his head and backing away. Victoria felt the loss of his warmth keenly but then she realized what she'd been about to do. *Again.* She kept her eyes averted from him as she hurried across her office, hastily rebuttoning her shirt as she answered the phone, privately wondering what the hell was wrong with her brain.

"Hey, Ms. Clemenceaux," chirped Ruthie, the cheerful evening security guard. "I got held up for a second, but I wanted to let you know that guy is on his way to your office. I got worried you might have already left and wanted to make sure it was all okay."

"Of course. He's here," she said, with a quick glance at Owen. Owen was still facing the door, hand pressed flat against it and his head hanging between his shoulders. He seemed to be breathing hard, and as she watched he curled his free hand into a fist. "And call me Victoria, okay, Ruthie?"

"Sure thing, Ms. Clemenceaux," Ruthie said playfully and hung up.

Owen finally turned around and grabbed his suit coat, face implacable. Still shaking from adrenaline, Victoria forced herself to straighten her spine and stay put, a safe distance from him. From here she couldn't breathe him in, clean and rich and masculine, and she'd be less tempted to run her fingers through his hair again. She wasn't sure what she wanted to say, whether she should laugh at how close they had come to danger, or to gently broach the subject of what the hell they were thinking, or even to simply pretend it hadn't happened.

Owen took in her hesitation and his face hardened. "I think we're done here," he said tightly and walked out, shutting the door firmly behind him.

Victoria wasn't sure how she made it home that evening. Working any later was out of the question, her mind spinning from whatever had happened with Owen, so she straightened her clothes and smoothed out her hair before throwing a few things haphazardly into her bag. She must have walked—her apartment wasn't far from Smorgasbord's headquarters—but she didn't remember any of it. One minute she was in her office, turned on and bewildered, and the next she was in her tastefully but sparingly decorated apartment. She changed out of her work clothes and ruined panties and picked at her dinner, unsatisfied, and decided to try and distract herself.

But it was no use. Victoria glared at the TV, barely cognizant of what she was watching. Her brain was fixated on Owen. They'd come so close to crossing the line twice today, and it needed to stop. She needed to get herself under control, yeah, but Owen needed to stop baiting her. She couldn't do her job if he kept looking at her like that, and she certainly couldn't represent her corporation to the best of her ability if she kept thinking about the way his palms felt on her skin. Her need to kiss him had overridden the rest of her brain, and that was unacceptable.

The more she thought about it, the more annoyed she got. This wasn't just on her—it was his fault too. Him and his stupid, annoying, handsome face. Owen needed to stop jerking her around, because she'd be more than capable of holding herself in check if he didn't say shit like *I've been thinking about these fucking thigh-highs all damn day.* What she really needed to do was tell him to knock it off.

The rational thing to do would be to take a deep breath and talk it over with someone. There was always at least one person in the chat who was available, and half the point of their group was to talk through each other's problems. Even if she ignored their advice, they would be good for a reality check.

But Victoria didn't want advice. She wanted answers, and she wanted to yell. She wanted to know why Owen had walked out on her without so much as addressing what had just happened, and she wanted to know why she *cared* about that lack of clarity. She was furious he had somehow managed to gain the upper hand.

The more she thought about it, the more annoyed she was. Their first hookup was a clearly mutual thing, and whatever happened in the stairwell earlier had been two people testing their limits. But what happened in her office crossed a line, and they needed to make sure it never happened again.

She slipped on a pair of sandals and grabbed her car keys. It wasn't a long drive to Owen's shabby bungalow on the south end of town, and before she knew it she was hammering angrily on his door. A shadow crossed in front of the big bay window and then the door swung inward, revealing a confused—and shirtless—Owen. His black sweatpants were slung dangerously low on his hips, revealing a smattering of reddish blonde hair that trailed down to the waistband. His eyebrows shot up. "What the fuck?"

"I could ask you the same thing," she said and barreled inside. She tossed her purse angrily on his kitchen table, which was just about the only clear space in the entire house. "What the hell was that earlier?"

He tipped his head to the side, eyes dancing. "I'm pretty sure that was a deposition. You know what a deposition is, don't you?"

"Cute," she snapped. "You know what I'm talking about."

Owen took a step towards her and for the third time today, her pulse spiked in response. "Do I? Use your words, Vee."

She swallowed hard and stiffened her spine. "Fine. I'm talking about the fact that you almost fucked me in my office today."

"There, was that so hard?"

"Screw you," she spat back, and he grinned. The son of a bitch was enjoying himself, and she narrowed her eyes at him. "We can't keep doing this."

"Seems like the sort of meeting that could have been an email," he said lightly.

"You really think it's a good idea to screw your opposing counsel in her office?"

"Maybe not a good idea, but it's certainly a fun one," he said, and this time she had to fight to keep an answering grin off her face. *God, he was infuriating.* It was even worse when he was being charming. "But is that really why you drove all the way here?"

"Of course it is. Why else would I be here?" she said, desperate to regain her footing. "You need to stop doing this."

"I'm not trying to be an asshole, I swear," he said, gazing at her steadily. "But *I'm* the one who needs to stop? From where I'm standing, you're the one who drove to my house at—" he glanced over her shoulder at the clock on the microwave—"ten o'clock on a weeknight to yell at me. If you didn't want this to happen anymore, you could have just told me over the phone."

"I just need you to stop . . . being you," Victoria said, waving vaguely at him. She'd never been this inarticulate in her life, much less during an argument. She should be in her element, but his bare chest—and the memory of what it felt like under her fingertips—kept distracting her.

"What, being handsome?" he said, and when she lost the battle and dropped her eyes to the trail of hair that led under his waistband, he grinned like he'd just been handed a summary judgment. "That's it, isn't it? You want me to look like a bridge troll so you'll stop being so attracted to me. But I'll tell you what, Vee," he said, pacing towards her and using her name like a lion tamer, keeping her mesmerized and frozen in place. "I'll stop being so damn handsome if you stop haunting my dreams." He glanced at her chest, taking in her loose white shirt and probably the bra underneath, the bra he'd seen just hours ago, before dragging his gaze back to hers.

"I haunt your dreams?"

"I think you know damn well you do," he said, his voice low and ragged. She kept looking at his lips, remembering how they tasted, and she had the irrelevant thought that it might be nice to just *kiss* him sometime, with no agenda or furious rush to orgasm. His lips could be soft and searching, and there was something sweet about the way he kissed her even when he was doing something filthy.

But kissing was the exact opposite reason she was here, and she needed to remember that. "At the very least we need to stop making out at work," she managed.

"Okay," he said slowly, like he was drugged. "Sure. No making out at work." He licked his lips. "This isn't work, though." He reached out and spanned her jaw with his hand, his touch scorching.

"No, it isn't," she agreed. This was another Moment. She could feel it, and she knew this all hung on her. Whatever she decided, Owen would accept.

Victoria sank to her knees.

Direct Messages: Nora @Noraephronwasagenius

@Lukethebarnyardcat
Sometimes, I think I'm the world's biggest idiot

@Noraephronwasagenius
Me too. Me fucking too.

Chapter Six

Victoria Clemenceaux on her knees was a powerful image. Owen was reasonably sure he was going to be seeing that whenever he closed his eyes for the next several months, and possibly forever. His house felt empty without her, her parting words of *there, now we're done* ringing in his ears.

She'd left five minutes ago; five minutes that he spent sitting blankly in the kitchen chair, half convinced he'd imagined everything. But no, it was definitely real, thanks to the lingering whiff of her perfume in the air. Owen shuffled slowly back to his couch. He ran his hands through his hair, elbows on his knees, and tried to think.

It was the last thing he'd expected tonight and yet it made perfect sense. Victoria was not the type of woman to just let him win. He couldn't tell you the rules of the game they were playing, but he knew he'd broken them when he left her office. He just hadn't expected her to go that far to rectify the situation.

He wondered if it was possible to change things between

them. They were already barreling down a track he knew would end in disaster. They could ignore the games they'd started to play, or at least redefine the rules. There was a moment earlier, just after he made her come with his face between her thighs, with Victoria perched on the edge of his kitchen table, where he realized he wanted to see her open her eyes first thing tomorrow morning, soft and hazy. He could have reached out and touched her cheek, coaxed her upstairs and made her fall apart on his tongue again and again until he was ready to be inside her. He could have convinced her to stay the night, work be damned. He didn't know why he wanted it, but he did, and so badly he had started to lift his hand. But instead he let her walk out, and now that felt like the wrong decision.

For the first time in his life, he wanted to fix something and had no idea where to begin.

Victoria poured herself a glass of Pinot Noir and settled onto her couch with her laptop. Twitter was open in her browser, like it usually was, and she turned on the TV for some background noise. She scrolled through her timeline, catching up on the news and tweeting out a few random thoughts. They usually revolved around the same topics: income inequality, misogyny, and terrible TV. But right now, the show she had on was an innocuous teenage drama, with a diverse-but-not-really-diverse-enough cast and snappy dialogue, and she didn't have much snark to share. She had a pair of pants she should probably be hemming, but she didn't feel like it. Several Owen-less days had passed, which was a blessing in that her libido was bound to get her in trouble sooner or later, and a curse in that she'd been feeling listless and adrift ever since she walked away from him even though every bone in her body screamed for her to stay. She hated feeling like this, like there was something going on under the surface and she didn't want to explore it. Or rather, she knew she needed to and wasn't sure how to navigate it.

A blue number one appeared above her messages and she got the usual pleasant thrill from seeing a notification from Luke.

@Lukethebarnyardcat
Planning on tearing anyone a new one tonight?

@Noraephronwasagenius
Eh, I'm not in the mood tonight. Might not even pick any fights at all.

@Lukethebarnyardcat
No fights? At all? Not even with an MRA or a Nazi?

@Noraephronwasagenius
Not even. Idk, feeling kind of contemplative tonight.

@Lukethebarnyardcat
What about?

@Noraephronwasagenius
Real talk?

@Lukethebarnyardcat
Real talk

@Noraephronwasagenius
I did something the other day. Something I'm not proud of, but I don't regret it. And I'm wondering what kind of person

that makes me. If I can do that and not care, what does that mean about who I am?

@Lukethebarnyardcat
Unless you murdered someone, you're probably in the clear
But in all seriousness, we all make compromises and there's nothing inherently bad about that. Is it a work thing or a personal life thing?

Victoria chewed her lower lip and thought. The case was a work thing, which made Owen a part of work, but "we keep hooking up" wasn't strictly work related. Nor was it something she felt like sharing with Luke.

@Noraephronwasagenius
Both. Kind of related, tbh. It's complicated.

@Lukethebarnyardcat
Nemesis related?

@Noraephronwasagenius
Exactly. I'm working on something and I'm just not sure I'm on the right side of it. But it's my job, and my duty is to who I'm working for. I want to say that I believe in what I do, but I'm not sure that's true anymore. Particularly in this case. And honestly, I wish I could quit.

She took a deep, shuddering breath. Writing that was almost as scary as thinking it. She'd worked so hard to get to where she was, and she hated it. She liked the paycheck, but the rest? It hurt. She loathed hurting people like her mother, and she absolutely detested having to pretend she wasn't sick to her stomach over it when she went head-to-head with Owen. She wished she could be on his side of it, but that sort of work paid peanuts and she had loans to pay and a mother to support. And Owen had a way of bringing up those conflicted feelings.

@Lukethebarnyardcat
Is he on the right side of it?

@Noraephronwasagenius
He is, and I hate that. He's holding it over my head, and he called me out the other day, and I think he was right. Which is probably the worst part.

Victoria's palms were unaccountably damp as she typed the words. Owen's accusations the other day had gotten under her skin because they were true. She wasn't extending a hand to pull up those after her. Sure, she had her responsibilities, but maybe working for Smorgasbord wasn't the most ethical thing she could do. Maybe there were other options out there she simply hadn't explored yet.

But, as honest as she could be with Luke, she couldn't bring herself to tell him she'd turned Nemesis into a hatefuck buddy.

@Lukethebarnyardcat
Tell me your side first

Victoria smiled to herself, because of course Luke would want to hear her side first. Not for the first time she considered just telling him everything, identifiable details and all, but she held off. She worried if she went too personal she'd lose the freedom she felt when she was talking to him and she didn't quite want to risk it.

@Noraephronwasagenius

You know how I grew up poor, right? Well, I had to take out a lot of loans to get where I am today, and the best way to pay them back is to get a corporate gig. But my corporation isn't always the most ethical, and Nemesis doesn't get how I can justify working for them.

@Lukethebarnyardcat

You can justify it because of what you just said. You can't fix everything, and going delinquent on your loans won't help anyone. He doesn't get to preach at you for that

Warmth settled around her ribcage and she sipped her wine. It was nice having someone like Luke in her corner.

Owen stopped with a spoon of yogurt halfway to his mouth and frowned. A faint buzzing noise sounded again, so it wasn't just his imagination. "Master Skywalker, have you seen my phone?" he asked, scanning the coffee table in front of him. "It could be Nora, you know." He hoped it was, because her anxiety about her job the other night had made him feel even more protective of her than usual. Luke's tail twitched but he stayed otherwise implacable, stretched out languorously on the couch. Owen paused the episode of *Parks and Rec* playing and lifted up the throw pillow next to him. One more buzz had him standing up, patting his pockets and moving the cushion behind him.

He stopped, eyes narrowed, and glared at his cat. "You're hiding my phone, aren't you?" Again Luke remained silent, uninterested in the needs of his human. Sighing, Owen scooped him up to grab his phone and check his messages. Unfortunately, the messages weren't from Nora.

Andy Lee
Quick question: which tie?????

What followed was no less than four photos of Owen's best friend in different ties for his upcoming wedding, two of which appeared to be exactly the same. Fortunately, Mark had replied already, saving Owen the trouble of deciding which indistinguishable tie the groom should wear.

Mark Olsen
#3
Trust me

Owen Pohl
I'd go with Mark's opinion since he maybe cares more about this wedding than you do

Mark Olsen
He's not wrong

Andy Lee
In that case would you make a playlist for the wedding? It's the one thing neither of us wants to do.

Mark Olsen
HELL YEAH I WOULD

Andy Lee
I'll send you me and Cassie's must plays.
I love you.

Owen Pohl
Why am I in this text chain? I feel unnecessary

Andy Lee
You're in it because I value your contributions.
Even if I should have just texted Mark directly since he's the one who has opinions on all things wedding.

Mark Olsen
Look I just wanna get married okay
But until I find someone I have to live vicariously through you

Owen Pohl
Vicariously is a pretty big word for you, bro
Did you get a word of the day dictionary?

Mark Olsen
Fuck you
Also yes

Owen snorted and Andy turned the conversation towards going out sometime soon, since the three of them hadn't gotten together in a while. Owen had met Andy during a summer internship at a white-shoe firm downtown in law school—Owen had gone to Harvard but interned in Minneapolis, while Andy had gone to the U of M—and Mark had been Andy's college roommate. But Mark was smart enough not to go to law school and instead was a high school gym teacher out in Apple Valley. They were the closest friends he had, save Nora, but Owen hadn't mentioned Victoria to them either. For one thing, Andy almost certainly knew her from law school—and if he didn't, his fiancée Cassie definitely did, on account of her only being one year behind Andy in law school—and for another, he didn't really feel like dealing with the trash talking that would ensue once they found out he had a fuckbuddy, even if it was good-natured.

A thought drew him up short. Was Victoria going to the wedding? Andy and Cassie were inviting half of Minneapolis and Saint Paul, it seemed, so she'd probably at least gotten an invite. But was she close enough to them to go? And why, now that he thought about it, did he desperately want to see her in a fancy dress, dancing and laughing? And why on earth was he imagining *himself* dancing and laughing with her? That wasn't part of their deal.

He shook his head like Cat-Luke when he was faced with ear drops. His imagination was really out of control these days.

Owen Pohl
Guys, I think I need a bro date

Andy Lee
Is everything okay?

Mark Olsen
Something wrong?

Owen Pohl
It's nothing major. But let's do something soon

Andy Lee
What about Saturday afternoon?

Owen Pohl
Can't. Sibling time with the girls

Mark Olsen
Give those little demons a hug from me

Owen Pohl
Will do

Andy Lee
What about the Saturday after that, then? At Lake Monster Brewing? 8pm?

Mark Olsen
Works for me

Owen Pohl
I'm in

Andy Lee
Then it's a Bro Date.

Direct Messages: Luke @Lukethebarnyardcat

@Noraephronwasagenius

Here's the thing about growing up poor: it never, ever leaves you. You can make as much money as you want, and your stomach will still drop into your feet when your landlord says rent is going up by 10% next year.

Never mind that you can easily afford it. You're just . . . always terrified that the money will disappear, and never really, truly secure in having it.

@Lukethebarnyardcat

Damn. That sounds really difficult to manage. I'm sorry

@Noraephronwasagenius

Thanks. It's one of those things I don't like telling people, because just about everyone I know grew up rich or middle class, and I just can't handle the pitying looks they give me.

@Lukethebarnyardcat

And why can you tell me? I'm really glad you can, I'm just wondering

@Noraephronwasagenius

Partially because I can't SEE you giving me those sad little looks.

And partially because even though you're basically a Rockefeller, I feel like you understand.

@Lukethebarnyardcat

Hey now, we are nowhere near Rockefeller levels of family money

We are Hearst family level at BEST

@Noraephronwasagenius

do you even hear yourself oh my god.

Chapter Seven

A warm summer breeze played with wisps of her hair. To her left a group of college kids tossed a frisbee back and forth, and to her right a young couple was having a picnic. Victoria turned the page on her e-reader and settled back against the tree. A few families ambled past towards the Stone Arch Bridge and the Mississippi River flowed sluggishly just below the park. She rarely gave herself days like this, where she put all thoughts of work aside and allowed herself to get lost in a romance novel, pretending she didn't have bills to pay and clothes to alter, not to mention a case to figure out how to win.

It was nice to sit outside in the dappled sunlight without any particular agenda. It was solitary, true, and her mother would probably scold her for not seeking out any other humans for companionship, but Victoria liked being alone. Or at least she didn't mind it. But then she felt, rather than saw, a presence over her shoulder, and turned.

A young girl with blonde pigtails was looking at her intently. Victoria wasn't good at placing children's ages, but this one was at least old enough to be out of diapers and maybe not quite old enough to be in school full-time. Small children unsettled her, quite frankly, mostly because she never knew how to act around them. "Your pants have holes in them," the little girl said solemnly.

Victoria glanced at her jeans, artfully distressed in the knees and thighs. "I know."

"Did you wear them on purpose?"

Victoria closed her e-reader to look at the girl more fully. She scanned the area but didn't see anyone looking for her, and hoped that whomever this child belonged to would come along sooner rather than later. "I did. In fact, I put the holes in them myself."

Her light blue eyes got big, and there was something vaguely familiar about the little girl. "Your mom let you do that?"

She smothered a smile and nodded. "She taught me how." Rich people would pay a lot of money to look poor, but Victoria had long ago figured it was cheaper to just buy an inexpensive pair of jeans and rip them herself.

The girl's eyes went even wider in awe, and in the distance Victoria heard someone yell the name *Olivia*. "Are you Olivia?" Victoria asked, searching the park for the source of the voice.

"How did you know my name?"

"Olivia!" someone yelled again, closer now, and Victoria craned her neck to see. "Because someone is looking for you," she explained.

"That's just my brother," Olivia said with a shrug, and plopped down in the grass next to Victoria. "What are you reading?"

Victoria furrowed her brow because the voice calling for Olivia was far too adult-sounding to be a sibling. "If they're looking for you we should find them," she said, hoping that if she said it confidently enough the girl would listen. She stood up, dusting herself off, and startled.

Because striding straight towards her, red-gold hair pulled back in an obnoxious ponytail, was Owen. Her stomach did a flip-flop before she even realized it was happening. There was something about him, between his laid-back attitude and unconventional but undeniably attractive looks, that got to her. He drew up short, another small blonde girl balanced on his hip. "Victoria?"

Olivia looked up at her. "Your name is Victoria?"

An unexpected flush crawled up her neck, caught between an innocent child and her not-so-innocent memories of the man in front of her. "Yep, that's me," she said in a slightly strangled voice. "I take it this one belongs to you?" She gestured down at the little girl, who was now looking interestedly between them.

At least Owen seemed as thrown as she was. "Uh, yeah. Olivia, when I said you could wait outside while I changed your sister's diaper, I meant *by the door*," he said, sternly but not unkindly. "Now let's not bother Victoria anymore."

"She wasn't a bother," Victoria heard herself say, and Owen's eyebrows shot up.

"Are you guys friends?" Olivia asked, and Victoria opened her mouth to reply and then closed it, because *fuck no* was probably not an appropriate thing to say to someone still watching *Sesame Street*. "Because he's talked about you." And now it was her turn for her eyebrows to shoot up, because *what*.

Fortunately, Owen came to her rescue before she had to try and figure out what *that* meant. "She works with me, sort of. Now let's leave her alone."

"I want her to come with," Olivia said stubbornly. She grabbed Victoria's hand and Victoria had to stop herself from flinching away, because there was no way Owen would ever let her live down hurting a little girl's feelings. He already thought she was cold; knowing she was uncomfortable around children would be handing over endless ammunition. The girl on his hip started squirming and Owen set her on the grass, watching Victoria carefully.

"I'm sure she's busy," he said, and Victoria saw it for the opening it was.

"Actually, not doing anything important," she said brightly, because fuck him, he didn't get to get out of this either.

Owen's eyes flashed with mild annoyance and Olivia clapped. "You said snow cones," she said to Owen authoritatively. "Victoria gets one too."

"Uncle Owen is buying us all snow cones?" she asked, amused.

"He's not my uncle," Olivia said, clearly disgusted. "He's my *brother*."

Owen looked at Victoria with resignation. "I guess I'm buying you a snow cone," he sighed.

She hefted her purse on her shoulder and the two little girls took off running, this time bolting toward a bright blue food truck with *sno cones* written on the side in white bubbly letters. "Sisters?" she asked.

"Technically half-sisters. Dad's third wife."

"She must be young," Victoria observed.

"She is. Went to high school with me, in fact."

Victoria blinked. "That's gotta be weird."

"It was, but I'm used to it now. Besides, *Ashley's* actually pretty cool."

It took a moment for that to land. "Ashley's your . . . stepmom?"

"Yep. And I've definitely never hooked up with her," he said tightly.

Embarrassment flooded her chest. "Shit, uh, sorry. I shouldn't have jumped to conclusions."

"Yeah, you really shouldn't have," he replied. He looked her straight in the eye, utterly serious. "I wouldn't do that, okay?"

"Okay," Victoria muttered, cheeks burning. There was a whole world of implication in that *okay* and she wasn't sure she could get her brain around it all.

The younger girl stumbled, her chubby legs not as fast as her sister's, and Owen jogged ahead to scoop her up. "This is Lily, by the way," he said, checking her for scrapes. His tone was easy, a sharp contrast to moments before. *Okay, so we're letting the whole Ashley thing go*, she thought to herself, relieved and a little surprised he was willing to extend her that much of an olive branch.

"Nice to meet you, Lily," Victoria said awkwardly.

The little girl ignored her and Owen snorted. "She's a two-year-old, not a managing partner."

Lily ran ahead again and Victoria rolled her eyes. "Whatever, I don't know any kids," she said.

"Why am I not surprised," he sighed, more to himself than to her, and to her everlasting shock, she decided to let his barb pass by without a retort.

They joined Olivia at the back of the line. "We're both getting blue," Olivia announced. Once again Victoria had to bite back a smile because this little girl was clearly going to be a CEO of something someday.

"Lily, did you want blue?" he asked. Lily grabbed his leg and hid behind his calf, peering up at Victoria curiously. The line advanced and he pretended he couldn't move with Lily attached to his leg, making her giggle. "Blue?" he asked again, and Lily nodded. "Vee?"

The gentle nickname continued to surprise her but she kept her face implacable. She peered at the chalkboard list of flavors. "Raspberry," she decided. Owen ordered—two raspberries, two blueberries—and she watched him pull out his wallet, wondering just what the hell she was doing. She'd agreed to come along mostly to put him in an awkward spot, but now she was in the awkward position of letting her opposing counsel buy her a snow cone like they were friends instead of mortal enemies slash . . . something.

But Owen handed her the cone as if this was normal, instead of the last thing she expected to do today, and fell into step beside her as they followed the girls back through the park, towards the bridge. "Nirvana, huh?" he said, with a nod toward her shirt. It was one of her mom's old shirts, and Victoria had taken it apart and put it back together so it was no longer a boxy black concert tee but instead a sleeveless tank that clung to her spare curves.

"You have a problem with them or something?'

"No, just doesn't seem quite your style," he replied mildly. Olivia paused and looked back for approval before running towards the pedestrian bridge, her little sister in tow. "I take it you don't have any younger siblings," he said, changing the subject.

"Nope." *Closest thing was an almost-stepbrother when I was twelve*, she almost added, but then she remembered this was Owen she was talking to and kept her mouth shut. "Are these two it for you?"

He shook his head, his lips a comical, deep red from the snow cone. "I have three former step-stepsiblings, two older and one younger."

"Big family," she observed. Ahead, the girls stopped at the railing to peer through at the muddy, foamy river.

"What about you? Big family?" he asked.

"Nope."

"Glad to see you're just as warm and fuzzy out of the courtroom as in it," he said drily.

Here was where she would normally snarl at him, but instead

she decided to put him off balance by doing the unexpected. "It was just me and my mom growing up," she said. "And one set of grandparents up in Fargo, but we never really saw them."

It worked, because Owen failed to have a snappy remark in response. They fell silent as they reached the girls. Their cones were long gone, the evidence all over their faces, and Victoria wiped surreptitiously at her own face, worried she might have followed suit.

"You missed a spot," Owen said, and she wiped her lips again. "Nope, still there," he said, holding his hand out hesitantly. He waited for her nod to touch his thumb to the corner of her lips. Her whole body went still, eyes locked on his, and he blinked slowly.

And then he grinned. "Kidding," he said, dropping his hand and pulling a surprised bark of laughter from Victoria. She shoved at his chest in mock-annoyance and he laughed too, her heart abruptly slamming against her ribcage.

Olivia reached for Victoria, breaking their momentary spell. Her hand was sticky with melted blue syrup but she took it anyway, crouching down to be at the girl's level. "Owen says this is the biggest river in the country," Olivia announced.

Victoria spared a glance for Owen, who was now trying—and failing—to clean off Lily's face, his ears perhaps a little redder than before. "He's right, for once," she agreed, hoping he didn't hear her, but an amused snort from his general direction told her he did.

Olivia looked down at Victoria's strappy sandals and poked at her bright blue toenail. "My mom says I'm not old enough to wear shoes like you," she said.

Victoria assessed her three-inch heels and had to agree. "You know, these are grown-up shoes. But when you're old enough no one can stop you from wearing them, no matter what, if that's what you want." Olivia grinned and Victoria turned to Owen. "I think you've got a budding fashionista on your hands," she observed.

Owen smiled fondly at his little sister. "You have no idea. Half the reason we're out here is because my other option was for her to make me play dress-up, and there's only so many times I can be Anna to her Elsa."

Victoria laughed delightedly. "Please tell me she makes you wear a dress."

"And braids my hair," he deadpanned, and broke into a grin. It was the damnedest thing, standing on the bridge with the wind ruffling her hair, laughing with Owen like they were friends. Her phone buzzed in her purse and she dug it out, her heart doing something strangely like falling when she saw the message and realized what time it was.

"Sorry, I actually have to get going," she said, surprised to find she meant it. "Meeting my mom for dinner and it's a ways away, so I'll have to head out now." She tugged Olivia's ponytail and crouched down to be at her level. "I have to go, Olivia. But it was very nice to meet you, and thank you for the snow cone."

Olivia was entranced by a set of ducklings paddling after their mama down the river, but tore her gaze away. "You're welcome," she said formally, and Victoria stood to go.

"Uh, thanks for letting me crash," she said, not really sure how to end this strange encounter.

But Owen, of course, took it all in stride. "Thanks for entertaining the little monsters," he said with a grin and a glance at his half-sisters.

Victoria started off the bridge, headed back towards her apartment building several blocks from the river, but she couldn't help but keep looking back over her shoulder, watching Owen talk animatedly with the girls as they shrank in the distance.

Direct Messages: Luke @Lukethebarnyardcat

@Noraephronwasagenius
Do you ever just get sad sometimes? Or feel lonely? Isolated?

@Lukethebarnyardcat
I think everyone does, yeah. But I'm pretty good about reaching out to my friends when I think I need some support, you know?

@Noraephronwasagenius
I need to get better about that.

@Lukethebarnyardcat
For the record, I'll always be here to listen
I'm sorry you're lonely, but I promise, you're not alone

Chapter Eight

Olivia was singing softly to herself in the backseat when Owen killed the engine. He gave himself a second to check his phone, but then Olivia was unbuckling herself and squirming out of her seat. He hefted the still-sleeping Lily against his shoulder and bumped the door closed with his hip.

Ashley, with her perfectly highlighted blonde hair, burst from the door to gather Olivia into her arms. "How was the park?" she asked. Owen walked across the cobblestone-paved drive and up the steps to the Cape Cod style mansion his father had purchased for his third-time's-a-charm wife several years ago.

"We met Owen's friend!" Olivia announced proudly.

"He does have some of those," Ashley agreed. "What's on your face? Paint?"

"Snow cone," Owen admitted. "Tried to clean them off but was only moderately successful."

Ashley shrugged. "We'll just toss 'em in the lake before dinner. How long has Lily been out?"

"Pretty much since we left the park. Half hour, I'd say?"

"Then she'll probably sleep a bit longer. Want to put her to bed and meet us on the patio?"

"Deal," Owen agreed, already climbing the sweeping staircase that led up from the foyer. Aside from his own mother, Ashley was oddly enough his favorite of his father's wives. Wife #2 had been fresh from her own divorce and desperate for a Brady Bunch existence, only with housekeepers and a vaguely garish home on the other side of Lake Minnetonka from this one. She brought her own three kids with her, which meant four teenagers living under one roof, three of them resentful of Charles Pohl for breaking up their parents' marriage and one of them who was just plain resentful of Charles Pohl, period. Judith had spent four miserable years trying to play peacemaker between the kids and Charles, and everyone—especially Judith—had been relieved when Charles decided to throw in the towel.

But when Owen was in his first year of law school, he flew home for Thanksgiving to find Ashley Kaminski beaming at him from his father's side, as if were totally normal for a twenty-four-year-old woman to be dating a fifty-one-year-old man. Owen had been pissed at first, mostly at his father for being a goddamn parody of a rich man having a midlife crisis. He and Ashley hadn't been close in high school, but they knew each other well enough, and Owen was sickened that his dad would take advantage of someone so goddamn *nice.*

He still thought Ashley could do better than his dad, but this was now Charles' second-longest relationship after his marriage to Owen's mother, so something about them worked. For his own sanity, Owen told himself it was Ashley's generous nature and not anything else, and he generally tried to think of her as a fun stepsister, rather than his actual, legal stepmother.

He settled Lily into her race-car bed without her making so much as a peep, and by the time he made it to the patio Olivia was already in her swimsuit, wading out into the water. Patio, of course, was insufficient to describe the sweeping expanse of stone that spread out from a set of French doors just off the kitchen. Lounge chairs dotted the space and a pergola with Pinterest-ready light bulbs woven through the lattice covered the far corner. Everything about the entire house said "we have enough money to hire interior decorators," but Owen knew Ashley was responsible for most of it. She had a good eye for color and design and was almost always elbow deep in some sort of minor remodeling project even though the house was practically brand new.

Immaculately maintained grass covered the stretch of land between the patio and the beach, and Ashley was standing barefoot in the grass, watching Olivia.

"Is Lily still out?" Ashley asked. She had two beer bottles dangling from her fingertips and held one out to him.

"Like a rock." He accepted the beer from her and twisted the top off. "Where's the old man today?"

Ashley shot him a warning look because despite Owen's opinion of his father—spoiled, lazy, rich jerk—Ashley seemed to genuinely like him. She had to, seeing as she was married to him, but still, Owen couldn't resist a few digs here and there. "Golfing and no, I don't want to hear you bitch about it. He sees the girls plenty, and he's taking them both out on the boat all day tomorrow."

Owen shrugged. Down at the lake Olivia was busy with a project that mostly seemed to entail filling up buckets of water, hauling them to the small, sandy beach, and pouring that water into *different* buckets. A beat of silence passed and Ashley spoke again. "Olivia was very impressed by your friend today.

Apparently, she now *must* have jeans with holes in the knees, or else she'll simply *die*, so thanks for that. I was hoping to steer her towards preppy chic, but I guess I have to get ready for the inevitable rebellion from her mother's wishes."

Owen gestured to Ashley's own jeans with several of their own rips. "That's not entirely her fault, you know."

"Yeah, but up until now I had managed to convince her that these were jeans for moms *only*, and your friend went and ruined that lie."

"Shoulda come up with a better lie, then," he teased, and she shook her head.

"Olivia also seems to think your friend's name was Victoria, but that is impossible because the only Victoria you've ever mentioned is practically a super villain," she said pointedly.

Owen sipped his beer to buy himself time. "No, it was . . . her."

"Any reason you're hanging around with, and I quote, a robot with no soul?"

Olivia yelled for their attention just then, and both of them dutifully applauded when she poured a bucket of water right onto the sand. "Olivia ran off while I was changing Lily's diaper and found her, and then insisted Victoria get snow cones with us. And you know how Olivia is when she sets her mind to something."

"I'm sorry, I'm stuck on the part where you let Olivia run away?"

"I didn't *let* her run away. She just did."

"That doesn't make it better."

"I got her back, which is the salient point," he replied.

Ashley sighed. "And this horrific, soulless corporate attorney dropped everything to hang out with a five-year-old she's never met?"

"Yeah," Owen mumbled.

Ashley lifted a perfectly manicured eyebrow. "Something going on there?"

"No," he lied, perhaps a little too sharply because Ashley tilted her head to the side.

"You sure about that? Come on, tell your old mom the truth," she wheedled.

Owen glared at her. "Don't call yourself that."

"Then don't lie to me."

"It's nothing, okay?" he said, and Ashley ran her tongue across her teeth. "What?"

"You have a way of . . . deciding things about people."

"Oh boy, this is gonna be good."

"Shut up, I know you pretty well. Once you make up your mind about someone, that tends to be it. You refuse any other information that might contradict the narrative you have in your head. Like with—"

"Don't say it."

"I'll say whatever I want. It's like with your father. He's not the man you think he is. He's better than that. He's changed, and he's determined not to make the same mistakes he made before."

"Can we not do the whole Dad thing today?"

"Fine," Ashley agreed. "I'm just saying, the asshole you grouse about constantly doesn't really sound like someone who would agree to spend her free time explaining fashion to a bossy five-year-old."

"Olivia's not bossy, she's authoritative, and I do not talk about Victoria *constantly*," Owen said.

"She's my daughter and she's bossy as hell," Ashley corrected. "I love that about her. But I'm just saying, I sort of feel like maybe you're missing something when it comes to Queen

Victoria, because you do, in fact, talk about her all the damn time."

Victoria's face flashed behind his eyelids, her lips swollen and eyes soft. "Maybe," he conceded.

"You haven't dated anyone in a while. What's up with that?" Ashley said, not-so-subtly changing the subject and yet not changing it at the same time.

"Busy with work."

"And your stupid cat."

"Luke is *not* stupid," he argued. "He's a gentleman and a scholar."

"You sound like a crazy cat lady."

"And that sounds like a gendered insult and you're better than that, *Mom*," he snapped.

Ashley shook her head with sisterly annoyance. "Whatever. I'm just saying, you should get out there more." She turned to face him, blue eyes sharp. "Unless there already is someone?"

"Not really."

"Not really? So there *is* something with Victoria!" she crowed.

"No, not her. I—Jesus, this is hard to say out loud, so you have to promise not to laugh."

"When have I ever laughed at you?"

"You literally just did."

"Fine, I promise."

"I . . . talk to someone."

"I didn't realize they still did phone-sex hotlines," Ashley said drolly, and then slapped her hand over her mouth. "Shit, sorry, forgot. I'll be nice, I swear."

Owen scrubbed a hand across his face, his palm damp with condensation from the beer. "I met her online. On Twitter, not a dating app. And we just . . . click."

"And I assume she lives in, like, Siberia or someplace incredibly inaccessible?"

"Chicago, actually. We DM a lot."

"What's her name?"

"She goes by Nora online but I don't exactly know her real name. We agreed to keep things anonymous."

"So you guys like, what, sext?"

"How do you manage to sound ancient when you say that?"

"Because I'm married to a boomer."

Owen shook his head and lost a battle with a grin. "No, we don't sext. We just talk. A lot. She wants to keep things anonymous, so we've never even exchanged photos."

"Think she's lying about who she is?"

"It's the internet, of course she might be. But I don't think so, for some reason. It feels real."

"Why not just make it real? Chicago isn't very far away."

"I dunno. Don't really want to change how things are right now," he said and drained the last of his beer. "But I should get going." *Before my dad gets back and we have to pretend to like each other for your sake.*

Ashley gave him a friendly pat on the shoulder and he jogged down to the lake to hug Olivia goodbye. She left a large wet splotch on his shirt from her swimsuit and a metric ton of sand on his neck, but he didn't mind.

Kimmy Clemenceaux, born Kimberly Clemons of Fargo, North Dakota, had the same lithe build as her daughter and the same dark, raven hair. The roots were a little silver nowadays, but in her mid forties she still had a sparkling smile and an infectious, throaty laugh. She was waiting at their usual table at Ron's Roadside Tavern, a tiny hole in the wall just off the interstate twenty miles south of Minneapolis. Ron's was sort of a shit hole, to be quite frank, with sticky floors and bad lighting and pitchers of cheap, weak beer, but it had the two things Kimmy and Victoria loved: wings and karaoke.

Victoria's favorite memories growing up involved singing along to songs with her mother—in the car, in the living room, at the grocery store; anywhere there was music, really. She'd inherited Kimmy's rich alto but with slightly less range; her voice wavered on the high notes the way Kimmy's never did. By the time she was eighteen Kimmy was helping her sneak into bars for karaoke night. Not to drink—she was far too strict for that—but the mother-daughter duo quickly became famous for their duets in just about any town they lived in. Ever since law school, Victoria had made the drive down to Ron's every few weeks for karaoke night, and it was usually her favorite night of the month.

"You're glowing, baby," Kimmy said when she rose to hug her. "Did you have a good day?"

The question threw Victoria for a loop, because she *had*. With Owen, of all people. "Just happy to see you," she evaded.

Kimmy already had their usual pitcher of cheap beer sitting in the middle of the small, unsteady table. "So how is work? You still killing it?"

"You know it," Victoria said drily. Her mother was her biggest cheerleader and closest non-internet friend, and she wouldn't have it any other way. "But I'm dealing with You Know Who again."

"Rich Dickbag?"

"Yep," Victoria agreed, although her stomach did something strange at Owen's assigned nickname. Because the Owen she'd seen today was nothing of the sort, and she didn't like feeling that way. It threw her off balance and Victoria *hated* being off balance. "He took over another class action, so I'll be up to my elbows in depositions with him for the near future."

"What's his angle this time?"

She shrugged. "The usual; Smorgasbord makes its managers work overtime against their contracts. And yes, I know they do that, but, you know."

"It's your job," Kimmy finished. "I get it."

Victoria let her mom pour her a beer and they clinked their glasses together. Up on the stage a middle-aged man was struggling his way through "Desperado" and most of the audience were politely pretending he was hitting at least some of the notes. "When are we up?"

"I think there's three more people before us."

"Are we doing the usual?"

"For our first round, yeah," Kimmy confirmed. "What did you do today?"

"Sat outside and read," Victoria replied, even though that wasn't the whole truth. But talking about the details of her day would open her up to a whole host of questions she didn't want to deal with. "What about you? What's new with you?"

"I think that guy from receiving might ask me out," Kimmy said excitedly. "The cute one with the tattoos."

"Oh, really?" Victoria said, and they settled into their familiar roles. Kimmy talked about a man at work she was interested in—she still hadn't given up on finding her one true love despite her very dysfunctional taste in men, bless her—and Victoria stayed as neutral as possible on the topic. Her mother's endless cycle of men was one of the reasons she wasn't bothering with dating, even though Kimmy frequently hinted she should "get out there" more. Men would inevitably let her down and it was best to either keep things just physical, like with Owen, or make sure he didn't know the real her, like with Luke. It kept her from getting sidetracked but, more importantly, it kept her from being disappointed.

When their names were announced they walked to the stage to a smattering of applause. Ron's had its regulars, and she and Kimmy were something of a minor sensation. The familiar opening bars of the Annie Lennox's "Walking On Broken Glass" kicked off, and Victoria picked up the mic.

They had it down to an art. Their voices wove around each other, harmonizing and soaring when the song called for it. Kimmy was a born performer; the spotlight loved her and she loved it back. It didn't feel quite as natural to Victoria as it seemed for her mom, but this was something the two of them did together and Victoria loved the feeling that came with smiling at her mom across a cheap plywood stage, crowd clapping wildly for them. Kimmy bowed and held out her hands towards Victoria, who dipped into a little curtsy that had the crowd whistling even more. They high-fived and walked back to their seats, flush with the attention and satisfaction.

Direct Messages: Luke @Lukethebarnyardcat

@Noraephronwasagenius

Did I ever tell you I taught myself how to sew? I mean, Mom taught me the basics, but I figured most of the rest out myself. I got sick of kids making fun of me for my clothes not fitting right, so I just did it myself.

@Lukethebarnyardcat

You're a really impressive human, I hope you know that

Chapter Nine

"Can we see the rings?" Mark asked. They were crowded around a hightop table at Lake Monster Brewing, the din of the crowd nearly drowning out everyone's voices.

"You've definitely seen Cassie's ring," Andy replied. "She's had it for at least a year and it's sort of hard to miss."

"It almost blinded me when I saw it the first time," Owen agreed.

"I meant the *wedding* rings, not the engagement ring. Weren't you shopping for them this weekend?" Mark said.

Andy sighed, running his fingers through his jet-black hair. It fell back into place, completely unruffled. "This one's mine," he said, pulling out his phone. He pointing to a silvery, plain band. "And this is Cassie's." He flipped to the next photo, revealing a delicate arch of emeralds supported by twining curls of white-gold.

"Ooooh," Mark cooed, picking the phone up to look more closely at it. His broad shoulders took up nearly half the table and Owen had to move over. "What color are the bridesmaid dresses again?"

"Champagne. But it's just Cassie's sister standing up on her side, and my brother on mine. We're going for small and elegant."

"Small and elegant and two hundred and fifty guests," Owen interjected.

"Exactly. We're going big on some stuff, so we have to go minimalist on others," Andy said, lifting his IPA. "That's how you know we're classy." Mark opened his mouth and Andy cut him off. "Can we please talk about something other than my wedding? It's all we've been doing this weekend, and with Cassie so busy at work I'm going to be dealing with the florist and photographer for the next couple of weeks and I'm burned out. Plus my mom has started hinting that we should do the Korean ceremony the night before, instead of during the reception, so it's all I talk about these days."

"We just want to be supportive, bro," Mark said softly. He had the thick neck and build of a pro-wrestler, but the heart of a turn-of-the-millenium J.Lo movie.

Andy clapped him on the shoulder. "I know, I'm just tired. What's new with you guys?" Both Owen and Mark shrugged at exactly the same time. "Aren't you suing Smorgasbord again?" Andy asked.

"When am I not suing Smorgasbord?" Owen replied. "I think this one has a real shot, though."

"Gonna bring them down single-handedly?" Mark grinned.

"Something like that." A woman at a nearby table flicked her gaze over at Mark for the fourth time in an hour, and Owen elbowed him. "Speaking of single, that woman has been checking you out," he said lowly. There had been a few women throwing looks his way too, but he ignored them, not really wanting to think about what it meant that *Victoria* was the reason.

Andy surreptitiously glanced over and nodded in approval. "She's pretty," he agreed. "You should go talk to her."

Mark's ruddy complexion turned several shades redder. "Too pretty, maybe," he said, glancing at the woman. She had long, dark wavy hair and satiny brown skin, and they made eye contact. She smiled at him over her drink and then looked away.

"Believe in yourself, man," Owen said, and nudged him.

"I don't know," he said, still bright red. "She's probably all smart and shit and out of my league."

"According to Cassie, sometimes the smart ones want a big dumb one so you're in luck," Andy teased.

"Does that make you a big dumb one?" Owen asked.

"No comment," Andy replied.

Mark looked over at her again. "Should I?"

"Yes," Owen and Andy agreed in unison, shoving him towards her.

"What about you?" Andy asked when Mark was safely away.

"What about me?"

Andy rolled his eyes. "Don't play cagey with me. You seeing anyone? You seemed kind of down the other day, in our text."

"Not really."

"That's not a no. Who is she?"

"You're worse than my stepmom, you know that? At least Ashley has an excuse," Owen grumbled.

"Just want to see you happy, is all," Andy said mildly. "Is she nice?"

Nice wasn't really how he'd describe Victoria, but then again, he was realizing he wasn't quite able to get a grasp on her anymore. He knew how he felt about her, past-tense, but wasn't sure about his present-tense feelings for her. She was interesting, if nothing else, and definitely not who he thought she was. "She's a challenge," he said finally.

Andy's face lit up. "Those are the best. Cassie was a challenge," he said, face going just a little bit dreamy. "Is she a lawyer too?"

"I've said too much."

"So she is. Do we know her?" Owen glared at him and Andy put his hands up in surrender. "Fine, fine, you can tell me when you're ready. Should we sneak out of here while Mark is busy? That'll give him a reason to keep talking to her, or else he'll bail too early and won't get her number. Besides, Cassie is probably home from work by now and I miss her."

"You guys are so fucking sappy," Owen teased.

"Yep. And it's awesome," Andy said proudly. "You should try it some time."

Safely back home, Owen toed off his shoes and scratched Luke's ears in hello. The house was blessedly quiet after the roar of the brewery, and his ears rang in the silence. He was sure Andy and Cassie knew Victoria from law school, but he wasn't sure exactly how he'd broach that. *There's this woman I sort of hate but also sometimes we hook up; what do you know about her?* But some instinct made him decide he'd rather keep whatever he had with Victoria close to his chest. Ashley's accusations rang in his ears, but puzzling out Victoria would likely involve spending significantly more time together, and aside from a few more scheduled depositions and then negotiations, he didn't see that happening. And depositions were hardly a situation where you could get to know someone. Unless he started pulling more stunts like the stairwell or her office, which he really shouldn't.

Luke bumped his face against Owen's shoulder for attention and he sighed. "Don't look at me like that, Rogue Leader," he scowled. "I'm basically between a rock and hard place here." Luke meowed, unperturbed, and he scooped him into his lap.

He checked his Twitter DMs to see a short, innocuous message from Nora. He should respond, but his heart wasn't in it. He wished he could see her in person, or hell, even know her real name. The anonymity was wearing thin for him, and deep down, he wanted what Andy had with Cassie—a real partner. He had half of one with Victoria and half of one with Nora, but that wasn't enough—with either of them. And that made him feel selfish.

Fine, he was lonely. He could admit that to himself, but only now, when it was late and he'd had enough to drink that he could face it.

His phone buzzed with a text message, but he ignored it. It was probably Mark, scolding him and Andy for bailing, but he wasn't about to let Mark get out of it that easily. His romantic-but-shy soul needed a push sometimes, and if he wasn't clicking with the pretty woman in the bar, he knew how to call an Uber home. Better to let Mark flail on his own a bit and make it up to him with lunch sometime in the next few weeks.

Owen checked Luke's water dish and flopped down on the couch. His phone buzzed on the table again, reminding him of the text, and he sighed, hauling himself up to get it. He looked at the screen, blinked, and looked again.

His mind was playing tricks on him. It had to be. Or else someone was pranking him, because there was no way—no fucking way—this text was real.

(507) 555-3901

It's Victoria. Don't freak out, I got your number from your email signature.

Are you up?

Owen scrubbed his hand across his face, still not believing what he was seeing. *Are you up?* He knew exactly what that meant, and he knew she did too. Those three words had precisely one meaning. He was partially surprised she hadn't gone with the even more informal and cryptic *wyd*, but then again, she probably didn't want to risk miscommunication. Because of course she was precise, even when setting up booty calls.

Are you up? He never expected to get this text from Victoria, and now he couldn't stop thinking about what it meant. It meant she was 1) awake, although that wasn't too strange since it was barely midnight on a Saturday, 2) awake and *thinking about him* at midnight on a Saturday, and 3) willing to hook up with him again, despite her stated intentions the other night.

It wasn't that the idea hadn't crossed his mind. It had, and with striking regularity. But he hadn't considered that she was thinking about it too, and all thoughts of turning in flew out of his head.

Owen Pohl
Yeah, I'm up

Direct Messages: Luke @Lukethebarnyardcat

@Noraephronwasagenius
When presented with a wide variety of choices, I am eerily good at choosing the worst fucking one.

@Lukethebarnyardcat
Are you me? Because this is very me

Chapter Ten

Victoria blew out a long breath. *Yeah, I'm up.* The four minutes between hitting send on that text and his response had been the longest, most excruciating four minutes of her life. She had stared at her phone for a solid twenty minutes before she sent it. This opened her up to him, put the power in his hands. She would be vulnerable the moment she hit send, and might remain so if he never responded. But she had been restless all day, unable to settle on anything. Day had dragged into night and by ten she'd given in and admitted she was horny. It took another hour for her to admit to herself her vibrator wasn't cutting it because there was one person in particular she wanted to sate her urges, and then another forty minutes of indecision while she told herself it was unprofessional and stalkerish to call up his work emails and steal his phone number from them.

But it had paid off—or it seemed it would, rather.

Victoria Clemenceaux
Wanna come over?

She made herself turn her phone over on the couch cushion so she wouldn't be tempted to track his response time. She had thought about offering to go to his place, but if she was going to open herself up like this she wanted to maintain some power and control. She picked at her cuticles until her phone beeped with a response.

Owen Pohl
Send me your address

After another long exhale she sent it to him, along with some instructions for parking. She'd hate for him to be towed during a hookup, if only because then she'd have to drive him to the impound lot. The more transactional they kept this, the better.

Victoria floated aimlessly around her apartment while she waited. She knew exactly how long it took to get from his house to her apartment—twenty-three minutes if there wasn't traffic—and there was no point in looking for him any sooner. She put her wine glass in the sink and brushed a few minuscule crumbs off the counter. She cinched her robe tighter around her waist and considered changing to something more provocative, but in the end she decided against it. A bralette and boyshorts were perfectly sexy on their own, and her robe just dusted the tops of her thighs. She had some lingerie tucked away somewhere but she didn't feel like wrestling herself into a corset just for Owen. Or maybe she wanted to see his reaction to her when she wasn't madeup. It wasn't a test, not exactly, but she was curious. Was he attracted to her as a *person* or just as a hot woman he got to have sex with? Some men took a lack of makeup as a personal affront, like she owed them that time and effort. She wanted to see what sort of man Owen was, deep down. Did he want to have sex with *her* or with a woman who was perfectly coiffed at all times?

She'd bang him either way tonight, but she wanted to know which type he was. For science.

She was considering pouring herself another glass of wine and bolting it down for courage when her intercom trilled atonally. The clock above the stove said it had been exactly twenty-seven minutes since her last text. She buzzed him in and unlocked her door, making one last haphazard circle around her living room because she literally didn't know what else to do. Owen knocked and she called for him to come in.

The door clicked shut softly. Victoria paused against the back of the couch and met his gaze across the room. She wondered if he had gotten dressed when she called, or if this was just what he'd been wearing today, but either way, her mouth went dry. The navy blue Henley stretched tight across his chest, and his jeans were molded to his thighs, the powerful muscles there bunching as he walked slowly towards her.

Victoria gripped the back of the couch for support even as she leaned nonchalantly against it. "I take it you found it okay?" she said, as if this were a totally normal thing she did with Owen all the time, instead of something terrifying and blatantly unprofessional. Although to be fair, they'd blown past that line several orgasms ago.

"No, your directions were terrible; that's why I wound up in Iowa instead of here in your apartment," he said wryly, his eyes dropping to her breasts. She tugged the end of her sash and her robe fell open, the silk sliding against her skin. He groaned softly and rested his hand on the curve of her waist. His other hand rose up to tug the band around her braid free. She tipped her face forward as he unraveled the strands, his fingers brushing her collarbone with each stroke. "Before we get started," he said, sounding more than a little dazed, "we should probably have some ground rules."

"Ground rules, sure," she said breathlessly. His thumb moved in a slow arc, back and forth across her side, and she threaded her fingers into his hair.

The hand on her hip drifted lower, flirting with the waistband of her shorts before sliding between her thighs. His palm cupped her mound firmly and she sucked in a sharp breath. "You don't get to kick me out the second we're finished," he warned.

She kept her hand on his jaw, his face just inches from hers. "Didn't take you for a cuddler," she said as lightly as she could. His fingers traced her folds through the cotton, the pressure maddening and enticing all at once.

"There's a lot you don't know about me. But even if this is just a quick screw, I'm not skulking out immediately like there's something to be ashamed of."

Her stomach flipped over at his words. "Fine. But you can't spend the night."

"No sleeping over, got it," he said, and ground the heel of his palm against her clit until she whined.

"Anything else?" she asked, impatient.

"Not at the moment, no," he said with a smirk.

Half of her wanted to wipe that grin off his face and the other half of her was going out of her skin, so Victoria cracked. "Then fuck me," she ordered, and sealed her lips to his.

She was going to kill him. His autopsy was going to read "Cause of death: Victoria Clemenceaux," and he couldn't even be mad about it because this was the way to go: her lips hungrily seeking his, her body soft and pliable against him. He'd never seen her like this and it was dangerous, because he liked her this way, vulnerable and undone. He suspected few people got to see Victoria like this and the possessive, prideful part of him preened.

He had always thought of her as a slinky nightgown type of woman but the way she looked tonight—a simple bra and panties and a robe that was hardly more than a scrap of silk—worked for her too. He'd been temporarily struck dumb when he saw her, entranced by the braid dangling over one shoulder and the way she clamped her lower lip between her teeth.

But now, with her hair loose around her shoulders and spilling through his fingers, he wondered if he'd ever really been alive before. Owen pulled her back to him, unable to resist tipping her face to his for another kiss. Twined together, they stumbled towards what he assumed was her bedroom, but he wasn't about to stop kissing her to check.

God, he liked kissing her. He took her face in his hands and tilted it to the side for better access, his tongue seeking hers languidly. She looped her arms around his neck and smiled against his mouth, nipping playfully at his lower lip and pulling back to make him chase her. He nudged her back against the mattress and followed her, covering her with the full length of his body before letting her roll them over.

It was so easy, being with Victoria. So easy and so, so good. They had left a trail of clothing behind them, and when she finally rid him of his underwear, her hand around his cock made him groan. Being inside her was better than anything he'd ever felt, and while she braced herself against her headboard Owen pressed his head into the pillows, letting her ride him. She was close, he could tell, so close her muscles were trembling and she'd lost the power of speech. Victoria dropped her hand between her thighs and he pushed it away, replacing her fingers with his. He wanted to be the one who gave her this, the need so strong and deep it felt like it had always existed.

She made a noise that sounded something like *please* and he kept going, pulling her with him until they both let go.

They collapsed into a sweaty tangle of limbs. Owen tugged her back to him, unable to resist tipping her face to his for another kiss. He hauled her half on top of him, rearranging them until her head was resting against his chest. She sighed and Owen kissed the top of her head, trying to remember the last time his heart felt so light and full at the same time.

"Remember, this was our deal," he said, but there was a note of humor in his voice and part of her was glad he was holding her to it. She let her leg settle between his and rested her head on the soft space between his shoulder and chest. Without thinking, she pressed a kiss to his skin and trailed her fingers up and down his arm.

"Just don't let me fall asleep," she mumbled, because already she could feel herself melting into him. There was a good chance she would be mortified by how defenseless she was later, but right now, all she wanted was to listen to the steady thump of his heart.

"Scout's honor," he promised.

Owen's arm came up around her back and he carded his fingers through her long, tangled tresses. His nails scraped at her scalp and she moaned softly. She felt, rather than saw, him smile in response, and he nestled just a little closer to her. "Tell me something about yourself," he said after several long moments had passed. "I feel like I know a lot about you, but I don't, really."

"What do you want to know?" she asked sleepily.

He shrugged with his free shoulder. "I dunno. Just something about you. Where'd you grow up? You said you had grandparents in Fargo?"

"Yeah, but I grew up all over," she said, yawning. "Mom and I moved around a lot."

"It was just the two of you?"

"Yep. Think *Gilmore Girls*, but make it trailer park."

Owen chuckled and then fell silent, frowning. "Hey, random question—do you have a Twitter account?"

Victoria froze. She had no idea what would make him ask that, but she knew she didn't want him to find her account. It felt too personal, even for someone who had made her come just a few minutes ago. "Nope," she said, hoping she sounded breezy. "Don't really have time for much social media. I've got a sorely neglected Facebook account but that's it."

Owen made a soft noise in response and dropped a kiss to the top of her head. She let out a long breath, willing herself to relax again, and snuggled deeper into his embrace. "What about you? What was your childhood like?" she asked.

"Very un-*Gilmore Girls* like, I'm afraid." She swatted at him and he laughed. It was a deep, rumbling sound, and suddenly she wanted to take back her earlier rule and ask him to spend the night, but kept that urge tucked away. "I grew up around here."

"I already knew that. Tell me something else."

"Something else," he murmured. His fingers were still working through the knots in her hair, gentle and deft. "Okay, how's this. I wanted to be a veterinarian when I was little, but then I found out it wasn't just playing with cats all day, so I decided to be a lawyer."

"How old were you?"

"Twelve, maybe?"

"You decided that young?" she asked, and he shrugged again.

"My dad hated lawyers, and I, uh, sort of hated my dad, so I figured that was it. And then I turned out to like it and be pretty good at it, so I guess it all worked out."

"Mmmm," she said in response, his slow, steady touches easing her dangerously toward sleep. He fell silent, and she might have been about to drift off when he spoke again.

"Hey," he said, moving his arm underneath her. "Hey—you said no sleepovers, remember?"

"Mmmph," she said this time, reluctantly rolling to her side to let him sit up. "I should—I should walk you out," she said, but a jaw-splitting yawn caught her off-guard.

Owen touched her cheek. "Don't worry. I'll lock up on my way out."

Part of her wanted just a little more time with him, but another part of her was already three-quarters of the way asleep, and when Owen pulled the comforter up around her shoulders, she let that side win.

Direct Messages: Nora @Noraephronwasagenius

@Lukethebarnyardcat

Sick days for me were a lot of *The Price is Right* and soup made by the housekeeper

@Noraephronwasagenius

Okay, I don't normally say this seriously, but poor little rich boy.

That is depressing as hell and makes me want to build a time machine and take care of you.

Chapter Eleven

Owen checked the phone number three times before hitting dial. It wasn't strictly something that needed to be done today—or at any point in the next three weeks, really—but he was just a mere mortal and Victoria was, well, Victoria. And maybe he felt like hearing her voice.

The phone rang and a young administrative assistant answered, his tone robotically professional but pleasant as he ran through the corporate-mandated greeting. "Victoria Clemenceaux, please," Owen requested.

"I'm sorry, she's out today—would you like to leave a message with me, speak to another attorney, or would you like her voicemail?"

"She's out?" he said, suddenly tripping over his words. "I was just calling to schedule—It doesn't matter. Is she sick?"

"She didn't say. Would you like to leave a message?"

"Uh—no, I'll call back another time," he said, and hung up. He looked at the time, debated briefly, and then decided to hell with it.

The soup from the deli was starting to cool when he arrived at her apartment. He had planned on leaving it with the front desk, but then he realized if she were sick, she might not want to walk all the way down there to pick it up. Instead he took the elevator to her floor and knocked softly.

But before she could open the door, doubt seized him. *Wait. This is creepy, isn't it? What if she isn't even here? Her secretary said she was out, maybe she's just at a deposition for another lawsuit or something. Oh fuck, abort, abort, abort*—He set the soup down in front of her door and was halfway down the hall, almost free, when he heard her voice.

"Owen?"

Slowly, he spun around. "Uh, hey."

"Is this . . . soup?" She appeared perfectly healthy, the cylindrical container clutched in her left hand.

"Yeah, uh . . ." He looked around, hoping a hellmouth would open and swallow him whole, but he was completely out of luck. "I—I called your office this morning and they said you were out, and I thought you might be sick, and I, uh, jumped to about fifteen assumptions that were clearly incorrect," he stammered.

Victoria bit her lower lip but couldn't quite smother her smile. "You thought I was sick so you brought me soup?"

"Yes?" he said, answering her grin with his own hesitant one.

She shook her head and gestured towards her door. "Come on in, then."

Victoria might not look sick, but she was far more casual than he'd ever seen her, save the other night. Her grey sweatpants molded to her body as she walked and a black sports bra poked out from the baggy neckline of her loose teal sweatshirt, while her hair was piled into a messy knot on the very top of her head.

Meg Ryan was frozen mid-sentence on her television, and her laptop and phone were scattered across her coffee table. "So . . . not sick then?" he said, leaning a little awkwardly against her counter.

Victoria pulled down two bowls from a cabinet and shrugged. The movement sent her sweatshirt further down her shoulder and he couldn't help but watch it intently. "Giving myself a mental health day to play hooky. Mom used to let me do it once a semester in school, and I kept it up. Sometimes she comes up and we go shopping, but today I just felt like doing absolutely nothing."

She divided the soup between the bowls. Owen rubbed the back of his neck, skin still a little flushed with embarrassment. "You don't—we don't have to eat that, you know. It was dumb."

She shrugged again, and she really needed to stop doing that because he was far too entranced by her collarbone to be healthy. "I was about to eat lunch anyway, and there's plenty here. Do you have any particular objections to *When Harry Met Sally*?"

"Only that the movie is based on the fallacy that men and women can't be friends when they demonstrably can."

"Oh good, you're pedantic. This'll be fun," she deadpanned. They pushed her electronics out of the way and set their bowls on the coffee table.

Owen stole a glance at her, wondering if he should just go with this—which was great, if weird—or ask what the hell was going on. In the end, his curiosity won out. "What, uh . . . what exactly is happening?"

Victoria crossed her legs and picked up her soup. "We're watching a movie and eating the lunch you brought me," she said drily. "What about that is confusing?"

"I mean, just that—well, you know—"

"We hate each other, except for when we're fucking?"

"Yeah, that," he laughed.

"You were the one bringing me soup," she countered. "I figure, if you're gonna do that, we can hang out. Why not, you know?"

"Why not," he agreed, smiling broadly.

"Next up is *While You Were Sleeping*," she announced, unfolding her legs. It was weird, sitting next to Owen on the couch like they were friends instead of . . . whatever it was they were, but when she'd seen him in the hallway, looking so goddamn embarrassed for having been caught caring about her, she couldn't help herself.

Even weirder, as the day wore on, she had absolutely no inclination to kick him out. They had moved from *When Harry Met Sally* to *Sleepless in Seattle* and now she was feeling like a slight change of pace. As it turned out, Owen was surprisingly a lot of fun to hang out with, even when his sisters weren't around. They were in their own little bubble, ignoring all of the outside world's complications. Like the fact that they were on opposite sides of a major lawsuit.

"And here I thought it was a Meg Ryan day," he said.

"It's a whatever-movie-I-want-to-watch day, and I want to watch Sandra Bullock catfish an entire family."

Owen wrinkled his nose. "That one's kinda creepy when you think about the plot, you know," he said from where he was lounging against the opposite side of her couch.

"So? Sandra Bullock is a goddamn gift to mankind, and her charm saves it," she argued. "Also, my day, my rules."

"Fine, but you're paying for the pizza."

But an hour later when the pizza arrived, he was just as into it as she was. "Peter Gallagher is a really underrated actor, you know," he said. "Between this and *The OC*, he really should be in more stuff. He's hilarious."

"And he was great in *Center Stage*," she agreed.

"I haven't seen that one."

"You're missing out, then. I bet your sisters would like it too—it's about ballet and finding yourself and god, it's just so good."

"I'll schedule a viewing," he said, putting the pizza on the counter.

Victoria scrounged up some plates and Owen pulled a couple of beers from her fridge. He paused closing it, frowning at the wedding invite she had stuck to the freezer door. "You know Andy and Cassie?" he asked.

"Went to law school with them, yeah. Are you going to their wedding?"

"Yep. You?"

Victoria sat down on her couch and picked up a slice of pizza. "Nah, I missed the RSVP deadline. How do you know them?" She adored Cassie but the wedding was up in Duluth, which meant paying for a hotel room and Victoria hadn't felt she could justify the expense.

"Interned with Andy one summer. It'll be fun; too bad you can't make it."

Victoria made a non-committal noise and they restarted the movie. Cassie's wedding sat heavily on her mind, because the money excuse suddenly seemed flimsy. It would be more expensive than she usually allowed herself, for sure, but Victoria genuinely liked Cassie, unlike most of her law school classmates. Most of them came from money, although probably not as much money as Owen. But they were the sort of people who were the richest kids in their high schools, and while they quickly accepted Victoria as one of them she kept most of them at arm's length. Cassie, though, had never made her feel awkward like that. She scrunched her face up in disappointment, feeling suddenly sheepish about how cheap she could be sometimes.

"What's wrong?" he asked.

"Eh, just having some second thoughts," she said with a shrug. "But what's done is done."

"So come with me," he said without looking at her, and her mouth went dry.

"Wait, what? Really?"

"I have a hotel room and a plus one, and Andy's one of my best friends. I'll just tell him I'm bringing someone. You wanted to go, and now you can. You can stay with me."

"Are you—are you sure?"

He glanced at her, a grin playing at the corner of his lips. "I've been inside of you. Pretty sure that's more intimate than staying in a room with two beds. And I can keep my hands to myself so long as you can, if that's what you're worried about." She narrowed her eyes and tossed a throw pillow at him, but he caught it easily. "Do you want to come?"

"I do, yeah."

"Then it's a date," he said, making her stomach flip.

Latest Tweets

@Noraephronwasagenius

Do you ever just wish you could take a weekend and escape from your life for a while?

@Lukethebarnyardcat

Every damn day

@Lukethebarnyardcat

But also there's this thing called "vacation" and you're definitely allowed to take one

@Noraephronwasagenius

oh my god I hate you.

@Lukethebarnyardcat

Do you? Do you really? Or do you love me and my rakish charm?

@Noraephronwasagenius

. . . I plead the fifth on that one.

Maddy H @MadisonHughes95

Keep your flirting in the DMs like RESPECTABLE MILLENIALS my god

@Lukethebarnyardcat

Sorry Maddy

Maddy H @MadisonHughes95

You better be jfc

Chapter Twelve

@Noraephronwasagenius
How goes things with Ice Princess?

Owen almost dropped his phone. He hadn't expected Nora to bring Victoria up, although in retrospect he wasn't sure why he was surprised. He used to make trashing Victoria a part-time job, but he had let that fall by the wayside lately. And now they had plans to go to a wedding together—a wedding out of town, no less—so he probably shouldn't badmouth her to Nora, even if Nora was an internet stranger, more or less.

@Lukethebarnyardcat
They're fine. Status quo, really

The lie sat awkwardly on his shoulders, even if it was nothing more than a little white lie in the end. He desperately wanted Nora's take on things, but it felt somehow dishonorable to share his feelings for Victoria with her. He was starting to feel like he was using Nora for emotional intimacy while having Victoria for physical intimacy, and that made him feel like a goddamn jackass. It wasn't cheating, not quite, but it made him feel like he might be.

Obviously, the answer was to come clean. Maybe not to Victoria yet—*I have an internet friend who I tell everything to and I care a lot about her but maybe I also care about you* was a tough sell to someone you knew well, much less someone with the history he had with Victoria—but he probably owed Nora something close to the truth.

But then Nora might think less of him, and that felt unbearable. Nora's good opinion mattered to him, and if she thought he was the sort of man who would string two women along, even if one was perfectly clear about what she wanted and it wasn't a physical relationship with him, he'd be crushed.

@Noraephronwasagenius
She's not giving you any trouble?

@Lukethebarnyardcat
Not any more than usual

Owen furrowed his brow and decided it was time to steer the conversation into calmer waters, waters that wouldn't make him feel like he was more like his father than he was comfortable admitting.

@Lukethebarnyardcat
Any plans for this weekend?

Victoria wrinkled her nose and stared at Luke's seemingly innocuous question. *Any plans for the weekend?*

She still hadn't told him about Owen and the upcoming wedding, because honestly, how did you explain that mess to someone?

Well, more accurately, how did you explain a wedding date with her hate-sex-semi-fuckbuddy-slash-mortal-enemy to someone she sort of had feelings for who was an internet friend she never intended to meet? She honestly didn't know how to explain it to herself, which was why she was doing her best to not really think about it.

And so instead of responding and continuing their conversation, she did the unthinkable.

She closed her laptop.

Victoria got up and paced around her apartment, rinsing out her wineglass and loading the dishwasher. *I'm not avoiding him, I'm just getting some chores done*, she told herself. Her phone beeped with a notification, and she closed her eyes, wondering what the fuck she was doing.

Not just with Owen, but with Luke. Part of her wondered if it was cruel to get so close to someone you were never going to meet, but then again, she had been up-front with him about it from the beginning, so it wasn't like she was leading him on or lying to him in any real way.

But still, it didn't quite feel right, especially now that she was . . . something with Owen. It felt unfair to have both men in her life like this, and she wasn't sure how to define what she had with either of them.

The longest she had ever gone without talking to Luke since their first couple messages was twenty-four hours over Christmas. Even if they just checked in with each other they always made time for each other, no matter what. But the thought of talking to Luke while spending the weekend with Owen made her stomach roil. She put her phone on Do Not Disturb, feeling like a piece of crap.

Direct Messages: Nora @Noraephronwasagenius

@Lukethebarnyardcat
What's on your mind today?

@Noraephronwasagenius
What do you think of marriage?

@Lukethebarnyardcat
Oh okay we're going big today, got it

@Noraephronwasagenius
Don't mock, I'm serious. What do you think about marriage?

@Lukethebarnyardcat
Like, as a concept?

@Noraephronwasagenius
Yeah.

@Lukethebarnyardcat
🤷🤷 I do want to get married. I just don't think I've met the right person, you know?

@Noraephronwasagenius
Same. I want to get married, but sometimes I wonder if I'm capable of being that selfless? I don't know, it seems hard. And I don't really have a good model for it. My dad was literally never around, and my mom's good guy radar has been on the fritz for a long time.

@Lukethebarnyardcat
Me either. Here's to being selfish assholes?

@Noraephronwasagenius
Clink clink, motherfucker.

Chapter Thirteen

Owen set his glass back down on the bar and checked his watch. The wedding wasn't due to start for another ten minutes, but Victoria hardly seemed like the sort of person who would cut things close. She had shooed him out of the hotel room a solid forty minutes ago to get ready, less out of shyness and more because he was *in her damn way.*

A few other wedding guests trickled out of the hotel bar and he fiddled with his cufflinks. By all rights a two-hour drive to Duluth with Victoria should have been at least a little awkward, but it wasn't. It was *fun.* Victoria had started out with a pile of work—not on their case, she had warned him almost immediately—but by the time they were out of the Cities and had hit open road, he had talked her into packing it away. She mocked his playlists but picked one anyway, and then Owen learned something unexpected:

Victoria had a gorgeous voice. It was low and sultry and he was, for the first time in his life, slightly self-conscious about his croaking, off-key singing. Normally he belted it out and damn the critics, but this time, he decided to listen. And when he turned into the hotel parking lot and his heart sank at the thought of turning off the music, he realized that this trip was a very stupid idea indeed.

It was something he had known on some level since he decided to try and play knight in shining armor by bringing her soup, and possibly for longer, but now it was utterly undeniable.

He had feelings for Victoria. Real, actual feelings; not just lust. He liked that she was prickly and complicated and he liked that there was a side of her that he had to work to see. He'd always appreciated a challenge, and Victoria was nothing if not that.

But he wasn't quite sure how she felt about him. It was entirely possible this was all just lust and attraction for her, even if she seemed to be lowering her walls for him just a little. Plus there was the Nora factor to consider, and he just didn't even know how to begin to untangle that.

"Ready?"

Owen turned and choked on his tongue. He thought he was prepared to see Victoria in black tie—leave it to Andy and Cassie to throw themselves the fanciest wedding of the year—but he wasn't. Not in the slightest. Her floor-length dress was nothing more than a simple, beaded sheath, but the deep purple hue set off her eyes like nothing he'd ever seen before, and it clung to her like a second skin.

She arched an eyebrow. "Owen? The wedding?"

"Right. The wedding," he sputtered. Leaving his glass on the bar he walked with her to the room in the back of the building where the ceremony was set to begin. Huge windows opened up onto Lake Superior, a deep blue on this late autumn afternoon. Trees framed the view to the left, orange and red on the spit of land that stretched out into the lake, waves crashing against the rocks below. The hotel itself was a Gilded Age stunner, but Owen hardly even noticed the gleaming floors or impressive chandeliers because when Victoria turned around he realized her dress had a long, draping neckline that left her entire back bare. His fingers itched to touch her skin but he curled his hand into a fist instead.

The ceremony was short but beautiful. Owen barely heard a word, even though these were two of his best friends getting married, because he kept glancing over at Victoria, wondering if she was real. She kept twisting the program into a tight cylinder and then unrolling it, and he once again had to curl his hands into fists to keep from weaving their fingers together. He had promised to keep his hands to himself, after all, and anyway, hand-holding was not a part of their deal, even if he wasn't completely sure what their deal was. They really needed to have a goddamn conversation about this.

But when they stood to go join the receiving line, Victoria shocked him by nonchalantly holding her hand out to him. He took it without comment, uncomfortably aware that his heart rate had sped up. Last time he had gotten this worked up over hand-holding he had been fifteen and worried Sarah Collins would notice his palms were sweating while they walked to third period math class. Victoria didn't seem perturbed by it at all, sweaty palms or no, and he let himself lace his fingers with hers as they walked. Every cell in his body screamed for him to pull her aside and ask her if they could talk about what they were, but the fear that she'd laugh at him and confirm that it was just sexual attraction kept him quiet. He allowed himself to rest his hand on her lower back while they searched for their table, her skin smooth and warm to the touch, and he was almost positive her smile lingered on him longer than usual.

Owen pulled out her chair just as Mark and Priyanka slid

into their seats. Mark and Priyanka had been nearly inseparable since that night at the bar, a fact Andy annoyingly took sole credit for in their group chat as often as humanly possible, completely disregarding Owen's protests that he deserved at least fifty percent of the credit. Owen hadn't told Mark he was bringing anyone, largely because he half-assumed Victoria would bail at the last minute. But for once in his damn life, Mark played it cool and stuck his hand out for Victoria to shake and introduced himself. "Are you a friend of Owen's?" he asked mildly, flicking his eyes toward Owen.

"I know him from work," she said vaguely, which earned Owen another pointed glance from Mark. "Are you a lawyer too?"

"Ugh, no," Mark said, wrinkling his nose. "Oh, shit—Sorry, didn't mean to offend you. But no, I'm a gym teacher."

"None taken. And what about you?" Victoria said, directing her attention to Priyanka.

"Grad student; English lit," she replied. She shifted her chair closer to the table. "I thought Owen worked for himself?"

"He does. We've just met through a couple of cases," Victoria said smoothly. "But grad school, huh? Are you doing an MA or a PhD?"

Priyanka launched into an explanation of her doctoral work on the colonialist underpinnings of eighteenth-century environmentalist poetry while they waited for their food. But Mark wasn't to be dissuaded. He waited until Priyanka was finished, watching her the whole time with a soft smile, and then turned back to Victoria. "When you say you know him from some cases, what does that mean, exactly?"

Owen glared at him, but Victoria took the bull by the horns. "It means I work for Smorgasbord. I'm their in-house counsel," she said, and Mark's eyebrows hit his hairline.

"But you *hate* Smorgasbord. And you hate—" Mark's brain caught up with his mouth and he broke off. "You hate, uh, big corporations," he finished awkwardly.

"Good cover," Victoria said drily. "You definitely weren't going to say he hates me."

"I wasn't—"

"You were, though," Priyanka chimed in, grinning at Victoria. "You're a really bad liar, babe."

"I didn't—I wasn't going to—" he spluttered.

"Sure you weren't," Priyanka said and patted his hand on top of the tablecloth. "But obviously, if you're here with him, Owen must not hate you that much," she added.

"Honestly, I think the jury's still out on that one," Victoria said.

"Are either of you going to let me defend myself?" Owen asked.

"No," Victoria and Priyanka said simultaneously, and burst into laughter.

Mark looked at him from across the table. "I think we're screwed, bro," he said, resigned.

Victoria and Priyanka shared another smile. "You are," they said in unison.

The rest of the dinner went quickly. Victoria seemed to genuinely like Mark, which warmed Owen's heart more than he could say, and Mark spent a considerable amount of time enthusiastically gushing over Priyanka's research. Mark was smitten, and Owen didn't blame him—Priyanka was smart and funny and sharp, and watching her and Victoria unite to tease him and Mark was his favorite part of the night.

The official first dances finished and Owen looked over at Victoria, surprised to find her shrinking back warily. She had been vivacious all through dinner, but now she looked hesitant.

Their table emptied out as people rushed to join the crush on the dance floor, and Owen lifted his eyebrow. "I don't dance," Victoria said.

"Everyone dances," he countered.

"Not in public."

"But you were getting along so well with Mark and Priyanka," he argued.

"Exactly. That makes it worse. They're your friends. Strangers, fine, but—" She broke off and chewed on her lower lip. This shyness didn't fit with the confident, fearless woman he'd met in the courtroom, but then again dancing was slightly different from litigating. Oddly enough, not wanting to dance in front of people she knew made him think of Nora, but it felt vaguely deceitful to both of them to be here with Victoria and thinking of her. Impulsively, he stood and held his hand out. "Come on, with me," he said, and when she slipped her fingers in his he wanted to crow with triumph.

It took a little more coaxing—and a lot of Owen's beatless flailing—before she fully got into it, but once she did, he was right: she was a great dancer. And she seemed to play to an audience, which didn't quite square with her earlier reticence, but he decided he would puzzle that out later.

A soft, lilting cover of "Can't Help Falling In Love" kicked in. Mark had his arms already wrapped around Priyanka's waist, sap that he was, and Victoria turned to go but once again Owen caught her hand and spun her back around. "Really?" she asked.

"If you're willing," Owen replied, but she was already stepping into his arms. This close he could smell her perfume, the subtle, rich scent stirring his chest. He closed his eyes and she leaned her cheek against his, sighing softly. In her heels, they were almost the same height. Owen readjusted his hand on her back, pressing her closer until she was molded against him.

"You know, as cheesy as it is, I prefer the Elvis version of this song," she said quietly.

"I'm never going to be able to pin down what type of music you like, am I? Nirvana, Elvis—nothing about you is what I expect," Owen replied.

"And that's the way it's going to stay," she teased. "Where would the fun be in knowing everything about each other?"

Owen was seized with the desire to say something completely stupid, like *I could spend the rest of my life learning about you*, but he caught himself just in time. "Good thing I like a challenge," he said instead, and she smiled against his neck.

"I feel like I should protest being categorized as a challenge."

"And I feel like you should recognize a compliment when you get one," he rejoined.

Victoria snorted and he tucked her against him more closely. "You're pretty challenging yourself, you know."

"Yeah, I know," he said, and he could practically feel her eyes roll.

"Are you always this exhausting?"

"Always," he said, grinning.

Victoria lifted her head and looked him in the eye. He couldn't remember her ever looking at him like this, soft and serious. "Thank you. For bringing me along."

"You're glad you came?" His throat was thick and he had to clear it a few times.

"Yeah, I am." Victoria said. She licked her lips, eyes darting to his mouth. He wondered if she could feel his heart pounding through his suit. "Thank you."

"No, thank you. You're a hell of a dancer," he said, steering them into much safer waters.

The heaviness of a moment ago lifted. "Well I'm certainly better than you," she laughed.

"That's not exactly hard."

"No, it really isn't," she said. Impulsively he brushed a kiss to her temple, and when she didn't pull away he swept his thumb back and forth across the delicate bump of her lower spine. She ducked her head to his shoulder again and they swayed in place, her hand coming to rest just above his heart with his own hand covering it. Slowly Owen dipped his head down until his lips met the juncture of her neck and shoulder. Victoria shivered and goosebumps broke out across her skin. She made a quiet noise in her throat and he wanted to curse the DJ when the next song began and it was "Shout" instead of another slow song.

Victoria pulled away reluctantly and silence hung awkwardly between them. They kept veering towards "acting like we're legitimately dating" and Owen couldn't tell how genuine it was on her part. He generally favored blunt conversations about feelings, but he had a gut feeling that would make Victoria bolt. "I'll go get us drinks," he offered, rubbing the back of his neck, and she nodded.

He was waiting for the bartender to finish pouring their drinks—red wine for him, a martini for her—when the groom shouldered in next to him. "Good to see you, man," Andy said with a genial clap on his back. "A white wine for me and a Scotch for the Mrs.," he added to the bartender. "Did my eyes deceive me or are you here with Victoria? When you said you were bringing someone I'd never have guessed it was her. Are you guys together?"

Owen shrugged, and when Andy raised his eyebrows he sighed. "It's a long story. She wanted to come but she'd missed the RSVP deadline, so I thought I'd . . . help her out."

"Help. Yeah. Definitely looks like you're *helping* her out there."

"Shut up," Owen grumbled.

Andy grinned. "When did that start?"

"Not exactly sure."

Now Andy cocked his head. "That sounds intriguing."

"It sounds like it's none of your damn business. Don't you have a brand new wife to get back to?" Owen asked, cracking a grin.

"Who do you think sent me over here to get the details? We're a nosy-ass family."

Owen shook his head and clinked his glass with his friend's. "Congrats, you know. I'm really happy for you both."

A misty look came over Andy's dark brown eyes as he found Cassie in the crowd, sitting next to Victoria at a table near the dance floor. "I'm pretty damn lucky, aren't I?"

Owen followed his gaze and once again his heart thumped painfully against his ribcage. "Yeah. You are," he agreed.

Direct Messages: Luke @Lukethebarnyardcat

@Noraephronwasagenius
What's the most reckless thing you've ever done?

@Lukethebarnyardcat
Honestly? My job now. I'm just Don Fucking Quixote, tilting at capitalist windmills

@Noraephronwasagenius
How do you handle taking risks like that? I know you're rich, but there must be some real brass balls behind that money to be this bold. Teach me your ways, because I don't know how you manage it. I can fake it, but with you it's the real thing.

@Lukethebarnyardcat
I'm a white male, Nora
The world is literally designed to make me happy
I don't really need to be brave. The world will pick up after me. So I'm just trying to do what I can to even the playing field for everyone else

@Noraephronwasagenius
I would hate you if I didn't adore you so much, you know.

@Lukethebarnyardcat
I know

Chapter Fourteen

Water hissed against the tiles, muffled by the bathroom door. The ride up to the room had been surprisingly quiet. Something had shifted between them during the dance, and Victoria wasn't sure she could put her finger on it, exactly, but things were different-with-a-capital-D. Even the bride had noticed, cornering her while Owen went to get drinks. *Since when are you and Owen a thing?* Cassie had hissed, and Victoria wasn't quite sure how to answer.

Because she honestly didn't know. They hadn't talked about it, but it was clearly more than she ever anticipated. She'd tested her theory earlier by seeing if he'd hold her hand when the ceremony was over, and the speed at which he'd accepted—and the way his thumb caressed the back of her hand—had seemed to answer it, but after their slow dance he had gotten quiet. *Regret, maybe, or maybe he doesn't want to send me the wrong signals?* But there was still that now-familiar look in his eye whenever he glanced at her, heavy and thick. *Lust. That's what makes the most sense,* she decided. *Not hate sex and not quite a relationship, but something in between.* It was more in their comfort zone than real feelings, although her heart sank strangely at the realization.

The easiest, most grown-up way of handling it would be to ask him, but she couldn't find the words. Owen had confessed that he needed to shower when they got into the room, his shirt soaked nearly through under his suitcoat, and she had been standing outside the bathroom door like a creeper ever since. Victoria pressed her forehead against the door and took a deep, steadying breath. She should probably wait, but she was impatient. And the longer she stood here thinking, the more fear worked its way inside her chest. If it was just lust for him that would hurt, even as she told herself that's all it was for her. The more she thought the tighter the tension in her lungs rose, and Victoria decided it was better to just get them back on their usual footing.

She knocked.

The answering pause was long enough to make her consider running downstairs, stealing his car, and driving all the way back to Minneapolis rather than face him. But finally he responded. "Yeah?"

"Can I come in?"

Another long pause. "Yeah," he agreed.

The bathroom was surprisingly modern for the old-fashioned building they were in, all glossy subway tile and chrome. The shower itself was glass, with a wide shower head sending gentle sheets of water cascading down Owen's shoulders. Victoria kept her chin up but the moment she saw the look in his eyes her knees went weak.

Getting back on track wouldn't be hard, with him looking at her like that. He wanted her, and she was powerless where that was concerned. She pointedly dropped her gaze, taking in the ridged planes of his stomach, lightly dusted with hair, and trailing down to the junction between his thighs. His cock was thickening against his thigh and he flexed his fingers as if resisting. "Mind if I join you?" she asked, dropping her voice to a sultry purr.

Owen lifted an eyebrow. "If you'd like," he said casually, but the slow, spreading flush on his neck told her more than his tone.

The dress slipped from her shoulders with a hiss. The beads clinked against the tile and his eyes darkened. Rent the Runway was a godsend, and not just because it let her go to a black-tie wedding without having to dip into her precious savings. She would be remembering the way Owen looked at her in that dress for years—decades, even. Her bra resembled a corset, secured at her lower back with just two clasps, the narrow band easily hidden by the waist of her dress. She sighed in relief when the black fabric released. Owen's hand flexed again, his dick now fully hard, but still he refrained from touching himself. Her hair came out of its coiled updo with a few tugs of pins, cascading down her shoulders.

Owen took a long moment to survey her. Clouds of steam billowed out of the shower and silence hung thick between them. Then he turned to face the water with a shrug, as if to say *it's all up to you.*

Good god, she loved that. He had a habit of turning things over to her in a way that made her feel powerful, even if she knew within minutes she would be under his control. Or maybe it was *because* she knew that was coming. The way they handed control back and forth, easy as breathing in and out, was unlike her experiences with any other man.

Victoria closed the glass door behind her and molded herself against his back, cheek against his shoulder. Water sprayed her skin, gentle and insistent, and Owen bowed his head. "Are you sure?" he said, so lowly she almost missed it.

Victoria decided to let her touch do the answering. He dropped his head back against her shoulder and their lips met in a sloppy, off-center kiss. Victoria slid her hand down his long, thick length, twisting her wrist when she reached the tip, the water raining down on them both. She only made it a few more strokes before Owen spun in her arms and took her face in his hands. This kiss was deep and needy, verging on desperate.

She sank to her knees without hesitation. Owen's hand came to cup the back of her head, not holding her in place but urging her on. She loosened her jaw and drew him deeper, making his hand fist tightly in her hair. More curses dripped from his lips. Victoria moaned, setting a rhythm she knew would break him, and break him she did. It was hardly any time at all before he was groaning and coming, spilling down her throat.

Owen yanked her up to stand and kissed her hard. "Fuck," he muttered against her lips. "Fuck. How do you—how do you do that to me?"

"Talent," she preened, but when he kissed her again she forgot to tease him. The way he kissed her—thoroughly, possessively, deeply—drove all other thoughts from her head. And when he pushed her back against the cool tile, his hand slipping between her thighs, she gave in to oblivion. She started begging—her, Victoria Clemenceaux, *begging*—for him to *keep going, don't stop, don't stop, please*, and he chuckled darkly in her ear as she came.

She'd barely caught her breath when he lifted her in his arms, her legs automatically wrapping around his waist. He was already hard again, pressing insistently at her core. Owen stepped out of the shower and set her down on the counter, roughly rummaging through his toiletry kit until he found a condom. And then he was inside her, and just like always, it was perfect. She braced her hands on the counter against his thrusts and he sealed his mouth over hers. Her world narrowed to the feel of him filling her and his fingers on her clit, coaxing her to fall apart one last time before he did the same.

He nosed at the side of her cheek, huffing out a laugh. "I think I might still have soap in my hair," he said, and she burst into laughter.

"We should fix that," she said, kissing the corner of his mouth just because she wanted to.

Owen guided her back under the warm, soothing spray and handed her a small bottle of shampoo. He kissed her forehead and just like that they shifted straight into domesticated intimacy. She washed her hair and he handed her the conditioner, and then she twisted out of the water to let him rinse his hair. But through it all they never let go of each other. It was gentle and easy, and it should have scared her instead of leaving her feeling fuzzy and happy.

When they finished the shower, Owen left her to finish taking her makeup off with the easy familiarity of a couple who had been together for years. But back in the room, the image in front of her drew her up short. Owen was stretched out in the bed in a soft-looking Harvard Law T-shirt, black-rimmed glasses perched on his nose and a thick book balanced on his chest. She had been planning on digging her own pajamas from her suitcase, but instead she grabbed a shirt of his he'd left on the floor—he really was a slob—and shrugged it on. "Whatcha reading?" she asked.

"*The Color of Money.* It's about income inequality and race," he explained, sparing her a glance.

There was a second bed right there. They hadn't discussed sleeping arrangements because they really hadn't discussed anything, but if she chose the open bed, the message would be clear. Here was another Moment, where everything balanced on a knife's edge.

Victoria slid under the covers next to him and he lifted his arm for her to rest against his chest. It was like they did this every night, and it struck her that she wished they did. "Sounds interesting." She nestled closer, arm possessively draped across his stomach, and waited.

"It is," he said, and to her everlasting surprise, Owen started reading. His voice rumbled against her ear and he ran his fingers through her drying hair, slowly and deliberately, and Victoria let herself be lulled to sleep.

The last time Victoria spent the night with someone was the guy she saw for a few months back in her 2L year. They were never very serious, but she sort of gave it a shot, even though she loathed trying to fall asleep with his arm crushing her ribcage while the rest of him twined around her body like a boa constrictor. She would wake up sweaty and annoyed, and after their fifth sleepover she developed an "allergy" to his dog and stopped spending the night. A few weeks later, they were done anyway.

So, it was a surprise to her when she opened her eyes and snuggled deeper into Owen's embrace. Normally she would roll away, maybe even get up and brush her teeth to avoid the awkwardness of trying to escape a morning cuddle. But this time, she simply buried her nose in the crook of his neck and waited for him to rouse. He did so slowly, with some muffled noises that made her bite back a grin.

She craned her neck up to kiss him, heedless of their stale

breath, and opened her legs easily when he rolled her onto her back.

The phone on the nightstand rang with an earsplitting shriek. They both paused, looking into each other's eyes, and when Owen grunted *fuck it* she kissed him deeply, glad they weren't going to be interrupted. The ringing stopped, only to start again a moment later, and he groaned impatiently. He rolled away from her and slapped blindly for the phone. "Yeah?"

Victoria attached her lips to the spot below his ear that seemed to make him putty in her hands. "What about—no, I, uh, yeah. That—makes sense," he stammered, distracted by her touch. "Yeah, do that. Yep, same card," he said, and hung up.

She'd been right before. Kissing Owen with no plan besides just kissing was almost as good as the sex itself. His weight pinned her to the mattress and his hands skimmed her sides and they kissed for so long she could have sworn the sunlight shifted before they broke apart.

It was only after they managed to completely disentangle themselves that she remembered. "What was that about?" she asked.

Owen sat up and pulled on his sweatshirt. "What was what about?"

"The phone call?"

"Oh, that," he said, leaning over and kissing the spot where her neck met her shoulder. "We missed checkout."

"What?" She twisted to look at the alarm clock, surprised to see it was already after noon. No wonder her stomach was growling. "Did you get us a late checkout?"

"Nope," he said, moving down to kiss her shoulder. "They didn't have that available but don't ask why, because I definitely wasn't listening. I just booked it for another night."

Victoria sat up straighter even though her muscles wanted

to dissolve under his touch. "I have to get back to the Cities tonight, though." *And I didn't budget for a second night.*

"Me too," he said, tugging the fabric aside to bare her upper arm to his lips. "But this will buy us a few hours."

"I can't—"

"You're not paying for it," he said firmly. "My decision."

"Only because I was distracting you."

"Yeah, that was a real hardship," he deadpanned. "How about this—I pay for the room if you pay for room service."

Victoria had never once in her life ordered room service. That was something that happened in movies where people worked as journalists but somehow had 2,000 square foot apartments decorated entirely from Anthropologie. Hell, that was something that happened when you stayed in actual hotels, something she hadn't done until she was twenty-two, unless you counted the incredibly depressing pay-by-the-week motel she and her mother had lived in near Fergus Falls for a month when she was nine, which she usually did her best not to think about. What Owen was offering was hardly a fair trade but somehow she didn't feel patronized. "Deal."

Owen guided his car through the maze of downtown skyscrapers in the early twilight to Victoria's now-familiar building, wondering how the hell he'd just had a perfect weekend with Victoria goddamn Clemenceaux.

It wasn't that he had invited her thinking they would have a terrible time, but he hadn't quite anticipated it being *that* good. Victoria materializing in a stunning dress like a heroine in one of her beloved rom coms, Victoria holding his hand tightly, Victoria dancing at the reception, Victoria undressing with her eyes burning into him and joining him in the shower, Victoria lounging on the hotel bed in his shirt like she was his fucking girlfriend, Victoria stealing the last of the room service coffee with a devious smile on her face. Hell, Victoria right now, snoring softly with her head rested against the window. She was wearing his sweatshirt for reasons he didn't even remember, and he hoped he would never, ever get that back because it looked so damn right on her it hurt.

She lifted her head, sleepy and bleary, when he pulled in front of her building. "Did I fall asleep?" she asked, clearly a little embarrassed.

"You might have been a little worn out, yes," he couldn't help but say. Between last night and then the second round after breakfast, he had an ache in his quads that he never wanted to disappear.

She rolled her eyes, grinning. Her bag was in the backseat and she grabbed it, hesitating with her hand on the door. "Did you—I know it's late, but did you want to come up?"

God, did he ever. He wanted to go up to her apartment, crawl into her bed, and never, ever leave. But Luke was waiting for him at his dad's and would probably revenge-pee all over Ashley's expensive rugs if he didn't come get him tonight. And then there was the whole never-wanting-to-leave aspect, which wasn't really a problem but probably wasn't something he should do quite yet, not when he still wasn't sure where he stood with her, romantic weekend aside.

Every bone in his body—especially that one—wanted to take Victoria up on her offer, but he shook his head. "I have a cat to feed, and there's a lot of work to get through still."

He saw the moment when she remembered they were opposing counsel, and wished he hadn't. Because as perfect as this weekend had been, there was still that minor mountain to get over, and he had a sneaking suspicion things would get worse before they got better. "Yeah, me too. Work, obviously, not the cat," she said a little stiffly, and he wanted to kick himself for bringing that elephant back into the room when they'd done such a good job of ignoring it all weekend. "Did you want this back?" she added, plucking at the grey fabric of his sweatshirt.

"It's cold outside. Give it to me some other time," he said, gratified when she smiled in response. She didn't fight him on it, so she was hoping for another chance of seeing him too. He'd take that. And when she leaned across the console to kiss his cheek, he dared to let himself hope that they could somehow magically make this work, for real.

Direct Messages: Nora @Noraephronwasagenius

@Lukethebarnyardcat

I just really, really love fall foliage. It's so beautiful and fall is easily my favorite season

Read: Yesterday, 4:03pm

Chapter Fifteen

Sincerely Your Bitches

@Noraephronwasagenius
It happened again.
The sex, I mean.

@Keanuisadreamboat
🎉🥳

@MadisonHughes95
🍆🍆🍆🍆🍆🍆
🍆🍆🍆🍆

@Neverthelesskararesisted
How/when/why

@Noraephronwasagenius
So remember how I went to a wedding this weekend?

It was with him.

Like, as a date? Or maybe not, we weren't very clear about that.

Either way, sex definitely happened, so 🤷‍♀️🤷‍♀️

@MadisonHughes95

🍆🍆🍆🍆🍆

@Keanuisadreamboat

So you just . . . went to town on each other.

@Noraephronwasagenius

More or less.

In the hotel room, obviously. Not like, on the dance floor or anything.

I have some self-control.

@MadisonHughes95

🍆🍆🍆🍆🍆🍆🍆

@Neverthelesskararesisted

Maddy please find your chill.

@MadisonHughes95

🍆🍆🍆🍆🍆🍆🍆🍆🍆

@Keanuisadreamboat

How are you doing with that?

@Noraephronwasagenius

Confused? I don't know what this IS and I don't know how I feel about it.

@Neverthelesskararesisted
Do you want it to happen again?

@Noraephronwasagenius
Yes? No? Maybe?

@Keanuisadreamboat
What is the reasoning behind each answer?

@Noraephronwasagenius
Yes: Sex is good. No: I hate his face? Or I did? Or I feel like I should, I guess? Maybe: But the sex?? So good?

Also I maybe stopped hating him a while ago but if I don't HATE him then what the fuck ARE we?

@MadisonHughes95
🍆🍆🍆🍆🍆🍆🍆🍆🍆🍆🍆🍆

@Keanuisadreamboat
Why do you feel like you should hate him?

@Noraephronwasagenius
Because I've hated him since the day we met. And by all appearances he's a fairly solid human, but he can be so IRRITATING, especially when it comes to work. Like, he's crazy rich and clearly assumes everyone else grew up exactly like him, and he's a dick to me for working where I do because we're ~evil~ and like yes, I am aware of that but some of us have BILLS TO PAY AND A LIFETIME OF LOANS THAT WILL NEVER REALLY BE PAID OFF. Every once in a while he seems aware of his privilege but then he just chucks it back in my face like CLASS ISN'T A THING even if yes, I am a

beneficiary of white privilege and I fully acknowledge that, but also sometimes I want to wear his sweatshirt and smell his sheets and guys I don't know if you know this but I AM A MESS.

@Neverthelesskararesisted
From twitter troll to Luke, where does he fall on the Men Are Garbage Scale?

@Noraephronwasagenius
6.5. 7 if I'm being honest.
Probably an 8 when he's going down on me. Maybe even 8.5.
I keep thinking with my vagina here and it's a problem.

@Neverthelesskararesisted
I'm going to point out that wanting to wear his clothes and smell him are not exactly vagina problems so much as heart problems, but you tell yourself whatever you gotta tell yourself to get through the day.
Has he ever done anything that made you feel dirty or unwanted or gross or just plain shitty about yourself?

@Noraephronwasagenius
Never.
Sometimes I think he might even be a Genuinely Good Dude but like, I cannot handle the implications of that.
And then we fuck in the shower, I guess.

@MadisonHughes95
🍆🍆🍆🍆🍆🍆🍆

@Neverthelesskararesisted
Oh my god you are a fucking mess.
But that sounds hot so good work.

@Noraephronwasagenius
WE ARE STILL NO CLOSER TO SOLVING MY DILEMMA.

@Keanuisadreamboat
I'm still not hearing a dilemma?
Good sex, decent human.
The major downside seems to be he's rich, which yes, capitalism has destroyed us all and it is time for the workers to seize the means of production.
But we'll handle that when the revolution comes.

@Noraephronwasagenius
You guys are no help.

@MadisonHughes95
🍆🍆🍆🍆🍆🍆🍆🍆

@Keanuisadreamboat
What Maddy said.

It was strange how much not being with Owen felt like she was missing something. Or someone.

Victoria kept thinking about their weekend at the wedding and how easy it was. It wasn't just the sex; it was everything else. How he made her feel part of the group, how he held her while they danced, and how outright happy he was the morning they woke up together. She'd been happy too, but as long as the case was going on they had to be careful.

But careful didn't give her butterflies and with things with Luke still awkward and stilted, Victoria found herself getting bored. After a week without contact with Owen—not even at work—she cracked. It was a beautiful, crisp fall weekend and she was itching to get out of her apartment, and she didn't feel like being alone.

Victoria Clemenceaux
What are you doing today?

Owen Pohl
Trying not to die
Wait maybe I'm already dead
I did shots last night and I guess I'm not 21 anymore? Who knew
Either way if you wanted to see me today you'll have to dig me out of my grave, because I'm so hungover I died

Victoria Clemenceaux
You are the most dramatic man I've ever fucked, you know that?

Owen Pohl
Ah, but you have heard of me

Victoria Clemenceaux
If you were trying to make a *Pirates of the Caribbean* joke there, it didn't land.

Owen Pohl
Don't blame me, blame my ghost
Because I'm dead

She pulled up in front of his house forty minutes later, Caribou Coffee to-go cups clutched in each hand while she awkwardly banged on his door with her elbow. She was back to not-thinking-about-it-too-hard when it came to wanting to see Owen, and she really hoped this didn't backfire on her.

It took longer than it should have for Owen to shuffle his way to the door, and when he opened it he blinked blearily at her for a long moment. "Vee?" he said finally, his voice hoarse. "What is this?" His skin had a faint greyish tinge, and his normally sparkling eyes were dull and watery. In short, he looked like hell.

"Payback for the soup," she said, holding out a cup. "One large drip coffee, with a splash of milk and *three* sugars because you're kind of disgusting." She grinned and looked at his bare feet. "Now put some shoes on, because we're going for a walk."

Owen slumped against the doorframe. "I can't, I told you. I'm dead," he whined. He took a sip from the coffee and closed his eyes. "Or maybe mostly dead? Either way, walking is definitely not in the cards." His cat snaked around his ankles and he toed it back inside with a quiet *tsk tsk*, stepping outside and shutting the door behind him. "Sorry, if I let him out he'll kill every bird in the neighborhood and pile them on my doorstep like some sort of barbaric English lord," he said by way of explanation. Victoria shrugged—she had always been more of a dog person, herself. Owen sat down heavily, running his fingers through his limp hair. "Did I say thank you for the coffee? I can't remember."

"You didn't, no," she said, sitting down next to him. "But now you can thank me for all of this in one go," she added, pulling the foil-wrapped breakfast burrito out of her purse.

Owen's jaw went momentarily slack and he snatched it from her hands. "Oh my god, how did you know?" He tore the foil off and took a massive bite, moaning as he did. "Marry me, Vee. I'm serious. I don't even care that sometimes you hate me, I'll marry you right here right now, on my front step."

She bit back a grin and rested her hands on her lap. "You know, I think that's my first marriage proposal, if you don't count Tommy Pierce in kindergarten."

"Fuck Tommy Pierce, he doesn't love you like I do," Owen said, and even though he was clearly joking—and half talking to the burrito anyway—her heart did a tiny little stutterstep at his words. He wiped his mouth with the back of his hand and looked at her. "Seriously though, why'd you do this?"

Victoria shrugged. "It's a nice day and I wanted to do something."

"And I'm something?" he teased. He still looked like death warmed over, but at least the spark was coming back into his blue eyes.

"I'd rather not get puked on, thank you," she said primly.

"Hey, I got all my puking done last night," he protested through a mouthful of burrito.

"I meant I wanted to go for a walk or something. And you came to visit me when you thought I was sick, so I figured it was my turn."

"So this is the Victoria Clemenceaux care package? A breakfast burrito and coffee?"

"It's actually the Victoria Clemenceaux Get Your Shit Together and Keep Me Company Package, but yeah, basically."

Owen turned his face to the sun, eyes closed again. "It is

really nice out," he agreed. "Don't know how many more of these we'll have."

"That was my thought exactly."

"You and every other Minnesotan," he said, gesturing at the steady trickle of people pushing strollers, walking dogs, and running past his house. "A whole state of people with chronic Vitamin D deficiencies, I swear," he grumbled. Victoria frowned, Owen's joke stirring something in her memory.

Owen crumpled the foil in his hand and pushed himself up. "For the woman who just literally saved my life, I think I can handle a walk. Let me grab my shoes and keys." He disappeared into his house and returned just a minute or so later, once again toeing his cat away from the door as he closed it. "You stay there, little one," he admonished the cat, and for the second time that morning she had to shrug away the uncomfortable resemblance to Luke. He had a tendency to dote on Cat-Luke in much the same way, half-exasperated and half-loving, but that was probably just how all cat owners were.

They fell into step beside each other, headed to the small lake that was just three blocks from his house. Thanks to a habit of scrolling real estate websites when she was bored, Victoria knew just how expensive a house in this neighborhood was, but for once she didn't feel the familiar stab of annoyance at how much money Owen had.

The walking path at Lake Harriet was relatively crowded, everyone making the most of an unexpectedly nice late-fall day. The trees were a riot of color against the silver-blue of the small lake, the sky above a deep, clear blue studded with faint wisps of clouds. Owen was walking slowly, clearly still feeling the effects of the night before, and Victoria idled beside him. "I assume Mark and Andy are responsible for the hangover?" she asked, sipping her coffee.

Owen chuckled. "Mark and Cassie, mostly. They called me and Andy chickens for not taking shots with them, and we couldn't possibly let that slander on our honor stand."

"Male bullshit, got it," she replied.

"I feel like Cassie would protest that characterization but . . . yeah, more or less. Usually we just grab a few beers, but last night got a little out of hand for no real reason."

"And Andy and Cassie are back from their honeymoon already?"

"Those two workaholics only took three days on the North Shore."

"How did Priyanka escape this fate?"

"By being smarter than the rest of us combined and refusing to participate."

"I knew I liked her." There was a faint sting in knowing they had all hung out without her, which caught her by surprise. It wasn't like she and Owen were on that sort of casual hangout terms, despite the sex, but maybe she wanted to be.

He threw his coffee cup into a trash can and took a deep breath. "Do you know why fall always smells like a bonfire?"

"Nope. But I love it," she agreed, and they fell silent for several paces. "I was thinking—" she started, but at the same time Owen said, "We should probably talk."

They both laughed awkwardly, and Victoria waited for him to speak again, heart abruptly pounding. "What are we doing, Vee? This is obviously not just a one-time thing anymore and the lawsuit could drag on for who knows how long, and I guess I realized the other weekend that we should, I dunno, maybe talk about . . . us?" Owen said, eyes on the path in front of them.

What she had been planning on saying was *I was thinking we could find a bench and sit down*, but now the conversation had taken an unforeseen left turn and she didn't know how to back out. "About that," she said, trying to figure out a way to word it so she wouldn't be divulging privileged information. Because on Smorgasbord's end, things were drawing to a close. She had worn Gerald down and was pretty sure she'd be getting the okay to send out a settlement offer to Owen's clients in the next couple of weeks, provided all the right people signed off on it. She would never tell Owen this because his ego was already enormous, but she wasn't sure Smorgasbord could beat him this time. After years of trying and countless lawsuits, he'd found one where his case was a lot stronger than even he realized. Sooner or later he'd find someone who would admit out loud what everyone already knew, and Smorgasbord would be screwed. The number she had pitched to Gerald was significantly less than Owen's clients deserved, but enough to make accepting a settlement not feel like a total loss. There would be NDAs involved to keep the press out of it and Smorgasbord could claim they had not broken any laws, strictly speaking.

This time, at least, she would be able to get out of it with a slightly less bruised conscience. Fifteen thousand dollars in back pay for each claimant was peanuts for Smorgasbord, but was just tempting enough for people living paycheck to paycheck. She knew how much that money would have helped her and her mother, at any rate.

But until she got the okay to send out a settlement offer, she couldn't tell Owen any of that. And she still didn't know how to talk about her feelings for Owen, so the longer they put that off, the better. "I wouldn't be so sure," she said finally, taking a deep breath. Victoria was not a gambling woman, but she was about to bet on Owen. "About things taking much longer, I mean."

Owen cocked his head to the side. "Is that so?"

"Possibly," she said airily. "So I don't know if we really need to discuss anything right now. Might be the sort of conversation that could keep. Maybe for a week or two, and we could see where things stand then."

"Interesting," he said, and his hand brushed against hers, so quickly she could have let it go as an accident.

Instead she slipped her fingers into his and squeezed.

Owen's heart should have been singing. Victoria had all but confirmed Smorgasbord was preparing to settle and she had her fingers laced with his while they walked, leaning towards him just enough to bump their shoulders together. Victoria was *holding his hand* while they walked, no ulterior motive on either side, and the romantic in him should have been winning this battle easily. But he'd accepted enough settlements from Smorgasbord to know what that usually meant: they were tired of paying the mediators and wanted him and his clients to just go away.

Except it never happened this quickly. Getting a settlement offer this early in the game meant there was more happening behind the scenes than he realized—this meant Smorgasbord was *worried.* And if they were worried, it meant there was something to be worried *about.* Which meant he had a duty to his clients to keep pursuing this, even at the expense of his own happiness.

And make no mistake: he should have been happy. Ecstatic, even. He had somehow melted the Ice Queen's heart and he hadn't even known that was what he wanted. He should have been wanting to sprint around the lake shouting for joy, or at least he should have felt a warm, melting feeling low in his belly. But instead his stomach felt queasy, and it wasn't just that fourth shot of fireball last night or the breakfast burrito he'd just inhaled.

His mind turned to Nora, wondering what she'd advise, and then suddenly he felt worse. He had to choose, one or the other, and since Nora didn't seem at all bothered by their utter anonymity, the choice seemed clear. Technically there wasn't anything official between him and Nora, but it didn't seem fair to Victoria to keep someone else as that close of a confidante-slash-flirt-partner without at least disclosing it.

Victoria peered at him sideways. "Are you okay?" she asked, slowing and tugging him off the path to let a couple runners pass them by. "You're looking pale."

Owen dropped her hand and wiped at his forehead. "I think the hangover just hit me again, is all. I need a second."

Victoria tucked her hands into her jacket pockets and lifted her chin back towards his neighborhood, her mood shifting slightly. "Should we head back then?" He could feel her withdrawing from him and he hated it.

"Probably," he agreed, wishing that just about everything about this fucked up situation was a little different.

Direct Messages: Nora @Noraephronwasagenuis

@Lukethebarnyardcat
Big day at work today

@Noraephronwasagenius
Same. See you on the other side.

Chapter Sixteen

All in all, Victoria was confident if not quite at ease with her choices the day the final settlement hearing rolled around. The only fly in her ointment was Luke, who was feeling ever more distant these days. She couldn't blame him, though, because she also found herself holding back for the first time in their friendship. It felt dishonest, being so open with him and falling for Owen, and part of her wondered if maybe their friendship had run its course. She hated to think that, because Luke was one of the first people to truly *get* her, on a level she didn't ever reach with anyone else, not even her group chat. And she wasn't sure she could ever reach that with Owen, or with anyone she met in person, even if she'd been spending less and less time online these days. She had too many walls, and too much practice at building them to know how to begin to tear them down.

Victoria set her bag on the conveyer belt at the courthouse and strode confidently through security. Maybe her dress was a little unfair to Owen, but she was coming to realize he really, really liked seeing her in purple. Her dark plum sheath was plenty conservative, but the slit up the back would reveal flashes of her legs when she stood, and he was a sucker for that too.

Owen caught her eye when she walked in, and she straightened her shoulders at the flash of heat that passed between them. But then an unfamiliar look crossed his face and he looked away, eyes on his phone as he texted. Disconcerted, she smoothed her dress and sat down to wait. She had been so relieved the day she got the go-ahead to email Owen the settlement offer. She dreaded just about any conversation about feelings, but this was at least one complication between them taken care of. They could handle their feelings later.

The judge entered from her chambers and everyone rose. The hearing began, everything clicking into place like clockwork.

"I hear you have reached an agreement," Judge Green observed.

"We have, your honor," Victoria said. "Smorgasbord is prepared—"

Owen stood, shoving his phone in his pocket, and Victoria broke off, puzzled. "Actually, your honor, my clients have rejected the offer."

"We already received notice that they accepted," Victoria interrupted.

"I know, but new evidence came to light and after a conference call this morning, my clients have agreed to pursue the lawsuit. I'm moving for an end to voluntary mediation; we'd like to continue this in court."

"What new evidence?" she replied sharply.

"A former team lead from the Alexandria store is willing to testify that retaliation for refusing off-books work is standard practice, as was acknowledged in the deposition of August twenty-fourth. I have her affidavit here."

"No such thing was acknowledged," she snapped. Her stomach felt tight, anxiety blooming. She recognized the look on his face now—Owen had a plan, and she was walking into a trap. To make matters worse, that deposition happened barely a week after he came over to her apartment, and she *knew* she'd been distracted that day. Her skin was buzzing with his closeness, and she could have easily overlooked something. She had coached her witness to be truthful but vague, never outright lying but careful not to give Owen an opening. But she couldn't say for certain if everything had gone to plan, because that entire day she'd been fighting a blush thinking about him between her legs. And every time she reread the transcript, she kept thinking about him and his stupid smile, or the way he looked at her when she made him laugh.

"Gustavo Lopez testified that managers are frequently asked to stay after hours for inventory, off-the-clock," Owen countered.

The walls Owen had been so close to toppling immediately realigned themselves and she sat up straighter. "Their contracts state that some work may be required after shifts, and all managers are aware of that before they begin employment. So long as they are free to refuse, it's allowed," she argued.

"But they are not free to refuse, as we see here." He handed her a copy of the affidavit and slipped one to the judge's clerk. "Debbie Spaeth of Alexandria is willing to testify that employees who refuse are immediately put on a list where minor infractions that otherwise go unpunished are written up, and are generally fired within three months. She will personally admit to firing four people in a two-year period for refusing off-the-clock work, and all four had all their infractions recorded after pointing out the illegality of required unpaid work."

Victoria blinked. It was exceedingly unusual for a team lead to come forward like this, since Victoria herself knew firsthand just how difficult jobs could be to come by in small towns. Most people grumbled and knew it wasn't right, but few would risk being blackballed at all Smorgasbord stores to come forward. There were usually clauses in team lead's contracts about what they could disclose and when. While most of that shit wasn't enforceable, like a non-compete clause that Victoria herself had argued in more than one meeting was ludicrous for a position like "assistant team lead of produce," it was usually sufficiently scary to keep people's mouths shut.

God, she worked for a terrible fucking place. But she did work for them, and as in-house counsel she had a legal and ethical duty to her client. "There's no corroboration here, your honor," she said, skimming the papers in front of her. "Debbie Spaeth could be a disgruntled employee, or mistaken, or there could be a whole host of other factors that caused these firings. Grocery retail is a high turnover business, and there's no reason to take one woman's word for it."

"Are you accusing her of lying?" Owen said, voice deceptively mild.

"I'm saying you're so obsessed with bringing down Smorgasbord that we might as well start calling you Captain Ahab," she snapped.

"Watch it," Judge Green reprimanded.

"Regardless, my clients have rejected the offer," Owen said, refusing to make eye contact with Victoria.

Realization barreled into her like a freight train. It had been a huge risk, hinting that an offer was coming, but she thought he would understand why she was telling him. Victoria had been trying to tell him their future was about to be a lot simpler, and instead Owen had screwed her over. He'd taken the information she gave him and went digging, knowing she wouldn't settle unless there was a real risk Smorgasbord could be found at fault.

Owen had used her, plain and simple.

Judge Green narrowed her eyes, her wire-rimmed glasses low on her nose and braids pulled back into a low ponytail. "Do you have a motion, counselor?" she interjected.

Owen pounced. "I motion for this case to be moved out of mediation. Smorgasbord has made their offer and it isn't sufficient."

Victoria's lungs tightened further. "This case belongs in mediation, as per the contracts of all listed employees. Smorgasbord can—"

"I'm inclined to agree with the plaintiff," Judge Green said swiftly. Victoria blinked, not believing what she was hearing. "There's more here than just contract disputes, and this no longer belongs in mediation. See my clerk about getting on the schedule," the judge finished.

She turned to her clerk and Victoria stood robotically, her brain feeling about twelve steps behind.

She'd lost.

Victoria never lost. A refused settlement was a huge fuckup in the eyes of Smorgasbord, and so far, she'd always succeeded. This was the first big loss of her career, and it was to *Owen*. Sometimes she would lose minor battles, but never the war. This was far from being over, but it was bad.

The clerk read out the next case number and Victoria fumbled with her bag, half numb and half furious. Owen was clearly trying to catch her eye but she was not about to let him talk his way out of this. She knew enough on both sides of the equation to know Smorgasbord did have a habit of asking employees to do work off-the-clock, and while they were very careful to never specifically violate the letter of the law, or at least corporate directed them to be careful, they were skirting a dangerous, fine line. One poorly worded request or one sloppily filled out infraction form, and they were toast, especially once it was out of the safe harbor of mediation. Maybe not in the courtroom specifically, but certainly in the court of public opinion.

Oh, this was bad. This was very, very bad. She was going to be in for the reaming of her life when she got back to the office, and there would be dozens of people assigned to this case from here on out. She'd probably lose her position as lead counsel, and honestly, she'd deserve it. She couldn't believe she'd been so careless, so sloppy. She couldn't believe she'd let Owen get under her skin, make her complacent and distracted.

She couldn't believe she thought she actually *liked* the snake.

The next attorney stepped forward and Owen was forced to vacate his table. She gave him a head start, stopping at the back row of benches to fix the buckle on her shoe, and then strode straight from the courtroom to the ladies' room at the end of the hall. She caught a glimpse of red-gold hair in the quiet scrum in the hallway, but by the time she emerged five minutes later—still pale and shaking with anger and surprise—he was gone.

Owen paced in front of Victoria's sensible Toyota Corolla. The scent of oil and gas and asphalt filled his nostrils, and to his left a county attorney he vaguely recognized climbed into a Subaru with a friendly wave on his way out of the parking garage.

He wasn't stupid. He'd known, from the moment he got the affidavit, that this would not go over well with Victoria. It was proof, in the best, most concrete form yet, that Smorgasbord was exploiting their employees.

He didn't regret doing it, of course. Whatever he had with Victoria, this case was bigger. His clients deserved fair pay for their work, and they deserved a right to a day in court. As much as he was falling for Victoria, it wasn't even a choice—between his personal life and his moral duty to his clients, his clients came first. Still, he hoped she'd let him apologize, or at least hear him out. She would have done the same in his position. In fact, she had done something similar in his first face-off against her, when she pounced on a minor, inconsequential paperwork error and made him look like a damn fool. Granted, they weren't sleeping together back then, but giving her a heads up about the new information would have been grounds for disbarment. His stomach twisted uneasily whenever he thought about the fact that her hint to him at the lake was what had sent him searching for another team lead to testify, but she had to understand. This wasn't personal.

Familiar footsteps echoed near the elevator and he stopped his pacing. He tucked his hands in his pockets and tried for an easy, friendly smile, but the second their eyes met all hope inside him withered up and died. "Don't fucking talk to me," she growled.

"It wasn't personal," he said anyway, because Owen was an idiot who never learned when to keep his damn mouth shut.

"It wasn't? Because that felt like getting fucked, something I am unfortunately well-acquainted with when it comes to you." She threw her bag in the backseat with terrifying force.

He stepped back to give her some space. "Hey, come on," he said, a little affronted. "You know I couldn't tell you."

"Of course not," she snarled, arms crossed. "But there's no fucking reason you had to pull this in court, like you were on goddamn *Law and Order.*"

"First of all, *Law and Order* doesn't do civil cases, only

criminal. Second of all, they only made the decision to reject this morning. I had less than an hour's warning."

"Bullshit. That was rehearsed."

"No, it wasn't," he said, unexpected anger flaring in his stomach. This was worse than he thought—she wasn't just mad, she thought he had set her up. He thought that after everything, he'd earned at least a *little* of her trust. But apparently, that was not something Queen Victoria extended to mere mortals like him.

She snorted. "Yes, it fucking was, because Owen Fucking Pohl doesn't think he's made his point unless he's also turned everything around him into a fucking circus. You like the spotlight, admit it."

"You think I did that for attention? And not in the best interests of my clients?"

"I think you engineered it so it would look like you had no choice when you were really just being a fucking showboat," she said with a bitter laugh.

"Of course you wouldn't be able to imagine someone acting in the best interest of someone who can't pay you," he spat, and saw the moment his barb landed. She paled, eyes still blazing, and he felt a half-second of regret before barreling on. "All you care about is money. You don't give a fuck that there are poor people out there trying to make a living, because all you care about is that your company can rig it so your shareholders make a profit."

"You don't know anything about me."

"I know plenty," he said, advancing on her. "I know you're a cold-hearted jackass. I know you're so obsessed with money that you'd sell out your own mother for a buck. You use people and then you move on, and you can't even muster up the compassion to feel *bad* about it." His blows were low and in some cases blatantly untrue, but anger was making him see red. Anger and betrayal, because he stupidly thought she would have given him the benefit of the doubt on this. They were in the same line of work—if anyone would understand, it was her. But no, she was determined to see the worst in him so screw it, he would see the worst in her. "Face it, Vee. You don't give a fuck about anyone."

She tossed her hair over her shoulder haughtily, and twenty-four hours ago, hell, even two hours ago, he would have melted at the sight. But now it made him even angrier, because he'd had her and now they were throwing it all away.

"No, you just can't imagine a world where people don't fall all over you like a white fucking knight. You're so addicted to being the hero that you think someone having a modicum of self-restraint makes her a cold-hearted bitch instead of a competent adult who can see through your crap. You think I'd sell out my mother? You'd push yours off a pier so you could jump in and take credit for saving her. You're pathetic, Owen. Pathetic. I can't believe—" She broke off and turned away, brushing at her cheek. The mere thought of Victoria crying over him, even angrily, should have broken his heart. Now it just turned it to ice. "I can't believe I thought you were who you pretend to be. You're just a worthless pretty boy playing with Daddy's money, and that's all you'll ever be." She stalked past him and threw open her car door, leaving him to stand speechless behind her as she drove away.

Direct Messages: Luke @Lukethebarnyardcat

@Noraephronwasagenius
Sorry for being so quiet lately, but not much is really new with me, you know?

@Lukethebarnyardcat
Yeah same

Chapter Seventeen

Victoria never cried at work. Never. Sometimes she got angry enough that tears would well in her eyes, but she knew that the second she showed that level of weakness, it was all over for her. She'd long ago learned to keep it locked away, and when tears threatened she would do simple math in her head until the urge faded. But no amount of *four plus five equals nine, nine plus seven equals sixteen, sixteen minus twelve equals four* could keep this torrent at bay. She made it through her report to Gerald—he was furious with her, as she expected—in one piece before she locked her office door and let herself sob, partly out of fury and partly out of pure, unadulterated heartache. Gerald's dressing-down was bad enough, but on top of that she felt . . . stupid. Used. Blinded by her dumb feelings for someone who clearly didn't care about her, and even worse, she felt bad for yelling at him. She would go to her grave remembering the look on Owen's face when she called him pathetic, and his own insults rang in her ears. She wasn't heartless, he just didn't know her. She wasn't obsessed with money, she had grown up poor, something someone as rich as him could never comprehend. She didn't do this job out of greed; she did it out of pure necessity. She was dedicated because she believed in giving her client 110 percent of her effort, even if that client was a piece-of-shit company that worked overtime to keep its employees below the poverty line. She couldn't help everyone, but she could help her mother, and this was how she would achieve that.

Mascara ran down her cheeks and her nose dripped, sobs wrenching her chest. She reached for a tissue and pulled out her phone, deciding that desperate times called for desperate measures. She'd break her rule about personal conversations on company time, because right now she was in crisis and there was only one person who would understand. Luke would never accuse her of being cold and unfeeling. He would support her no matter what, and she abruptly felt silly for neglecting her friendship with him while she was distracting herself with bad choices named Owen. She'd been such a coward, hiding from Luke when he was the exact sort of understanding, caring man she wanted.

It was time to fix that.

@Noraephronwasagenius

This is going to be completely out of the blue and I apologize, but promise you'll hear me out.

I have a confession to make: I don't live in Chicago. I honestly can't even remember if you ever straight out asked or I just implied it, but I have this weird thing about internet privacy and I don't reveal my actual location. I've never had a bad experience or been stalked or anything, I'm just happier if I keep some things to myself. And I have never lied about anything else—not my feelings, not my past, not my job. I keep things vague sometimes, but I have never, ever lied to you and I wouldn't.

I live in the Twin Cities. Minneapolis, to be exact, and I think you (and Cat-Luke) might live here too. I don't know what you do, exactly, but I'm a lawyer and I suspect you might be one too. Which means maybe we've met in person? I don't know, I feel like I would know if I met you, because well, you're you. I know everything about you and you know everything about me, but I was sitting here today thinking and it's just wild that we've never (officially, to our knowledge) met in person. And I know that's almost entirely due to me and my hang-ups, and you've been so awesome and understanding and that's why I think it's time.

Victoria took a shaky breath, her hands clammy and her armpits sweating like crazy. There was officially no going back now.

@Noraephronwasagenius

We should meet. In person. Maybe a date? If you live nearby, I mean. I don't know if you'd be into that, and maybe we should wait and see how things turn out after we meet in person, but fuck it. You're my best friend and even though I've never seen you, I think I have feelings for you. Real ones. And I think we owe it to ourselves to give it a shot, assuming you feel the same way. (And I think you do? Oh god if I'm wrong I am going to die of humiliation, but please do not agree to this out of pity. I'm a big girl who can handle rejection just like anyone else; with copious amounts of alcohol and poor decision making. And now I'm rambling so please put me out of my misery.)

If I haven't driven you away yet, here's my proposition. We could do things the millennial way and just exchange selfies and Facebook information so we can sufficiently stalk each other before meeting, but why do things the easy way? I'll be at the coffee shop on the corner of Washington and Fourth downtown on Friday at 7 p.m. Hell, I'll even have a pink rose sitting out on the table so you'll know it's me. Meet me there?

PS and for fuck's sake, if Friday at 7 doesn't work for you but some other time DOES, please tell me and we can rearrange things. I'm dramatic, not delusional, and I know you probably have a schedule and plans and all that shit.

And if you don't want to do this, uh, sorry for vomiting all of this on you. I will do my best to resume my chill, I promise.

She wiped her face and tried to steady her racing heart. Now there was nothing to do but wait.

Sincerely Your Bitches

@Noraephronwasagenius
I did something reckless.
Very reckless.
Someone sedate me.
I swear to god one of you assholes had better be awake.

@Keanuisadreamboat
Oh honey what's wrong?

@Noraephronwasagenius
Okay so you know how I pretend to be from Chicago on the internet?

@Keanuisadreamboat
Yes, we're all aware that you're basically catfishing all of us.

@Noraephronwasagenius

Well, I'm actually from Minnesota, and so is Luke. I think. I'm like, 99% sure.

@MadisonHughes95

I knew you were a fucking Minnesotan

I knew it

I don't know how I knew but I knew

Next you'll be telling us your REAL NAME

@Noraephronwasagenius

Oh god I'm a terrible friend, aren't I?

@Keanuisadreamboat

You're a little overly tightlipped about your personal details considering you also tell us whenever you have sex, yes.

But you've said that being anonymous is what lets you be honest, so we love you and accept you.

So you told Luke your real name?

@Noraephronwasagenius

Not yet.

I asked him out.

I went with the incredibly dramatic approach of suggesting meeting him in a coffee shop, sight unseen, with me having a pink rose on my table.

@MadisonHughes95

That is so cute I want to vomit, and also OH MY GOD WHEN IS THIS HAPPENING?!!

@Noraephronwasagenius

Friday.

I also told off Nemesis for good.

We're through.

I can't say exactly what happened, but he pulled a dick move in court and we sort of had it out.

I just cannot deal with his ego and need to be the Good Guy At All Times.

It's exhausting and I'm done and I'm going to give this thing with Luke a real, honest shot.

@MadisonHughes95

wow everything's really happening at once for you, huh

@Neverthelesskararesisted

Gentle question: so you're pissed at one guy and decided to go all in on another? That's not maybe a little reactive?

@Noraephronwasagenius

It is 100% reactive and I don't give a shit. I've had a decent guy in front of me all along, and I was too busy thinking with my vagina to give him a real shot. So Vagina Brain is on time-out, Real Brain is taking over.

@MadisonHughes95

We support you, boo

Latest Tweets

@Lukethebarnyardcat
Getting ready!

@Noraephronwasagenius
👀

Chapter Eighteen

Owen had never been more nervous in his life. Even taking the bar exam paled in comparison to this, the thought of meeting Nora in person.

He couldn't believe his eyes when he opened up Twitter and saw her messages. She lived *here*, not in Chicago, and she was a lawyer. For one heart-stopping second he wondered if she was Victoria, but the warmth and vulnerability exuding from her messages—and so soon after Victoria's ice queen act in the parking garage—made that completely impossible. Her timing couldn't have been better, either, as he had been dangerously close to pouring himself a vodka on the rocks and texting Victoria a few more choice insults that he hadn't managed to get in.

But then Nora asked him to meet, and he could tell himself he didn't give a shit what Victoria did with her empty, miserable life. His thoughts had strayed towards her more often than he'd like in the last few days, but now he had this date to drag himself back into a happier mindset. Sometimes he wondered what Nora looked like—he was betting on a blonde, although for no particular reason—but mostly he wondered how it would feel to be able to talk to her in person. A few months into their friendship they had stayed up almost all night, talking about everything and nothing until he fell asleep and dropped his phone straight on his face. He hoped it would be the same, and he had deliberately rescheduled plans with his sisters from Saturday to Sunday so he could spend the night with Nora if it came to that. Not sex, necessarily, but he wanted to be sure he had absolutely nothing standing in the way of his time with her.

He paced back and forth just around the corner from the coffee shop, too terrified to walk in. Snow dusted his hair and shoulders. What if she hated him? What if he didn't live up to the sparkling wit he could manage online? What if the magic just wasn't there, and he lost his closest confidante? He tapped the roses he'd purchased against his thigh, heedless of the obstruction he was causing to the people trying to walk past him on the sidewalk. *Maybe the roses are too much. Maybe she won't remember that we talked about how much she liked them. It's not stalking to remember something someone said to you, right? It's thoughtful, not creepy. Maybe. She's going to have a pink rose on her table so it's like, a theme, right?*

Owen had a habit of getting a little clingy in relationships, as no fewer than two ex-girlfriends had noted. He could go a little over the top in trying to show his affection, and he wondered if he should dial it back. But then again, Nora knew him inside and out. She knew him at his most vulnerable, and he had to just believe that she would accept him.

He looked up, ran his hand through his hair, and squared his shoulders. But at the door to the coffee shop, his courage failed him again. He walked back halfway down the block, shook his head, and turned around. *This is fucking ridiculous. Wait much longer and she might walk out.* He crept back towards the building and paused at the edge of the coffee shop's bay window.

Christmas decorations were out in full force now, despite it being barely November. Garland surrounded the edge of the window, and inside was a border of fake, sprayed-on frost. A faux pine tree took up the center of the shop, and just to its left he spotted a pink rose on the corner of a table. His heart stuttered.

She's here. Oh god, she's here. Of course she's here, idiot, this was her plan. You're the one who keeps chickening out. He needed to stop stalling and just go in; no need to make a scene. Victoria's barbs from the parking garage had lodged deep under his skin. He was acutely aware of his more attention-seeking qualities these days, and he didn't want to do anything to prove her right. But Victoria had no place here tonight. Tonight was about Nora; sweet, funny, insightful, kind, intelligent Nora. Victoria and her cold heart were a thing of the past. Nora was his present.

He squinted and craned his neck. He couldn't see the owner of the pink rose thanks to another patron—a middle-aged woman with a sensible haircut—who seemed to be conversing with whoever was sitting at the table. The other patron shrugged and shifted her weight. *Move, lady. Please. Just let me see her and then I can walk in*, he thought, but then he got his wish and his heart promptly plummeted down through his feet and splattered on the sidewalk.

It was Victoria. He'd barely gotten a glimpse of her arm and profile before he spun away from the window to hide, but he'd recognize that long dark hair and sharp, elegant posture anywhere. Sitting at the table with an unmistakable pink rose was none other than the woman he'd yelled unforgivable charges at just four days ago.

Nora was Victoria. Victoria was *Nora*.

Maybe he was wrong. Maybe it was a weird coincidence, and Victoria was there with a pink rose on her table in a random coincidence. He inched over, careful to stay behind the tree so she wouldn't see him, and scanned the rest of the coffee shop. No other roses, and only one other woman roughly his age and she was there with two other men, all three of them grouped around a laptop. She clearly wasn't waiting for him.

Which left Victoria. There was no other option. This was really happening. The door to the coffee shop opened and she sat up straight, her head whipping towards the tinkling bell. The woman talking to her moved away, presumably to her seat, and Victoria noticeably wilted when the new customers proved to be a college-aged couple. He watched disappointment etch itself in her brow, and she looked down at her phone as if checking the time. He was not quite ten minutes late yet, but if she was waiting on someone, that would be enough to put her on edge.

Reality set in. The woman he adored and the woman he hated and the woman he sometimes fucked were all the same woman, who was *also* his main opponent in the biggest case of his career. He turned away from the coffee shop and leaned against the solid brick wall of the building next door. How was this possible? How could the woman he opened himself up to every night and most days also be *Victoria*? Victoria was fun in the sack and, fine, maybe they had been getting closer lately and maybe he thought he was falling for her, but she had proved just this week that it wasn't that deep for her. She saw him as a good lay and that was it, while Nora made him feel understood. And yet they were the same, and his brain could not process that fact. Would not process it, even. He roundly rejected it, because it just simply wasn't possible.

His phone buzzed with a notification.

@Noraephronwasagenius

I know it's only been ten minutes but I'm a little jittery here. Everything okay? Traffic? Car trouble?

Owen fought the urge to throw his phone into oncoming traffic. *Fuck. Fuck fuck fuck fuck fuck.* He had to make a decision. Nora was waiting on him. *Victoria* was waiting on him. He could walk in there and see how it went, try and figure out how the hell he'd gone and fallen for a version of her that Victoria never bothered to let him see. He could walk in and yell those last few insults in her face, because the petty, competitive side of him was furious he'd let Victoria get the last word, but that would probably leave her wondering where the hell Luke was, and he just didn't know if he could bring himself to admit to her face that it was him.

A new, horrible thought occurred to him. What if, knowing that he was Luke, her opinion of Luke changed forever? What if she hated him-as-Owen enough to start hating him-as-Luke? Even worse, what if she was disappointed? What if he walked through that door and her face fell? He would probably never fully recover from that, quite frankly. He wasn't exactly taking this news well, and he had the ability to hide his face from her while he processed it. Nora-Victoria would have no such luxury, and he knew both women well enough to know he would be able to pinpoint the exact second reality set in.

And disappointment was inevitable. With the way he and Victoria had left things, there was no way she wouldn't be upset. That was probably a best-case scenario, even. She'd probably be upset, and hurt, and a dozen other emotions that were swirling through his chest right now. He would have to see them all play out on her delicate, finely molded features. He would see her face fall and then contort into inevitable rage and betrayal, even though he hadn't lied to her. Hell, she was the one who lied to him, and that realization stopped him cold. He had straight out asked her if she had a Twitter account the night she made a joke that sounded like Nora, and she had said no. If she'd admitted the truth then, maybe he wouldn't be in this position. They would have been on the same page so much earlier, and so much could have been avoided.

In fact, if it wasn't for Nora's insistence on anonymity, they probably would have figured this out before they'd ever hooked up. This whole mess was her fault, whether she knew it or not. He wasn't sure he would have even gotten in this deep with Nora if he'd known up-front that she was Victoria, and he certainly never would have antagonized Victoria until they hatefucked a few months ago. Everything would be different, and he didn't know exactly how, but he knew it would be. And the fact that it was the way it was right now was on her, not him.

But still, he had a choice to make. Go in and blow it all up, or walk away and let it blow up on its own. The latter choice would at least leave him the option of telling her something had come up so he could think of a way to defuse the situation. He wasn't sure he even wanted to defuse the situation, but going inside meant it was only going to end one way—with anger and disappointment and probably shouting, given their performances early in the week. Walking away meant maybe it could be salvaged, if he decided he wanted to salvage it. And it would mean preserving his ego, which probably couldn't take the blows Victoria was about to level at him.

@Lukethebarnyardcat

Hey sorry, was just about to message you. Something came up and tonight won't work

He pocketed his phone and walked to the corner. The flowers went in the trash and he stuffed his hands in his pockets, shoulders hunched. Not only was he a coward, he hated that it dovetailed perfectly with Victoria's accusations earlier this week. He did like being the center of attention, and he did like being the hero. And maybe facing Nora-Victoria was the right thing to do, but it would make him look terrible, and he hated that. He already hated that she was pissed at him, even though he was just as pissed at her. He liked being liked way too much.

Traffic streamed past. Owen shuffled his feet, waiting for the light to change, and once again abruptly changed his mind. The flowers might be lost, but he could run back in and explain everything; prove to her that he wasn't who she thought he was—and conversely, that he *was* who she thought he was, when he was online.

He walked confidently towards the coffee shop. So confidently that he didn't even see Victoria until she barreled right into him, her arms crossed and body curled protectively against the wind.

She bounced off his chest and his hand went out to steady her automatically. He caught a glimpse of tear tracks on her cheeks and his heart cracked. He had never thought Victoria would be the type to cry, but Nora—Nora might. "Oh for fuck's sake," she grumbled, wrenching her arm away. "Could today get any worse?"

She brushed past him and he trotted after her, not sure where he was going with this. "Is everything okay?" he asked, more to get her to stop walking than anything else. He needed to fix this and he didn't know how, but he was at least going to try.

She scoffed without turning around. "Why do you give a shit?"

"Because." *Because we were both out of line after court. Because you're Nora. Because I want you to understand I care about you, even if I'm terrified about what that means.*

Victoria drew to a stop and her eyes went straight to the trash can. There lay his roses, clearly freshly discarded. They rested there like an ugly scar, proof that Luke had been here and walked away. Her face paled, her eyes went cold, and she rounded on him. "Go away. I had a shitty night, and you—you are not going to make it any better." *There goes that plan.* He couldn't very well admit he was Luke now, not when she knew Luke was a fucking coward. He would have to figure out a better way to come clean.

"Let me try." The words were out of his mouth before he could stop himself. He couldn't fix this if they were permanently broken, after all. But maybe he could cheer her up a little, make her remember why she liked the Owen version of him. Then he could figure out a way to tell her so she wouldn't hate the Luke version, either.

"How?"

He glanced around and his eyes landed on the Depot. "Let's go ice skating."

Victoria stared at him, dumbfounded. "I've never been ice skating."

"Never?" Owen asked.

"Never." There wasn't much money for activities that weren't free when Victoria was growing up, and ice skating wasn't a necessity like learning to swim. By the time she had the disposable income to try it, she was far too afraid of falling and cracking her head open to bother. She blinked back the tears that had been slowly tracking down her face since she found out Luke wasn't coming and lifted her chin. She wasn't about to let Owen see her weak like this, not after what he pulled in court.

"Well then there's no time like the present," he said, and held out his hand.

When Victoria woke up this morning, she was sure of two things: Owen Pohl was a piece of shit, and she was about to start something wonderful with Luke. And now, with the evidence of Luke's disgust sitting clear as day on top of the nearest trash can, all of that was upside down. And Owen kept looking at her meaningfully, like there was something more happening here, when just a few days ago she thought they were completely out of each other's lives for good.

Here was another Moment. She could walk away and be done with both of them or she could throw caution to the wind and accept Owen's offer, which would at least salvage some of her ego.

Against her better judgment, she took his hand. He pulled her along for a few paces before doubt hit and she dug her heels in. "Hold on, I don't know if I'm up for this," she protested.

"Let me guess—you got stood up by some asshole and you want to go home and brood about it."

She dropped his hand. "I also got reamed out at work this week because of a dirty trick one of the opposing attorneys played on me, who then went on to accuse me of being a heartless bitch. Don't make this all about some asshole guy." Calling Luke an asshole hurt, but it also felt right—she didn't want to mope about him, especially if he was going to be one. Victoria was self-aware enough to know that she was pretty damn good-looking, objectively speaking. The blow to her ego went deeper than that. If he didn't think she was hot enough for him, then Luke wasn't the guy she thought he was. But if he thought she looked vain, or shallow, or high maintenance, well, that would hurt. A lot. More than Owen's words in the parking lot had, and those had cut deep.

Something unreadable flashed in his eyes. "Fair enough. But brooding on all of it isn't going to help."

"Plotting a way to get away with your murder might," she argued, and he grinned.

"Also fair. But are you in?"

Suddenly, she didn't hate Owen as much as she hated Luke. This was an unexpected turn of events to say the least, but if she couldn't prove Luke wrong to his face, Owen would have to suffice. If he thought she was a cold-hearted robot, she'd show him otherwise. "I'm in," she agreed, and once again let him take her hand and tow her down the street. If nothing else, it would be a good distraction from the shitshow of tonight and keep her from checking her phone obsessively.

But once she had the skates strapped to her feet, doubt seized her. She wobbled precariously on the narrow blades and sat immediately back down on the bench, ready to take them off. She had insisted on getting figure skates instead of hockey skates, but when he stood up without a trace of wobble she wondered if she'd chosen wrong. "It's not the skate, I promise," he said, reading her mind. "I'm better at hockey skates, but figure skates should be easier for you to learn in." His eyes glimmered and he leaned closer to her. "If you're really scared, they have walkers available. You know, to lean on as you learn."

"Har har, very funny."

"They do! I can get you one, if you want. If you'd rather not hold my hand, that is."

"Any chance we can just get hot chocolate and say we went skating instead?"

"You chickening out on me, Vee?"

The nickname got her. In just a few days, she'd somehow come to miss the way he teased her, half out of admiration and half out of pure, natural competitiveness. "Just worried you're going to screw up while teaching me and I'll end up dead. And then I'd have to haunt your ass," she replied. "Possibly with that walker."

"I promise, learning to ice skate is a low-fatality endeavor."

"Not if I murder you."

"Do I need to be worried? This is the second death threat you've made tonight," Owen said, even as he held out his arm for her to lean on as they awkwardly hobbled towards the gate to the rink. She saw the stash of learning-to-skate devices lined up near the boards, but she ignored it. Owen's arm was steady enough and despite it all, she did trust him. The ice smelled sharp and fresh, and there were dozens of people out there, traversing the rink in a counterclockwise circle. The windows of the old train depot opened out onto the busy downtown streets, lined with a thin layer of ice and slush.

"That depends. Are you going to stand me up?" she threw back, and he winced. But then he stepped out onto the ice and held out both his hands, waiting for her.

"I'm here, right now," he said seriously, as if he was trying to tell her something else. "Do you trust me?"

"Honestly, jury is still out on that one," she said, but slipped her hands into his.

It was terrifying and exhilarating at once. She fell half a dozen times, bringing Owen down with her in a tangle of limbs at least three of those times. But each time he would laugh and pick himself back up, unshakable and ready to try again. He talked her through keeping her balance and taking tiny steps, and pretty soon she was only loosely clasping his hand as they skated side by side. They were slow—an elderly couple and several small children kept lapping them—and she could tell he was holding himself back, speed-wise, but it was fun. She didn't even need to hold his hand after a while, but she did anyway. It was warm and steady and she needed that tonight.

"When did you learn to skate?" she asked.

"I don't really remember learning, but my dad must have taught me. He played hockey in college."

That was an unfortunately similar story to one of Luke's, but she shook it off. Most guys in Minnesota played hockey, after all. "Did you?"

"In college? No. But I did in high school for a bit."

"Were you any good?"

"Pretty good. Not great, but good enough."

"So modest," she teased, sneaking a glance at him.

His lips curved up and it seemed like he was about to say something, when the loudspeaker announced it was time for the Zamboni break. The music stopped and they joined the scrum at the gate while the Zamboni slowly approached. "Now it's time for that hot chocolate," Owen declared, and she let him buy it for her because after the fiasco with Luke, it felt good to have someone paying attention to her. She itched to pull her phone out of her pocket and send off a satisfying, lengthy screed to Luke, but as long as she was with Owen, she could refrain. They tucked themselves in a corner and wrapped their hands around the flimsy paper cups, and inspiration struck her.

"Okay, my turn," she announced. Owen lifted his eyebrows in question. "I've never been skating before. Have you ever done karaoke?"

"I went to college, so yes."

"I mean on your own. Not with fourteen of your frat brothers."

"First of all, I was never in a frat and I'm appalled you think I would be. Second of all . . . okay no, I've never done it solo. Is that a requirement or something?"

She crumpled her cup and threw it in the garbage. "It is now."

Owen was not prepared for a whole lot of things that had happened in the past few hours, but nothing—nothing—could prepare him for the sight of Victoria up on a small stage in a dingy bar, belting out "Come As You Are" by Nirvana. She came alive, her face glowing while she tossed her hair and growled the lyrics like Kurt Cobain's long-lost baby sister, and Owen leaned back in his chair and took it all in.

The rest of the crowd was clearly enjoying it too, because Victoria could work an audience like none other. He watched her wink at a table of guys sitting in the corner and they all howled in response, clapping and cheering so loudly it drowned out the next few bars. He wanted to see her like this all the time, alive and sexy and uninhibited. But as soon as he told her the truth, she'd hate him. He needed to find a way around that.

The song finished and she dipped into an elegant curtsy. Owen pushed her beer across the table as she dropped into her seat with a flourish. "Nirvana really is your favorite band, isn't it?" he said, and she grinned at him over the pint glass.

"My mom was a die-hard. Pretty sure 'Heart-Shaped Box' was my first lullaby."

"That's dark."

"That's teen parenting," she laughed. " 'Black Hole Sun' was another staple."

"So all grunge, not just Nirvana."

"Kurt was her first love, but yeah, she was into that whole sound. All music, really."

He remembered something Nora had said about radio singalongs with her mom and winced internally. The pieces had all been there; he should have put it together sooner. He needed to tell her, but he wanted to enjoy this a little bit longer before throwing them back into the arena. "So what's the rules for this? I have to go solo?"

"I should make you go up alone and sing 'Purple Rain' to a Minneapolis crowd after the shit you pulled this week. They'd tear you to pieces if you screw up Prince," she grumbled. "But I'll be nice. We're up in two more songs. All you have to do is not embarrass me."

"That might be kind of a big ask," he admitted.

"Tone deaf?"

"Worse, if possible. I tried singing to Olivia once and she held a hand over my mouth until I stopped."

"Well, we're doing 'Living On A Prayer,' so try and keep up," she said. "It's an easy one, so long as you don't try and get fancy. The crowd usually loves it and sings along, so it's less work for you."

"I thought this was about me paying my dues."

"Baby steps," she replied. Up on stage, three women in their early twenties were collapsing in giggles while they tried to get through an Ariana Grande song, missing half the words and screeching loudly on the high notes, of which there were many.

"You plan on taking me out again?" Owen asked, trying to hide his surprise.

"Don't push it," she said dismissively. "I'm mostly doing this because some asshole stood me up tonight and I just can't take any more rejection."

Owen shifted uncomfortably. Now was his chance, so he opened his mouth to admit the truth. "About that—" he started. But the DJ called their names, and she tossed down a napkin.

"Later," she said, and jumped to her feet.

The best he could say was it wasn't a massacre. But the moment he croaked the opening lines her eyebrows shot up, and she took over. She let him fade into the background, which was unusual for him, but compared to her talent he felt a little exposed. Fortunately, crowds are far more forgiving of men sucking at karaoke than they would be of a woman, so most people just laughed whenever his voice cracked.

The song was mercifully brief, or at least it felt that way standing next to her. Seeing her from the crowd was one thing, but watching her from the stage was something else. She was vivacious and warm and so beautiful it hurt to look at her, and he resolved to tell her the truth.

At the end of the night.

It had been a crappy week for her, mostly because of him, and he wanted her to have at least one fun night. Which was ridiculous because it wasn't like he was going to tell her she had terminal cancer or something, but he did want to give her this. And he was selfish too, because she was smiling at him while they settled their tab and he never wanted that to end.

"I assume you're a regular here?" he asked as they fell into step outside. She lived close, but he wasn't about to walk quickly. He was not quite so melodramatic as to think he was on death row, but he did feel like he was on borrowed time.

"Not there necessarily. Usually my mom and I go to a shitty one south of the Cities. It's closer for her and more our speed. But I always know where there's karaoke, in case one of us needs to blow off some steam."

"I thought that was rom coms and skipping work?"

"That's a scheduled mental health day. Karaoke is more like, the guy you were dating turned out to be a piece of shit and you want to torch his car but instead you just sing a lot of Shania Twain."

Owen winced. "Was that a common occurrence?"

"What, torching cars? We never actually got that far, but for her . . . yeah, there was a fair bit of heartbreak. She's sort of a hopeless romantic, and she's always assuming guys have a hidden gem inside of them that she just needs to find. Means she spends a lot of time in the dirt with nothing to show for it."

"I notice you don't mention your dad much," he ventured.

"You noticed right. He walked out before I was even born. If he's not going to pay attention to me, I'm not going to pay any attention to him."

"That's fair," he said carefully. "But what about you? Anyone whose car you want to torch? Aside from the guy tonight, I mean."

She snorted and stuffed her hands in her pockets, but her arm was pressed close to his. "That would involve me giving guys a chance. I don't tend to let them get close to me, if you noticed."

The penny dropped. *Wow, I am the world's biggest piece of shit.* Luke was her safe space, the person she let see her vulnerable. And knowing that meant asking him to meet in person was an even bigger deal than he had realized, because it meant she was giving him a real, honest-to-god chance. He had seen Nora's vulnerability and Victoria's hard-as-nails exterior, but he hadn't considered what that meant when they were the same person. And he'd blown it, because he was worried about how it would make *him* feel. He took a deep breath, because now was the moment.

They approached her building and drew to a stop. "Did you want to . . . ?" she asked, jerking her head towards the door.

"Weren't you just threatening to murder me maybe an hour ago?" he joked. He hoped she wouldn't notice how fake his smile was now, and his heart pounded as he frantically tried to come up with the right words.

"Chicken," she teased, but she didn't seem too upset. "Wouldn't think a little threat of murder would keep you from getting laid."

"What can I say? I'm very attached to this whole 'being alive' thing."

"Then I should probably . . . get going," she said, but she was stalling. And he knew why, but he also knew he needed to not kiss her and just rip the band-aid off. Because if he kissed her, he would lose his nerve, and if he lost his nerve he would never forgive himself. He had to tell her the truth. Victoria shuffled her feet and moved closer, chin tilted up and lips level with his. She leaned forward, mouth parted, and for half a second he almost gave in.

He took an unnecessarily large step back. "There's something we should talk about," he said in a rush, exhaling heavily.

Her expression crumbled. "You know what? Forget it. Whatever it is, I don't want to hear it. This whole week has been shitty, and I don't need anything else to make me feel like crap," she said, and the resignation in her voice hurt more than any of the insults she'd thrown at him the other day. She turned and walked towards the door, only stopping when her hand was on the handle. "I don't need your pity, or your—whatever. Just leave me alone after this, okay?"

And then she was gone.

Chapter Nineteen

Humiliation and sadness blinded her. Victoria didn't remember walking into her apartment, or locking the door or throwing her purse across the room. All she remembered was a loud, insistent pounding in her ears while her cheeks burned with shame.

She was a goddamn idiot. She had gone and fallen for Owen's charade again, thinking he genuinely felt bad about the shit he pulled in court rather than just pitying her for having had a bad day. There was only so much humiliation one woman could take in a night. Luke bailing had stung, but Owen seeming to want to make it up to her had been just sweet enough for her to shove it to the back of her head for now. She figured if Owen wanted to be with her tonight, she might even be able to forget about Luke and his rejection for a whole twelve hours.

But now, not only was Luke not interested in her, neither was Owen. That felt like a particularly pointed slap, since physical chemistry was the one thing she could always count on with Owen. Even when he didn't like her, he wanted her.

But now, he liked her but didn't want her, which was apparently the same problem Luke had. Someone who had been interested in her before, who then abruptly changed his mind once he saw her. She stared at herself in the bathroom mirror, trying in vain to find what hideous flaw had driven them both away tonight. There was nothing in her teeth, her hair was bouncy and perfect, and her clothes were immaculate.

No, they were just assholes. Victoria had spent so long trying to convince her mother of that very fact: men suck up all available emotional energy and give nothing in return, and she was furious that she'd allowed herself the fantasy of believing that not one, but *two* men weren't utter pieces of shit. This was what she got for opening herself up. She knew better, and she was not about to make that same mistake ever again.

Now was when she should turn to someone—her mother, the girls, anyone—to talk her down, but she didn't want to be talked down. She wanted to destroy Luke, the same way she felt destroyed. It was what he deserved.

In flagrant defiance of Owen's earlier prediction and direct contradiction of her own wishes, she left the wine bottle on the top shelf. Opening Twitter on her laptop was easy, and calling up the most recent DM from Luke was even easier. Just the words *tonight won't work* were enough to send her heart rate spiking, and anger began clouding her vision again. Her armpits started sweating and her hands were trembling visibly when she placed them on her keyboard.

@Noraephronwasagenius

Okay look, I don't know what the fuck happened tonight. And don't give me any stupid excuses, because I know you were there. I saw the roses in the garbage. Don't tell me it's conceited of me to think those were for me, because there's a reason I picked having a pink rose sitting out on the table and I know you knew why I chose that. You know everything about me, including shit I've never even told my own mother. You know my favorite movie and my favorite food and my favorite color and yes, my favorite flower, so don't fucking bullshit me. Another customer said she thought she saw someone standing outside the window with a bunch of roses looking in right before I got your message, okay? I was so nervous I asked her if she'd seen anyone waiting outside, and when she said she saw a man with roses I was so happy I wanted to cry.

And then I got your cowardly ass message, and realized you don't deserve my tears. What the ever living fuck, Luke? Really, truly—what the fuck? After all these messages, you don't have the courage to just tell me you're not into me to my face? You couldn't even bring yourself to walk through the door and let our complete and utter lack of chemistry be hint enough for me? You had to pretend like something "came up"?

No. Fuck you. Fuck you and every dude who has ever pulled something like this. Fuck you for making me think you cared, and then turning out to be a shallow, pathetic jackass just like every other dirtbag out there. What was it about me? Was I not hot enough for you? My tits too small? My nose too big? Or was it the other way around and you thought I was too hot for you? My clothes and makeup make me look too high maintenance? Worried your bros would mock you for dating out of your league?

Guess what, asshole? None of those fears give you the right to treat me like this. You owed me a face-to-face conversation, if nothing else. Hell, even a longer DM would have been acceptable, had you been man enough to just lay it all out there. I know it was sudden and you didn't know I lived here, but to do this to me? Fuck. You.

I'm done with this and I'm done with you. Don't bother to reach out, because after you get this? You're blocked. If you make a new account to try and contact me, I'll block that one. You don't ever get to talk to me again, because you fucked this up. I'm not interested in explanations or apologies. Just leave me the hell alone.

Breathing heavily, she hit send with far more force than necessary. The check mark showing he'd received it showed up almost instantly, and she had to get up and pace around the couch, the urge to reach through her screen and punch him too strong. It felt good to get that out there, but it was a loss too. A loss of something she didn't realize she'd cherished until just now—a possibility. As long as she had Luke online, there was always the hazy, future possibility of a real relationship with a man who understood and supported her. Owen had seemed like it too, with his stupid jokes and stupid smile and habit of making her skin burn whenever he touched her. And now, with both Owen and Luke dead to her, all of that was gone, and she was stupid to have put her hopes in either of them.

She clicked through to Luke's profile—his stupid fucking cat, as always, staring serenely up at her—and hit block with vicious satisfaction. He was out of her life, for good.

"What's gotten into you?" Ashley asked. Her eyes were glued to the astroturf field where Olivia was determinedly chasing down the soccer ball.

"It's nothing." Owen clapped for Olivia, who had now come to a complete stop and was staring at her coach for directions. She kicked the ball straight to a member of the opposing team, and the field dissolved into momentary chaos. "I feel like indoor soccer is a bit much for five-year-olds, don't you?" But watching this was better than what he had been doing, which was moping around his house, annoying his cat and trying to forget how monumentally he'd fucked things up with Nora.

He had managed to go from having two perfect women to none in record time, and it was all his fault. Her fuck-you message kept running through his head, the accuracy painful to admit. He did owe her a face-to-face conversation, but he hadn't been able to bring himself to do it, and that was entirely on him.

"You try running a five year old ragged in the winter," Ashley said. "There's only so many times she can go sledding, and this doesn't require a snowsuit, which means when she has to pee it's not a national emergency. But really, what's your deal?"

"No deal," he shrugged. Ashley waited patiently and he caught another parent looking askance at them. "I assume most of the parents think there's something scandalous going on with us, right?"

"Guaranteed." Out on the field, the ref blew the whistle and the girls hustled and stumbled towards the sidelines for half-time. "I mean, I'm already the dumb bimbo married to a man old enough to be my dad, so of course I'd be sleeping with his son too." Ashley tossed her hair over her shoulder and looked him fully in the face. "But nice try with the distraction. Spill."

"You know, you're worse than my actual mother."

"That's because your actual mother is an academic who gets lost in her work, which is not a criticism, just an observation. You and I also grew up together, which means I have a unique perspective on you."

"Would you stop bringing that up? It's creepy," he whined.

She crossed her arms. "Is it that girl?"

"Victoria?"

Her eyebrows shot up. "I was talking about the other one; the internet one. Was there something with Victoria?"

Owen shoved his hand through his hair in annoyance. Ashley had a way of weaseling everything out of him one way or another. "Sort of. It's complicated."

"And we have at least five more minutes before the game starts and I return to superfan mode, so spill."

"So Victoria and I were sort of seeing each other."

"You were fucking, got it."

"Don't be crass."

"Don't be such a prude."

He sighed. "Anyway, it *was* complicated. She was opposing counsel on my Smorgasbord case, and—"

"She was? As in, isn't anymore?"

He shook his head. He'd gotten word she was off the case a week after he'd gotten Nora's Dear John: Fuck You message, and he didn't know if it was Victoria's decision or if a higher-up was upset with her. He hoped it was the former but feared it was the latter, and even though things were fifteen different kinds of screwed up between them, he didn't want her job to be in jeopardy.

So much about Victoria had fallen into place now that he knew she was Nora. Nora had grown up poor and was fiercely, fiercely committed to making sure she was never in a place where she or her mother wanted for anything ever again. Owen didn't understand what that was like, not really, but he admired Nora's dedication and now saw it in Victoria's uncompromising position. She worked for Smorgasbord because they paid better than most, and her position wasn't just prestigious—it was safe. It meant enough money to pay off what were probably enormous student loans, and if she was supporting her mother, even partially, it would be a stable, steady income to rival even the biggest white-shoe firms in the area. It also meant that unlike what he'd assumed, she didn't get it because of who she knew. She'd gotten her in-house position on raw talent. And if he'd put her job in even the slightest bit of doubt, he felt bad about it, even if he didn't regret it. His clients deserved justice and Smorgasbord was standing in the way of that, Victoria alongside it. Fifteen different kinds of screwed up, indeed.

"She's off the case for now, at least. And I did what was right by my client to get the case pushed into litigation, but in the process I may have been a little . . . showboaty."

"You? Never," Ashley said drily. She spared a glance for Lily, who was playing with another little girl just off to the side of the bleachers, and then turned back to Owen.

"Yeah, well, she was pissed. Rightly so, for some of it, but then she jumped to some conclusions about my motives, and I got pissed, and it was bad."

"So she dumped your ass."

"More or less, yeah."

"And now you're moping about it, instead of apologizing and trying to fix it."

"There's more, and it makes apologizing a hell of a lot harder," he said, and spilled the rest of the story. The coffee shop, the realization that she was Nora, his own cowardice, the ice skating, the karaoke, and finally his inability to kiss her because it felt like a lie—which it would have been—leading to Nora's epic goodbye message.

Ashley let out a long breath and shook her head. "Wow, you really blew it," she said, patting his knee sympathetically. "But also, there's a pretty obvious solution here. You have Victoria's phone number. Text her or slide into her DMs or whatever, but tell her the truth. She deserves that."

"Except she doesn't want Luke to have anything to do with her. Shouldn't I honor that request?"

"You can be honest with her without expecting her to engage

with you. This is a pretty big thing for you to know and for her to be in the dark on, so no, I think you've got a duty to come clean no matter what."

"She'll hate me."

"She already hates you. You'll live. Besides, it sounds like you really like her, so if there's even the slightest chance of you guys working this out, you can't do it under a cloud of lies. And it's the right thing to do, so just nut up and do it," Ashley said. Out in front of them, the game resumed and Ashley turned her attention back to the team, leaving him with a lot to think about.

Chapter Twenty

Victoria's phone was a lot quieter these days. Without her messages from Luke she was spending way less time on Twitter, which also meant far fewer notifications popping up on her phone during work. The group chat was constantly checking in on her, but she was being vague and not really answering their questions. They knew things had gone poorly with Luke, but she wasn't up to explaining everything quite yet. It made her feel like too much of a failure. And throwing herself into work wasn't necessarily a bad thing, especially given how much shit she was in for letting the case slip from arbitration to litigation, but it did make the workday drag. A notification popped onto her screen from her personal email account and she glanced at it, barely registering it before her brain caught up.

PaVang@reprojustice.org RE: In-House Counsel Position

Reproductive Justice has an opening? she wondered with a jolt. They were a national feminist organization that handled discrimination suits with an explicit intersectional mission. Victoria had volunteered for them for one semester in law school, but aside from lobbying for Smorgasbord to sponsor their 5k and attending a few fundraisers, she hadn't had much contact with anyone there since then.

She opened her email and read so quickly she wondered if she was hallucinating.

Dear Ms. Clemenceaux,

We have an opening in our in-house counsel in Minneapolis, specifically for someone with experience with litigation. I understand if you are happy with your position at Smorgasbord, but you come highly recommended and I hope you would consider applying for the job. I have attached the details and if you have any questions, please don't hesitate to ask.

Sincerely,
Pa Vang

Human Resources Director
Reproductive Justice
(612) 555-4982 extension 233
761 University Ave
Saint Paul, MN

You come highly recommended. Victoria wracked her brain trying to think of who she would know with connections at RJ, coming up empty. She hadn't worked there long enough to leave a lasting impression and she didn't know anyone who had gone into the nonprofit world after law school. Owen was the only one involved in progressive causes who she had any sort of interactions with—and he certainly wasn't going to be recommending her for jobs right now, not after everything.

Her heart lifted. Reproductive Justice wanted *her*, and it might be a way out of the Smorgasbord trap. But when she looked at the details, her heart sank. Annual compensation was higher than she was expecting, but not enough. It was flattering to be wanted, but in the end that's all it could be. She had dreams and plans and responsibilities, but those required a certain salary and that meant staying at Smorgasbord.

With a sigh, she closed her email app and returned to work.

Owen snagged a glass of wine from a passing waiter and scanned the crowd. Ashley had badgered him into coming to her latest charity gala, even though it meant time with his father. So far, Charles was safely tucked into Ashley's side on the other side of the country club ballroom, which meant he had some time to brace himself—or to get good and drunk, if necessary. He had promised Ashley he would be civil, at the very least, and he was determined to live up to that promise.

But for now, he had some mingling to do. A familiar blonde head caught his eye and he broke into a grin. "How's married life treating you?" he asked, hugging Cassie with one arm.

"Pretty damn awesome, I gotta say," she replied.

"Where's the husband?"

"Off making white people uncomfortable with his jokes, I'd imagine," she laughed. "Someone from our law firm pulled him into a conversation about golf and I barely managed to escape with my life. Where's Victoria?"

Owen tried and failed to hide his wince. "Not here, obviously."

"Oh shit, sorry. I thought—you guys seemed so solid at our wedding, I assumed—god, sorry," she stumbled.

Andy materialized to her left and plucked the wine glass from her hand, downing it in one. Their intimacy made his heart ache, remembering how easy things had been with Victoria for that short amount of time. "I swear to god, what is it about lawyers that makes them want to talk about golf? Have you ever golfed, Owen?"

"I grew up rich and white in the suburbs, so yes, I have."

Andy shook his head, black hair gleaming under the chandelier. "I'm so glad I escaped that particular rich man disease. Anyway, how are you? How's—"

"Tell us more about the golf conversation," Cassie interrupted, eyes wild as she tried to silently communicate with her husband.

Owen managed a chuckle. "It's fine, Cass. Victoria and I aren't together anymore," he told Andy.

"Ah, damn that sucks. You okay?"

"It's fine," he dismissed.

"Which one of you fucked up?" Andy asked, and Cassie elbowed him very unsubtly. "What? It's a legit question."

"I did," Owen admitted.

"That sucks, man," Andy said, touching his arm gently. "Any chance you can repair it?"

"I don't know," he admitted honestly. "It was pretty bad." *Plus I'm keeping a fairly big secret from her and I don't know how she'll handle it.* He knew Ashley was right, but he figured Victoria needed a little time to cool down. If he tried to apologize now, he risked making everything worse. Better to let her heal a little on her own, then explain.

Cassie wrinkled her nose. "Then I assume it's pointless to ask if she heard from Reproductive Justice," she said. Andy threw his arm around her casually and once again, Owen wished he had handled everything differently. It would be so nice to have Victoria here, to whisper in her ear when things got boring, to touch her whenever he wanted. From the stage in the corner, the boring jazz band that worked all of Ashley's galas started to play quietly.

"About what?"

"Oh, their in-house counsel is leaving for a job in DC, so I mentioned to their HR director that Victoria would be kickass at that. I don't think she's really looking to leave Smorgasbord, but I figured it'd be worth a shot for them."

Owen couldn't suppress a smile at the thought of Victoria working for RJ. It was the perfect job for her—progressive, feminist, and plenty disruptive. She would be filing suits and tearing old white men a new one on a daily basis, and he genuinely hoped she'd gotten an offer. "Yeah, I don't know about that. But I do know she'd be perfect for it, so let's hope they manage to poach her."

Out of the corner of his eye he saw his father and Ashley wrap up their conversation and start walking in his direction. He steeled himself and bid goodbye to the newlyweds, making sure to grab himself another glass of wine before his father finished crossing the room.

Charles Pohl looked exactly the way a multimillionaire in his early sixties would look if he were the star of a movie—square-jawed and handsome in a salt-and-pepper way, with an impeccably tailored suit and just enough tan to his skin to tell you he had a second home just outside Hilton Head. He was an exacting, unforgiving man, or at least he had been when Owen was a kid. Ashley claimed he had softened of late, and it did seem the girls were growing up with a slightly looser set of rules. Charles liked lawyers when they were working for him and making him rich, but he loathed the sorts of lawsuits Owen tended to bring, feeling they disturbed the invisible hand of the marketplace. That got in the way of making money, and that was an offense Charles couldn't forgive.

They shared a handshake and Ashley visibly stifled an eye roll. "How are you, Owen?" Charles asked formally.

"I'm great. Suing Smorgasbord again."

A beat of silence. "How is that going?" Charles asked, and Owen wondered if Ashley had made him practice for this conversation. She probably had.

"Pretty good. I'm taking them to court, and we should be doing the pre-hearing motions next week."

"Ah. That must . . . be what you hoped for?"

"What I hope for is for them to stop exploiting their workers but yeah, this is a decent start."

A familiar muscle twitched in Charles' jaw, one that Owen recognized from childhood when his father would walk into his complete disaster of a bedroom and start ordering him to *put your damn things away or else*. "Then I'm happy for you," Charles said stiffly.

Ashley patted his arm and nodded to a server. "I have to go check in with the caterer," she said, leaving the two Pohl men to stare awkwardly at each other over their drinks.

"Ashley says you're doing well," Charles offered. "That's good. I'm glad."

"Are you?" Without Ashley there to soften his edges, Owen's old habits with his father came roaring back.

An unfamiliar look crossed Charles' perfectly weathered face. "Of course I am. I know I made mistakes when you were young, but—"

"But what, you think a couple of conversations because your wife told you to try will fix them?"

"Of course not," he said, unexpectedly soft. "I just wanted to apologize. According to Ashley, that's the first step toward repairing our relationship."

Owen blinked in surprise. "And you want to do that? Or she's making you?"

"I want to," he said, still in that same gentle tone. "I never wanted—I know I was absent and harsh, and there's no excuse for that. I thought I was doing what you needed to push you to succeed, but Ashley and the girls—I've realized what I did back then wasn't right, and I'm sorry. I can't fix that, but I can try and be better going forward."

"Damn, Ashley's really done a number on you," Owen muttered, shaking his head.

Surprisingly, his father smiled. "She really has. In a good way, I hope."

Against all of his instincts, Owen smiled back.

Nora @Noraephronwasagenius

I'm bored. What should I do? Live-tweet a rom com? Join a dating app and post all the terrible "hey beautiful" messages I get sent within the first twenty minutes? Tweet something with the hashtag feminist and see how many men pile into my mentions to scream at me?

Victoria hadn't posted like this publicly in a while, preferring to save her salt for the group, but she felt like being a little feisty. She waited for the responses to roll in, which they predictably did within seconds.

Kara Hates Nazis @Neverthelesskararesisted

You know you're bored when you consider baiting MRAs into a fight.

Nora @Noraephronwasagenius
I'm bored AND feeling like a fight.

Reiko @Keanuisadreamboat
Yeah yikes girl, are you sure that's wise? :o

Maddy H @MadisonHughes95
I vote live-tweet a rom com, if only because that's the least likely to get you death threats. Sidenote: men are garbage and I hate this planet

Nora @Noraephronwasagenius
What if I feel like making men feel like garbage? Maybe it's worth the death threats.

Maddy H @MadisonHughes95
You are a braver woman than I

Victoria got up to pour herself a new glass of wine, and by the time she was back on her couch with her laptop, Kara had already slid into her DMs.

@Neverthelesskararesisted
Okay seriously, everything okay?

@Noraephronwasagenius
Pissed at Luke still.

@Neverthelesskararesisted
Did you want me to do some light stalking? Or is the blocking working for you?

She still hadn't fully explained the whole mess to them, but they'd at least gotten the highlights. It was the most she could bring herself to do, with the irrational shame from being rejected still burning the back of her throat whenever she thought about it.

@Noraephronwasagenius

I dunno what's worse. Knowing he's moved on from me and doesn't give a shit or that he's just sitting over there, moping.

Moving on would sting, but if he's moping that would be infuriating, because he had his fucking chance.

@Neverthelesskararesisted

I could also try and track him down and like, slash his tires or something.

Just saying, it's an option.

Victoria sipped her wine and frowned. There was also the Owen complication to deal with. She was a little embarrassed by how she had reacted to his rejection—he was allowed to not want to hook up—and the more she thought about it, the more she realized her reaction in the courtroom had been at least partially ego-driven on her part.

Victoria never lost cases. She never got ruffled and she never got surprised, and the fact that Owen had pulled off all three in one go was more a reflection on her than on him. She had let her guard down around him, and that made her vulnerable, and she had forgotten that they were opponents. He clearly hadn't, and that wasn't a flaw—that was proof he was a good attorney willing to go the distance for his clients. She had been so relieved to see him that night Luke stood her up, despite everything. She realized she'd gone too far in judging him earlier, but the combination of rejection from Luke and rejection from him had sent her spiraling.

Before, she had been in the weird position of having feelings for two men, unsure of where to concentrate her affections. And now she was in the position of missing them both, furious at one and too ashamed of her behavior to apologize to the other.

@Noraephronwasagenius

Question: what if I have another guy problem to tackle too.

@Neverthelesskararesisted

Fuck Buddy?

Also girl I know you're tight about privacy but giving some actual first names would be helpful for your friends.

@Noraephronwasagenius

Yeah, it's fuck buddy. Long story short, I got mad at him for some shit. Some of it was his fault and some of it wasn't, and I didn't react super well to either, in the first instance because I was feeling like I'd fucked up and in the second because I had literally just been rejected by Luke. Like, only hours before.

@Neverthelesskararesisted

And an apology is out of the question why?

@Noraephronwasagenius

Because I hate apologizing? Lol, but really, I do, and he makes me all discombobulated.

There's also the fact that he might have recommended me for a job? Like, I would kill for this job, except the pay just isn't quite what I need it to be, but he wouldn't know that. But they said I come highly recommended, and I was checking out their website and he's like all over it. Looks like he goes to a lot of their fundraisers and is buddy-buddy with the board.

So now I'm in the weird position of having been a massive dick to him and knowing he did something super nice for me AFTER that, and I have to apologize and my ego straight up can't take it.

@Neverthelesskararesisted

You know you literally answered your question, right? Like, just fucking text him. Say "Wow I was a dick and thanks for the job rec." And then when you're done with that, you and me are going to have a discussion about your financial anxiety, because I know it comes from a very real place but it sounds like your job is killing your soul. I grew up poor too, so I get it, but I think you're putting some undue pressure on yourself.

Victoria's frown deepened, but she knew Kara had a point. That job at Reproductive Justice was so perfect for her, and it wouldn't come with Gerald making her feel like an idiot every time she poked her head out of her office these days. Things had been tense at Smorgasbord ever since the case shifted to litigation, and she had been reassigned to a lower priority case almost immediately. It wasn't quite a demotion, but it was a crystal-clear warning. She was on thin ice with them, and one more screwup could mean her job.

The problem was, she didn't really care that much. All she cared about was the paycheck, so she'd already started looking into other jobs that paid the same. Cassie's firm might have an opening, even though that would mean going to billable hours and entering the endless, soul-sucking race to be partner. It was just as crappy as her job, but maybe she would hate herself a little less. She'd be more removed from the worst of it, at least, because if she worked for a big firm she would be working for people who were hired to make rich white men and corporations money, as opposed to working for the corporation itself.

The Reproductive Justice job would require giving up the dream of buying Kimmy a house, and even though Victoria knew her mother would never, ever ask her to trade her happiness for something like that, it was Victoria's dream. She had vowed to buy that damn house when she was only thirteen, and she had spent half her life working towards that goal. Giving up would be surrender, and she flat-out refused to do that.

And apologizing to Owen also felt like a bridge too far, if only because her feeble attempts at vulnerability kept blowing up in her face. She felt too brittle, too fragile, and if this one exploded on her, she wasn't sure how she would ever get the courage to try it again. Maybe it was just better to let herself heal for the time being, and apologize later. It would be cowardly, just like she accused him of being, but maybe better late than never.

She returned her attention to Twitter and thanked Kara for her advice, changing the topic to Kara's pug, better known as her baby and the cutest dog in the universe. While Kara DMed her pictures of Teddy she announced she wouldn't be picking a fight tonight but rather live-tweeting a cheesy looking Hallmark movie, and settled more comfortably into her couch. She would apologize to Owen.

Eventually.

Chapter Twenty-one

"Now, no parties," Ashley admonished. Their luggage was piled near the door and Charles was trying to coax Lily into her jacket while Olivia was sitting cross-legged on the ground, Luke clambering all over her.

"You mean like the time Taylor's parents went to Cabo and someone broke their pool table?"

"Yes, exactly like that," Ashley laughed.

Charles smothered a smile and pushed himself off the floor, picking up Lily as he went. She clung to his neck and Owen blinked, looking away. It was strange to see his father genuinely parenting. There was a pang of loss that went with it, but it wasn't overwhelming. He was glad his dad was getting a second chance with the girls, if only because the girls deserved that.

"You know, sometimes I wish I didn't know stuff like that," Charles said genially.

Owen bit back his usual poisonous retort and let Ashley handle it. "That's what you get for marrying your son's classmate," she teased gently, and then tugged on Olivia's braid.

"Come on, kiddo. If you get into the car you can watch part of *Moana* before we get to the airport." That got Olivia off the ground, much to Luke's dismay, and Owen scooped him up to keep him from trying to hitch a ride on one of the suitcases. "Come on, Son of Skywalker, just you and me this weekend," he crooned, and caught his father's eye. Charles wasn't a fan of pets, but he wasn't making the expected snarky comment.

He's trying, Owen reminded himself. *He's trying, and that might not fix anything in the past but it counts for something if I want it to.* And truth be told, he did want it to count for something. Knowing his father could change, even slightly, meant something. Owen was enough of a softie to root for him, however distantly.

"Thanks for watching the house," Charles said. He hitched Lily a little higher on his hip and made steady eye contact. "It's a big help."

It was an excuse, is what it was. Ashley and Charles had groundskeepers who could let themselves in to water the plants, and their security system was probably more reliable than Owen sleeping like a rock in the third guest room. But Ashley asked him to come watch the house while they took a trip to Sanibel Island for a week, and Owen knew this was Ashley's attempt at nudging him and his father towards a reconciliation. It meant seeing him today and the day they returned, so hardly a massive time investment, but that was more than he had committed to in years.

"It's no trouble," he assured his father. "Thanks for letting me bring the kitty."

Hesitantly, Charles reached out and scratched behind Luke's ears. "Of course. He's not half bad, this cat of yours."

Personally, Owen felt Luke was perfect but that might be a little too gushy for his father, so he settled for patting Lily on the top of her head and making her giggle. "I like him almost as much as I like my sisters," Owen said, and then it was a crush of confusion and bodies as they tried to get everything out the door and into the SUV with entirely too many seats for a family of four.

Their taillights disappeared down the driveway and Owen let his fingers trail idly across the granite countertop. The house was eerily quiet without the girls running around like mad, and Luke hopped from his arms to pad slowly towards the fire, where he curled up with an elegant stretch.

He was lonely. That was probably why he had agreed to house sit all the way out in Minnetonka. It made the fact that he wasn't going out seem purposeful rather than a symptom of his listlessness. He still hadn't figured out a way to tell Victoria the truth. He wanted to, but it felt presumptuous to email her out of the blue and confess, because that assumed she wanted to hear from Luke again, which she clearly didn't. She'd blocked him on Twitter, and her group of friends—who used to sometimes interact with him—had all built a wall of silence around him, if they hadn't blocked him themselves. The message was clear as a bell, and he wondered if this was his penance—to just pine for her from afar, knowing who she was and unable to tell her the truth about himself.

He flopped down onto the leather sectional, feeling absurdly small on the massive sofa, and turned on the TV. Beside him, his phone buzzed and his heart suddenly tumbled straight down into his stomach.

Victoria Clemenceaux
I still have your damn hoodie, you know.

The ellipsis appeared and disappeared several times. Victoria bit her lip, Owen's hoodie piled on the coffee table in front of her.

Owen Pohl
And here I thought that was lost forever

She scrunched her face up, annoyed that he was being just as difficult to read as she was being. She had been hoping he would be his old self, transparent and open, while she slowly felt him out again.

Victoria Clemenceaux
I mean, I can keep it if you'd rather.
Or I can return it.

She waited with bated breath. The more she'd thought about it, the more the job offer felt like Owen doing something kind for her with no expectation of anything in return. She was still annoyed with him for what happened in court, but if the situations were reversed she honestly couldn't say she would have done anything different.

Owen Pohl
If that's what you want
But I'm housesitting for my dad and stepmom out in Minnetonka this weekend

Victoria Clemenceaux
So what you're saying is I really have to want it.

Owen Pohl
That's exactly what I'm saying

Victoria grinned to herself at how quickly he responded to her flirting. They still had some work ahead of them—she needed to apologize to him for one, and he had some apologizing to do too—but maybe they could pick back up where they were before she lashed out.

Victoria Clemenceaux
Then I guess I'll need that address.

Owen sent it over and she put it into her maps app, slipping on his hoodie as she grabbed her keys. She wasn't exactly being subtle here, but then again neither was he. She had never in her life driven a half hour out of town for a hookup or whatever this was, but she was justifying it because it wasn't just a random guy—it was Owen.

The further she got from downtown the more the cloud that had followed her around for the last few weeks lifted. She had started getting ready to apply for other jobs, particularly at firms that would let her do a good amount of pro bono hours. It wasn't perfect, but that was the way things were for the time being. She was young—she would have time to do more later. Once she bought that house for her mom she could relax a little; consider something lower paying.

The voice on her GPS told her to turn right into the driveway for her destination, and Victoria did a double take. She knew Owen was rich, but knowing it was very different from seeing it in the flesh. She'd had rich friends before; friends with summer homes or cabins up north and shiny, expensive cars that told her they weren't at all concerned about a car payment on top of student loans, since they had neither. She'd even been to various expensive houses for fundraisers for Reproductive Justice, but all of that looked solidly middle class compared to Owen's father's house.

The driveway was cobblestone, for one. *Cobblestone.* And

long—she had to sweep all the way around to the right before it curved back up to the left, the house perched on top of a hill like a castle. The cedar shingles and steeply pitched dormers made her think of movies set on Martha's Vineyard. A memory of telling Luke about her Martha's Vineyard misunderstanding threatened to surface, but she shoved it down. Luke had no place here tonight. Warm lights blazed from a room to the right of the front door, which was itself illuminated by faux gas lanterns on either side of the beveled glass and wood. The landscaping was barren this time of year, past Christmas and still far from the spring thaw, but she could tell it was immaculate. Orderly hedges lined the walkway, with space for what she imagined were flower beds that were riots of color in the spring and summer.

She killed the engine and stepped out just as Owen emerged from behind the front door. "Holy shit," she called, her breath steaming in the cold air. He looked relaxed, casual; like he'd stepped out of an ad for clothing worn exclusively by people who owned boats. Which, she realized belatedly, he probably did. She looked up at the massive three stories looming above her and then back at him. "Did you grow up here?"

"Not here. Across the lake, in a slightly less massive place."

"Define slightly."

"Five thousand square feet instead of six. And an outdoor pool, not an indoor one."

"This place has an indoor pool? Are you kidding me?"

"Indoor pool and a wine cellar the size of most apartments. Oh, and a sauna."

"God, I hate rich people," she said.

He grinned. "Me too." Owen crossed his arms, only in a thin sweater despite the winter air, and trotted down the front walk toward her. "You came a long way to return a sweatshirt," he said, and her stomach fluttered at the familiar dark tone in his voice. But she lifted her chin and pretended it didn't affect her, because that was how they played this game.

"Apparently, I came a long way to get a tour of a freaking mansion, because holy shit, Owen," she said, brushing past him blithely. "How good is this wine cellar?"

"How expensive is your taste?"

"I usually buy one step above boxed wine, but I've had the good shit at work parties." She paused with her hand on the doorknob. "Wait, before I go in—what's the decor? Classy New England cottage-on-the cape? That weird, overly patterned rich-people look from 1995? Full-on rococo gold and peach nightmare?"

He laughed, and her stomach leapt. She'd missed that sound more than she realized. "You do not pull any punches, do you?"

"You said you didn't grow up here, so what do you care? I want to be prepared to be as judgy as possible once we're inside."

Owen stepped close enough to her that she could feel the heat radiating off him. "You could just go inside, you know," he said, his lips tantalizingly close to her ear.

Victoria turned and grasped the doorknob behind her back, grinning. "Just upping the anticipation," she teased, gratified when his eyes flashed.

He reached around her, his hand warm over hers, and turned the knob. "Then let's give you a tour," he murmured.

Victoria dropped her jacket and purse in a pile beside the door. "Go on, booboo," Owen said when a lithe grey cat emerged to sniff her things. "Back in the living room." He nudged the cat away and stuffed his hands in his pockets. "Where do you want to start?"

She looked around at the grand, sweeping staircase and the polished floors. This entryway alone was as big as some of the apartments she had shared with her mom. "Kitchen," she decided.

She let out a little moan when they entered, because the kitchen was gorgeous. A central island had its own sink, and the range was big enough to cook Thanksgiving for a small army. The fridge hummed softly in the corner and recessed lights under the cabinets gave the butcher-block countertops a warm glow. "I'm so jealous right now," she muttered, randomly opening a cabinet to find a giant stand mixer.

"Do you cook?"

"Only out of necessity. But if I had a kitchen like this, I could. Or I could stand in it and *look* like I cook, which is just as good."

"I feel like you'd like Ashley," he said with a half-grin. "I'm pretty sure that was her rationale for this kitchen as well."

"I bet she's got an awesome Instagram."

"It's very good at making people jealous, yes."

"Smart woman," Victoria replied. "She's around our age, you said?"

"Yeah, just a year older. I went to high school with her."

"And you get along?"

He leaned his hip against the counter and crossed his arms. His biceps bulged through the thin sweater he was wearing, and she let her gaze linger appreciatively. "We do. Better than I do with my dad, actually, but we're working on it."

"Sounds like there's a story there."

"It's depressingly ordinary. Workaholic dad, kid feels neglected, takes it out on him by becoming what he hates the most."

"A lawyer?"

"A progressive. Dad's pretty committed to being a Rockefeller Republican, which is to say he considers himself a fiscal conservative and is sure that he earned everything he's made completely on his own. He thinks law firms like mine represent whiners trying to steal from people who worked hard."

"Did he? Earn all this, I mean."

Owen snorted. "No. My grandpa owned a bank and he grew up solidly middle class. Not rich like this, but certainly not poor. But he thinks because he had to get a job in college that means he came from nothing."

She nodded, searching for the right words. Old bitterness rose in her, but it wasn't Owen's fault his father was rich. "And you have a trust fund, right?"

"I do," he sighed. "And the fact that he didn't try and take it away from me when I opened up the firm is probably a sign that he's at least okay with me trying to right some of his wrongs, even if he finds me obnoxious."

"And where does your stepmom fall in this political tableau?"

"She sides more with me than with Dad, which is probably a generational thing. She knows enough people with loans to get that our generation has a different financial situation, and she's smart enough to realize that when you're born white and middle class, you've got privileges others don't have access to. I wish she'd do more, but she has managed to shift his philanthropy from like, country club improvements to urban music programs, so it's a start. Not much, but better than nothing."

"And where does Smorgasbord fit in?"

"What do you mean?"

She rested her forearms on the breakfast bar and cocked her head. She watched his eyes track her movements, dwelling on her neck and the sweep of her hair. "You're not just trying to right some cosmic wrongs, here. You hate Smorgasbord pretty specifically."

"I don't, actually. It's just the biggest target around. The headquarters are here, which means I can depose higher-ups, and it's one of the biggest employers in the country. If I focus on them, I can do the most good possible. Or at least, that's what I'm trying to do. I haven't been too successful until recently." He took a deep breath and she shook her head, forestalling him.

"Don't. What happened in court happened. We don't need to relitigate it. Honestly, I probably would have done the same thing."

"You're off the case, aren't you?"

"Yes, and not by choice. But I didn't react well in the moment, and I'm sorry about that."

"Don't apologize," he said, unexpectedly fierce. "You have nothing to apologize for. I'm a showboat, and—you were right to call me out about that."

"Where does that come from, by the way?"

"What, being a dick?" he asked, and god, she had missed this banter.

"Needing to be the center of attention at all times."

"Probably my mom," he said, looking down and tracing a pattern on the countertop. "She's fairly dramatic."

"And where is she these days?"

"Teaching at a university in Shanghai. She's an art professor—mostly sculpture, although she's done some absolutely mortifying performance art."

"That bad, huh?"

"Honestly, it could be good, but when you're fifteen and your mom is doing spoken word poetry about menstruation, it's . . . not ideal."

Now it was her turn to snort. "God, that does sound painful."

"What about you? Embarrassing high school moments from your mom?"

"Actually, everyone loved her, because she was so much younger than the rest of the moms. She was definitely the Cool

Mom, even though she desperately wanted to be the mom everyone was scared of. Mostly the embarrassment came from people assuming she was my sister, which sucked. But she always encouraged me to be myself, and even took me to my first feminist protest—a sit-in against the local radio station carrying Howard Stern, because she absolutely hated him," she chuckled. "I was maybe five."

Owen ran a hand through his hair and took an unsettlingly deep breath. "I wanted to talk to you about something," he started, and she shook her head. She wasn't ready to talk about the job offer and the accompanying vulnerability that would come with that, because it meant Owen knew her well enough to know how desperately unhappy she was at Smorgasbord. He understood that she wanted to do something better, and what's more, he believed she could. But the apologies they'd just managed were hard enough for her, and she hated having to talk like this—she would rather show him her appreciation than actually say it.

"Not now. Tour is just getting started," she said. He hesitated and she shook her head. "Please, Owen, not—not yet. Whatever you want to talk about, it can wait." He frowned but followed her into the next room. Each room was somehow better than the last—tasteful and expensive, but not without warmth. There was a small study, complete with leather chairs and dark blue accents, and a den that had been converted entirely into a fairy princess play land. Owen's cat snaked in and out of rooms, clearly preferring to stay close to him.

"So what is your stepmom like?"

"Like I said, she's pretty cool."

"And what drew her to your dad?"

He winced. "I have no idea, really. But she's on a mission to liberalize him and chill out the rest of his social circle, so I'm all for that. She even got him to utter the words 'white privilege' the other day, or so she says. And she's a great mom."

"You seem pretty close to your sisters," she ventured, and Owen lit up. He was a doting brother, that much was for sure, and he walked her through the rest of the first floor while regaling her with tales of dance recitals and soccer games. It was adorable, seeing how much he loved them, and it reminded her of that day in the summer, watching him be completely at their beck and call and loving every second of it.

The fact was, Owen had a way of getting under all her defenses. He was so open, so loving, that it was hard to resist. She wanted a little bit of that for herself. It reminded her of Luke, in a way—the good parts of him, at least. The way he seemed to be able to draw her out, crack the walls she had so carefully built. She missed that with Luke, but maybe she could find it with Owen.

Victoria spotted a staircase that led downstairs. "Is the wine cellar down here?"

"Wine cellar, pool, and sauna."

"Then that's where the tour goes next," she said, deciding. She would show him how she felt because words might be failing her, but their bodies never did.

The lights under the pool were bright enough to light up the area without Owen bothering with the overhead fluorescents. Humid warmth surrounded them and the scent of chlorine bit his nostrils, while the windows facing the lake carried an ever-present sheen of condensation. "A pool," Victoria said under her breath. "A goddamn pool, while you live on a lake. What's the point?"

"Well, for one thing, that lake is mostly frozen solid right now," he pointed out. "And for another, some people think lakes smell bad and would rather not swim with the weeds."

She wrinkled her nose. "What sort of stuck-up jackass thinks that?"

"This one," he admitted with a laugh. She wandered across the tile floor and peered down at the water. It threw reflections across her face, lighting her up until she seemed to glow. He had been relieved when she reached out to him, excited to finally have a chance to clear their slates and start again on even footing. But he hadn't accounted for how much she threw him off guard, and how much he craved her adoration. Making her laugh, seeing her smile—those were his favorite things before he knew she was Nora, and now that he did, it made it all the more potent to know that this was the same witty, kind, open woman he had fallen for online.

And she was wearing his hoodie. It made him feel like a high schooler to be giddy over that, but he had noticed it the second she shed her jacket and couldn't stop staring. He wondered if she had worn it a lot over the time they were apart, or if this was a new thing. He hoped it was the former, and that her scent would linger when she gave it back to him. Or she could keep it—he was fine with that too.

"Do you swim here often?" she asked, and maybe it was his imagination, but it seemed as though her voice dropped an octave.

"Occasionally," he replied, measuring her reaction.

"That's a shame. Seems like a waste of a pool, especially with the house to ourselves," she said, eyes suddenly dark.

Her hand lifted to the zipper, currently nestled between her breasts, and she eased it down. The noise seemed unusually loud in the echoey pool room, a metallic click for each tooth of the zipper. "I forgot to give you this," she announced, her voice throaty, and shrugged out of it.

Owen barely caught it before the sweatshirt hit him in the

face. Underneath she was wearing a blue jumpsuit. The halter neckline showed off her shoulders, and a slit of fabric down her sternum revealed a tantalizing slice of skin. She reached for the strings at the nape of her neck and his lungs completely stopped working.

It took forever for her to unravel the knot, or maybe he had just lost all grasp of the time-space-continuum. With one last tug it came undone and the bodice of her jumpsuit fluttered down to her waist, the material fluid and soft. She was wearing a tiny black bra underneath, more lace and strings than anything else, and she unzipped something at her hip to let the rest of the jumpsuit fall away.

Owen swallowed and dug his fingers into his palms, desperate for something to ground him. This was going faster than he anticipated, and he still had some rather big things to reveal. But then Victoria stepped out of the fabric with a flash of legs, and his brain ran straight into a brick wall.

Her black panties matched her bra—of course they did, this was Victoria—and she looked at him over her shoulder. His eyes trailed down the curve of her back, helpless, and she dove into the water with a dainty splash.

"You coming in?" she asked, resurfacing.

His hands were already gripping the hem of his sweater. "That was an impressive dive," he observed, kicking off his socks and undoing his belt.

"My mom was a varsity swimmer, before—well, before I showed up and screwed it all up for her. But she taught me well."

"She sounds like fun," he said, hoping if he kept the subject light and neutral it would keep the situation from getting too charged. *You have to tell her. Tell her now.* Down to his boxers, he walked to the shallow edge and stepped onto the stairs, wincing.

"Are you kidding me? You're going to walk in?" she groused.

"The water's cold," he whined. "I've never been able to do the whole cannonball-in thing."

"On no planet can this water be considered *cold.* My god, growing up on a lake was wasted on you," Victoria retorted. With two strokes she was into his side of the pool and stood, water cascading down her shoulders. *Bad idea, bad idea*, his brain squawked. Even the water washing up his legs did little to cool the fire building in his veins.

"You're telling me," he agreed. He had finally reached his waist and he realized the water wasn't going to do what he hoped it would, because it really wasn't that cold—cooler than the surrounding air at first touch, maybe, but Ashley and Charles kept it warm enough for the girls, which meant it was actually quite pleasant. Victoria waded over to him, her nipples tight under her bra. Owen quickly redirected his gaze to her face, but that didn't help either—her eyes were dark with lust, and a wave of his own threatened to draw him under. "One time, when I was thirteen, I—" he started, babbling, and she pressed her finger to his lips.

"I'm sure whatever story you were going to share is either very touching or very funny, but I'll be honest, I don't give a shit about your childhood right now." Slowly, deliberately, she peeled her bra off and tossed it to the side.

Owen swallowed hard. Her hands wound into his hair and left droplets of water sliding down his cheeks. "What if—what if there's other things we should talk about?" he asked, but his traitorous body stepped closer to her and his hand came to rest on her waist. God, he'd missed the feel of her skin, warm and smooth under his palms, and suddenly he was skating his hands everywhere, remembering every curve of her body.

Victoria rested her forehead against his. "I don't know if we have the best track record when it comes to talking," she said with a shivery sigh. She pressed against him, arms tight around his neck.

"Still though." He cleared his throat, losing the thread before finding it again. "Maybe we should."

"Later," she whispered, and kissed him.

If touching her had reminded him of what he was missing, it was nothing compared to this. Kissing Victoria meant bursting into flames, a wildfire racing through his bloodstream that no amount of water could quench. She nipped at his lower lip and he growled, crushing her against him as his tongue traced the seam of her mouth. When she granted him access he was lost, the brush of their tongues replacing every coherent thought in his head and the taste of her lips driving out any hope of regaining control.

Her nails scraped his scalp and she hitched her leg around his hip, rocking her core against him. But that wasn't enough—nothing would ever be enough with her. Owen hefted her into his arms and let her wrap her legs around his waist. She whimpered, limbs going soft, and Owen spun them around so he could sit on the narrow ledge that lined the pool just a foot or so under the water.

He loved this. He loved bringing her to the edge like this, making her crazy with want. It wasn't a power thing for him, it was just knowing that she wanted *him*. She could have anyone, but she wanted him, and that was enough. But he didn't get to want this, not yet. He slowed his movements, gentling a hand down her back and pulling away for a breath.

"Does it count as dry humping if we're in a pool?" she joked, lips on his jawline.

Owen nosed at her cheek until he found her mouth. "Just how pedantic do you want me to be?" he replied. His erection was pressed between them, but guilt reared its ugly head and he softened slightly. Victoria reached her hand down but he intercepted her, lacing their fingers together and diverting her hand away. He cleared his throat. "And I know we don't have the best track record at talking, but we probably should."

She heaved a sigh and tempered it with a sloppy kiss to his temple. "Fine. But I want wine first," she announced, and climbed elegantly out of the pool. His own movements were clumsy, his fading erection making him awkward. Victoria padded across the floor in nothing but a tiny scrap of fabric, water streaming after her, as if she owned the whole place. She snatched a towel from the cart Ashley always left loaded by the wall, and after a second she took a thick, terrycloth bathrobe as well. "Are these for guests?" she asked.

Owen nodded and shrugged into one himself. "Wine cellar is that way."

She led the way down the hall, feet slapping against the wood slats. She drew up short when they entered the wine cellar, because it really did need to be seen to be believed. The arched ceiling was stucco, and the mosaic floor was straight out of Pompeii's ruins—which was no coincidence, as Ashley had hired an artist to recreate murals to that exact specification. Racks and racks of wine bottles surrounded them, amounting to several hundred thousand dollars in alcohol alone. Warm, yellow lights glowed from a chandelier hanging from the apex of the dome, and the faint hiss of the climate control unit told him they were letting in too much humidity from the pool. The room was almost a thousand square feet, with cabinets for glasses and decanters on the left and a granite-topped island in the center, complete with padded leather stools for people to sit on. This wasn't just a storage room, it was a room meant to be seen by guests who would then sample the wine right there. Ashley and Charles sometimes had tasting parties down here, and the nearest liquor store had someone who called them whenever a particular vintage came in. Wine had never been Owen's thing, probably because he would do anything to avoid being his father, but he knew that this room was special to Charles and Ashley.

"You've got to be kidding me," she said quietly. "You know, there are people out there on food stamps."

"Believe me, I know," Owen agreed. "It's over the top."

"And here I was picturing, like, a really big closet. Holy shit," she muttered, spinning slowly on her heels. "Where do you even start?"

"At random," he admitted. "I know there's a method to how they store it, and they keep the really special stuff in that rack, but beyond that I'm just as lost as you," he said, nodding to the floor-to-ceiling honeycomb on the far wall. "But anything we pick is going to be good, because that's one advantage of rich people. We can usually be counted on to have hired someone to tell us what to buy. What's your go-to?"

"Red," she laughed. "But, um . . . Cabernet Sauvignon? Usually? Is that too pedestrian? Should I ask for a Bordeaux?"

"I have no goddamn idea," Owen said, scanning the rack nearest him. "Okay, here's a Cab Sav. There's supposed to be a whole process with pouring it into a decanter and letting it breathe, but honestly, the wine police won't arrest us if we don't bother."

Victoria found some glasses in the cabinet and he fished a corkscrew out of a drawer in the island. The rich scent wafted out of the bottle and she closed her eyes in pleasure at the first sip. "Damn, that's good. What else is this house hiding?"

"The top floor has a view of the lake," Owen said. "It's pretty damn spectacular."

"Lead the way," she said, but this time, she slipped her hand into his as they walked.

Chapter Twenty-two

Victoria gasped with delight when they reached the third floor loft. From up here, they were above the trees and had an unobstructed view of the lake. Moonlight glinted off the ice, and on the far side of the bay house lights shone warm and inviting. "Being rich must be so nice," she said, without any real heat, and he laughed.

"There's really not a downside," he agreed.

"What, you're not going to tell me some sob story about being a poor little one percenter?" She sipped her wine, warm to her very bones. Now was her chance to say thank you for the job recommendation, but she didn't want it to seem like she was here to pay him back for that. She had to find The Moment, was all. She definitely wasn't stalling or anything.

"Hey, we're not like, billionaires."

"I'm sorry, but how many homes do you guys own?"

"Technically, Dad and Ashley only own this one."

"Technically?"

He shrugged. "They sold the house in Hilton Head a little while ago. But I see your point."

"I'm stuck on this, though—growing up, did you know you were rich?"

"I guess? Everyone else I knew was pretty wealthy, and I knew we had more money than them, but I never really thought much about it."

"That must be nice," she said, only slightly bitter. She had started keeping specific, itemized budgets in sixth grade, not because her mother was irresponsible but because it helped Victoria to feel more in control. Even now, she rarely bought anything that wasn't the generic brand in the grocery store, and her splurges were always meticulously planned. She could tell Owen down to the cent how much she had in each account at this exact moment, and she would bet he only had the roughest idea how much he was worth.

"Believe me, I understand how lucky I am," he said, and when she met his gaze she knew he was serious. "That's why I'm trying to do some good with what I've got. I know not everyone can take on my sort of clients without significant financial risk, so I'm doing what I can."

"So it's not just to piss off the old man?"

"That's just the icing on the cake."

She turned back to the view and tossed her slowly drying hair over her shoulder. "You know that's why I'm at Smorgasbord, right? I need the money?"

"I know, and Vee—I get it. I'm sorry if I was a dick to you before I knew you. I thought you were like me, and that's—that's not an excuse. I was an asshole."

"You were, yeah. But so was I," she agreed. "I think we can safely call all of that water under the bridge." She set her glass down on a narrow bookshelf to her left and tugged him closer by the belt of his robe. "Bygones?" she said, once again stepping close enough to him that she could feel his heat.

He sighed, carding her hair back from her face. "There's . . . one more thing you should know."

"I know," she said, hating that she felt awkward about this, like she owed him something. She didn't want to feel that way and she didn't want him to feel like there were secrets between them. "I figured out it was you a while ago."

He blinked rapidly and stepped back. "You—you did?"

"You were the only person who made sense," she shrugged, pulling him back toward her. "We don't have to get into it," she added, but when she kissed him, he didn't respond right away.

"Wait, you—you knew?" he stammered. "Since when?"

"The internet is a really useful tool, you know. You can find out all sorts of things there," she said drily and this time, his mouth opened to hers.

"You knew," he said, breathless and a little too shocked for her liking.

It's just a damn job offer, she wanted to say, but the moment was spiraling away from that anyway. "Yeah, I know," she agreed. She plucked at the belt on his robe until it fell open, and his jaw went slack when she curled her hand around his cock.

She drew his earlobe between her teeth and slowly jacked him, enjoying the way he seemed to harden further with each twist of her wrist.

He blew out a breath that turned into a groan. "Wait, the—" he gestured helplessly at the windows even as she shrugged out of her own robe.

"We're pretty high up," she said, still stroking him. A bead of pre-come pearled at his slit. She brushed her thumb across it and a tendon popped out on his neck with the strain of staying still. "Do you really think anyone can see us?"

". . . Drones, maybe?" he said in a strangled, amused voice, and she laughed.

"Yes, sounds like we should be very concerned about that," she teased, but nevertheless she stilled her hand. "Did you want me to stop?"

"Fuck no," he growled, cuffing his hand around the back of her neck. This kiss was bruising for them both, clashing teeth and sloppy, messy angles, and his hips thrust forward with each stroke of her palm.

He broke away from her and pressed his forehead to her shoulder, panting. "I'd fuck you against that window right now but I don't have any condoms with me," he rasped. "And I am not about to raid my dad and stepmom's stash."

"There's one in my pocket," she said, giving his dick one more stroke and nodding towards her robe.

"What are you, a witch?"

"Just prepared," she said, kissing the corner of his mouth. "I grabbed it on our way up here—I had a bunch in my purse."

"God, you're amazing," he said, so devoutly she had to laugh.

"Any other objections?"

His hand palmed her ass and he smirked. "None whatsoever."

He was delirious with happiness, and it wasn't just because Victoria's hand was working his shaft. *She knew.* He didn't know how, exactly, or when, or why she didn't just *tell* him she knew he was Luke, but she knew. The burden was off him, and anything he had left to apologize for—like standing her up that day at the coffee shop—could come later. He was so happy he couldn't stop kissing her. They could enjoy themselves without the veil of secrets between them, and he was so goddamn relieved he wanted to jump for joy.

He walked her backwards down the hallway to the third-floor bedroom, not willing to break the kiss even to talk. She clung to him with each step and eventually he lifted her into his arms, her legs wrapping around his waist. Her heat against his aching dick was almost a relief but not enough, and he had hardly deposited her on the bed before he yanked her underwear down. She was so wet already, her scent as indelible in his mind as his own name, and he swiped his tongue through her folds, eager for a taste.

Her hands knotted in his hair, pulling him towards her, and he let her, enjoying the way she would take charge when she wanted it. He sucked her throbbing, tight nub between his lips, and the moan it wrenched from her lips was almost as delicious as she was. He gave her two fingers to clench down on, and the vise of her around his fingers made his vision waver at the edges. Suddenly she was falling apart, her thighs shaking and her back bowing with the strain.

He didn't give her time to recover, just rolled the condom on and thrust inside her. Her arms wrapped around his neck and she urged him down, her mouth chasing him while his thrusts set her breasts bouncing. He nuzzled at her neck, kissing her jaw and nipping at her ear, and with each thrust he felt himself go deeper and deeper into her until he had completely lost himself in her.

Victoria's nails dug into his backside and he growled, half-feral. He pushed her thigh up and out so her knee was almost at his shoulder, and when he saw the look in her eye he knew it felt as good for her as it did for him. The shift in angle made her drag just right against him, and he watched her fingers start drawing tight, perfect circles over her clit. "Fuck, again?" he gritted out, and she nodded helplessly.

He wanted to feel her come again so badly he slowed down, just enough to lessen the heat building at the base of his spine. "No no no no," she whined. "Faster."

He was powerless against her commands, and sped up. "Like this?" he managed, and she nodded, closing her eyes and pressing down hard. Her peak came just as his was approaching, and when she clamped down on his cock that was all it took.

Owen managed to catch himself on his elbows before he crushed her, but only barely. His body was limp and his mind was floating, and he didn't know how long they stayed like that before her gentle touches brought him back to himself.

She was stroking his back, murmuring nonsense into his ear, and he slowly regained full consciousness. He pulled out, tossing the condom into a trash can near the bed and foggily reminded himself to empty it before the rest of the family came home. Victoria clawed back the sheets and helped him under them, and even though he knew there were still things to talk about, she had worn him the fuck out.

But Victoria didn't seem to think there was anything left to discuss, because she simply curled up against him and tangled their legs together. It was like being back in the hotel room, close and peaceful, and just as he was drifting off he felt her press a soft kiss to his shoulder.

Chapter Twenty-three

Waking up with Owen felt right. Victoria stretched languidly before curling back against him, eager to chase his warmth. Owen made a sound halfway between a sigh and a grunt that made her grin. She nuzzled his jaw, breathing in his clean, masculine scent. "You know, I don't think I actually said thank you," she realized out loud.

Owen preened. "For the multiple orgasms? You're very welcome."

She laughed and let him pull her half across his chest. "No, I meant for suggesting me to Reproductive Justice."

A beat of silence fell. "What?"

"I got a job offer from them. Or an offer to apply, I guess. I can't because I still owe so much on my loans, but I know you suggested me to them even though we weren't really getting along, so thank you." She frowned and craned her neck. "I told you I knew."

All the color drained from Owen's face. "Wait, what?"

"It's not a big deal, I just appreciated the olive branch," she explained. "I've been really unhappy at Smorgasbord, and if things were even just a little different, RJ would be perfect for me, you know? So thanks for thinking of me, even if it didn't work out." She pushed herself up to look at him.

But Owen was inching away. "So wait, last night, when you said you knew, you were talking about . . . that?"

"What else would I be talking about? And I don't know anyone else who's all over RJ's Facebook page like you."

"It was Cassie," he mumbled, swiping a hand across his face. "I didn't have anything to do with that. But—oh, fuck. I thought you knew." He looked terrified and it sent her stomach tumbling.

"Wait, what were *you* talking about?"

"The night—the night we hung out. Went skating, karaoke."

"The night you wouldn't even kiss me goodnight for no apparent reason," she said, now clutching the sheet to her chest. It wasn't a very good shield, but it was better than nothing. Dread built in her throat and she didn't know why, because this morning should have been perfect. But something was going wrong, everything sliding sideways out of her control. "Owen, what the hell is going on?"

"Maybe we should get dressed," he said, no longer looking at her. "This wasn't—I shouldn't tell you like this—I thought we—"

She reached out and caught his face, making him look her in the eye. "You're making it worse," she pleaded. She wasn't sure how she had gone from happy and peaceful to falling apart in a matter of seconds, but whatever it was, she needed him to stop stammering and just tell her.

Owen's eyes were inexplicably sad. "I thought you knew," he said again. He took a deep breath. His hands fisted the sheet and he looked her straight in the eye. "I wouldn't have done this if you didn't know, I need you to know that up-front. I was going to tell you last night, but then you said you knew, and I—I should have checked, or clarified, or whatever, and that's all on me, but—"

"Owen. Say it."

"I'm Luke."

The words hung in the air, inexplicable. "What?" It wasn't adding up. How would Owen even know about him?

"I'm Luke."

Her heart plummeted. "You're—you're—what? How?"

"I don't know," he said miserably. "You were in the coffee shop where Nora told me to come meet her, and when I saw the rose I knew you were her, and I . . . panicked."

"You panicked," she echoed. Bile was bubbling in her stomach, thick and acrid. She thought she was done with Luke, had shut him out of her life completely, but instead she went and slept with him. And Owen had known the whole time.

Because Luke was Owen.

Her mind was reeling, trying to keep up.

"I knew I would walk in and you would be disappointed, and god, I'd fallen so hard for you—Nora you, and, uh, you-you—and after our fight at the courthouse I didn't think I could take it."

"So this is my fault?"

"I never said—"

"No, you just did. *You* couldn't take me being mad at you some more, so you, what, ran off? Then decided to be the hero and make me feel better about myself, even though you were the one who made me feel shitty?"

"That's not how it went," he said, but she was already standing up and searching for her panties. Her jumpsuit was several floors below them, but she needed *something* on to make her feel less naked, both figuratively and literally.

"No? Then how did it go? Please, tell me, because you've been apparently keeping a whole lot of shit from me."

"I did not do that deliberately," he said, an edge creeping into his voice. "I wanted to tell you. I *tried* to tell you. You were the one who said we don't do well when talking."

"And it would appear I'm right," she spat. She stalked out of the room and picked up the robe. "Besides, what prevented you from telling me *that night*? You know, the night you realized it and then spent several hours with me, letting me believe Luke stood me up?"

"I told you, I was worried you'd be disappointed and—"

"There it is again—your feelings. It's all about you, isn't it?"

"I didn't mean—"

Victoria had enough experience arguing with Owen to know she had to keep him from building up to his argument. As long as she never let him finish a thought, she would maintain the upper hand. She needed that control right now, and badly. "Tell me, do you ever think about someone besides yourself? Doesn't it get exhausting, needing to be the good guy that damn much?"

His face twisted; she'd hit a nerve. "All of this could have been avoided, you know," he said, roughly shoving his arms into his robe. "You were the one too paranoid about privacy to agree to meet me. But it's not just privacy, is it? You just can't bear to let anyone in. Are you even capable of that?"

She felt like he'd slapped her. She had let him in. And now he was throwing it in her face. She was safest behind her walls. That was the only way she knew how to open up, because—well, she honestly didn't even know why. It was just how she was, it didn't have to be from some long-buried trauma or childhood secret. She didn't like people knowing her business, and when they did it was easier if they didn't know her name.

Not everyone could be like him. Owen walked around with his heart on his sleeve and barely seemed to notice when it was bruised. Maybe it was his privilege, or maybe he was just a more secure human being than she was, but she resented that he expected her to be like him when she just couldn't.

"I'm perfectly capable of letting someone in," she said acidly. "But only once I'm sure they won't disappoint me. Clearly, I miscalculated when it came to you." She wasn't fighting fair, pulling out fears he had confessed to her as Luke, but then again, neither was he.

"That was low," he whispered.

"So was fucking me without telling me the truth," she threw back. She started down the stairs, debating what would be more humiliating: going all the way to the pool room to retrieve the rest of her clothes or simply driving home in a goddamn bathrobe.

"I. Thought. You. Knew," he spat, chasing after her. "Why the hell would you say all that shit about a job recommendation? How was I supposed to put that together?"

"Because I don't let anyone help me," she nearly shouted. "I don't let that happen, and you knew it. And if you're Luke, you *really* should have known it." She could feel the tears threatening but wouldn't let them drop, not yet, not like this.

His cat jumped from out of nowhere and twined around her ankles just as she reached the second to last stair. Victoria tripped over him and nearly fell the rest of the way down, only saved by Owen grabbing her arm at the last second. His hand was sure and strong, and she hated that she still liked how that felt.

She wrenched free of him and straightened the bathrobe with as much dignity as she could muster. Owen looked at the cat and then fixed her with a glare. "You never put it together? That Luke has a cat named Luke and I have a cat named Luke?

It never once occurred to you that we might be the same person?"

She narrowed her eyes. "I have never once heard you call that cat by his actual name, so no. And it's a grey fucking cat, Owen. How the hell was I supposed to know?"

"I don't know, but if you hadn't lied when I asked you if you had Twitter, maybe we could have worked this out way earlier."

"Wait, so it's *my* fault you lied to me?"

"You lied first," he said, arms crossed.

"Not like this," she said. "That was—that was nothing like this. I didn't tell you about a Twitter account but you—you lied about who you were."

She turned away, only to have him tug her back around. "Vee, come on—we can work this out."

"We can? How? You fucking lied to me."

"Just—"

"No, no 'just' here. You lied, and you think because everything has always worked out for you, it always will. You don't understand what it's like for the rest of us."

"What the hell is that supposed to mean?"

She threw her arm out, gesturing wildly at the walls. "All of this. You grew up with it, and yeah, you know that not everyone did, but you don't *get* it."

"My family's money has nothing to do with this," he snapped.

"Except it does. You've always had a safety net, and so you just—you assume everyone else feels as secure as you do. You always assume you'll get a second chance, or that things will work out, because you can afford to. I can't."

"So your problem is with my money? You didn't seem to have a problem with it last night," he said nastily.

Victoria screeched in frustration. "It's everything, okay?

You thought you could get away with lying to me because you think you can get a second chance any time, and I—god, you don't know what it's like to *not* assume that. And I just—I can't. I can't forgive you for that. For any of it."

His face shifted abruptly. Anger melted away and sadness took its place. "Vee—"

"Don't," she said, and decided that her jumpsuit and bra were an acceptable loss. At least her shoes were still by the door, so she shoved them on. "You and me? We're over. Once and for all. I don't want your apologies or your . . . your whatevers. Just leave me the fuck alone."

The door slammed loudly behind her. Outside the morning was still, the air too cold for any birds to be chirping yet. The chill went straight through her bathrobe and she turned the heat on full blast, shivering with cold and rage as she blindly drove down his driveway. Halfway home, she realized it was already far too late in the day to make it all the way from her parking garage to her apartment unnoticed, wearing literally nothing but her underwear and a bathrobe.

She didn't really have many other places to go. All her internet friends lived in different states, and she wasn't sure she was close enough to anyone to show up half-naked and crying on their doorstep. Kimmy would probably be at work and she knew where her mother's spare key was usually hidden but what she really wanted right now was a friend. Someone close by, her age, who could hug her and tell her everything was going to be okay.

But instead, she drove home alone to drag herself into the tub and cry.

Chapter Twenty-four

It was a long few days waiting for everyone to get home. Owen thoroughly cleaned the house, removing all traces of Victoria before the Pohl Family 2.0 returned from their vacation. He wasn't sure what to do about her bra and clothes, but they were freshly laundered and packed into his duffel bag anyway. He also spent a lot of time lying flat on his stomach on the living room floor, staring into Luke's unconcerned eyes, wondering how the fuck he was supposed to move on from this.

Because that was his only option. He'd gone and lost everything, just when he thought it was finally working out. He should have known it was too good to be true, should have listened to the tiny voice of doubt in him when what she was saying didn't fully match up to what he was thinking. He was too optimistic, too naive, too full of himself and confident that the world would work out in his favor. Victoria had been right about so many things, but that in particular stuck out.

He had put so much effort into thinking his family's wealth didn't matter. He knew it did, in the abstract, and he was proud of himself for recognizing that he had a lot of what he did because of his father's money, not his own efforts. But who he was? His personality? That much he thought was independent of his upbringing, or as much as it could be. It never occurred to him that he was able to be optimistic because there were never any serious consequences to him either way. He could risk playing the hero because if he failed, he was still a rich kid. He had understood when Nora would talk about making necessary moral sacrifices to pay her bills, but he had never extended that courtesy to Victoria, nor had he thought about what that type of life might cost.

He could see now how her walls weren't just a method of protection, but a necessary byproduct of her life. She kept him out because that was safest, and because her safety net wasn't anywhere comparable with his. That extended to her emotional safety too. She was so much stronger than him in so many ways, and he'd been so, so blind.

And now she was gone, and that was his fault. He'd lashed out at her because he wanted it to be an equal fuckup. If it was both their faults, maybe it could be repaired.

But it wasn't.

He handwashed the dishes from his pathetic pasta dinner simply to have something to do, and wondered if there was any possible way to fix this without trampling all over her wishes yet again.

He couldn't think of anything, and for the umpteenth time in the past few months, he was relegated to trying to imagine the rest of his life without Nora *or* Victoria. He'd been there already, but only now was he really, truly realizing what that meant.

No more late night talks with Nora. He wouldn't ever get the thrill of seeing a notification from her, or laugh at her jokes or ache at her vulnerability. He wouldn't get to spill his own secrets to her, secure in knowing that she understood, or hear her own and know that he was being trusted with something precious.

There would be no more seeing Victoria laugh unexpectedly, either. No more watching her carefully rearrange her long, silky hair over her shoulders. No more Victoria biting down on her lower lip in unconscious thought, no more seeing her try in vain to fight a smile at him being funny. He would miss her softness and sweetness but more than that he would miss her sharp edges; the way she never, ever compromised herself. She was the type some would call high maintenance, but he just saw her as put-together and in charge, her armor visible but crisp and tailored. He'd never get to wrap his arms around her shoulders and kiss the nape of her neck, or nuzzle the spot just behind her ear. He'd never again wake up with her, eyes hazy and soft, and he would never get to tell her he loved her. Not like the way he'd joked about on his front step, but in a real way, whispered soft and low when they were curled up together in bed.

A plate slipped from his fingers with a clatter. He was in love with her. He'd been in love with her for a while now. The realization was like getting broadsided by a speeding car. "Did I really not know that until now?" he said aloud, and Luke meowed at him in response. "Fuck. I really, really screwed this up, didn't I, bud?" He meowed again and Owen set the plate aside to drain.

He had only been in love once before. His college girlfriend, a spitfire of a Boston girl who never understood his desire to move back to the Midwest. He had loved her and then they fell apart, and he had spent a sad, bleak few months missing her when he moved back to Minnesota, but that was that. This felt different, like a gaping wound that no amount of scar tissue would cover.

He picked up Luke against his yowling protestations and wandered towards the large French doors. In the fading twilight he could see thin patches on the lake where the ice was slowly thawing. He opened the door and caught the first faint hint of mud on the breeze, wrapped in a bouquet of frost and slowly melting snow. The world was mostly grey, spring's colors too far off and winter's austere sharpness slowly bleeding into greys and browns. It was a landscape that matched his soul, he thought, and then chided himself for being so damn melodramatic. But there was a sort of poetic justice to it, he mused, with the outside world matching the bleakness in his chest.

Victoria was gone, and he was going to have to deal with it.

Sincerely Your Bitches

@Noraephronwasagenius
Is everyone around right now?

@Neverthelesskararesisted
Present.

@Keanuisadreamboat
Here, although only halfway through my coffee so only like, half here mentally.

And the boyfriend's boxes are still fucking everywhere, so I'm also half about to snap.

@MadisonHughes95
I have not slept in weeks of course I'm here

@Keanuisadreamboat
Maddy, grad school seems really unhealthy and I am worried about you.

@MadisonHughes95
You and me both, friend

@Noraephronwasagenius
How do you guys feel about Skype?

@MadisonHughes95
As a general concept or as in, you're going to Skype us all right now?

@Noraephronwasagenius
. . . The latter?

@MadisonHughes95
!!!!!!!!!!!!!!!!!!!!!!!!!!!!!!!!!!!!

@Keanuisadreamboat
You mean we get to see your face??????????

@Neverthelesskararesisted
YES DAMMIT DO IT NOW

Victoria straightened her shoulders and quickly set up the Skype call. Her breathing was a little too fast considering she was just going to be actually talking to the women she chatted with every day, but then again, her ego had taken quite a blow. After everything, it felt so silly to hide so much of herself. It wasn't the anonymity that made her able to open up to them, it was *them*. Their love, their friendship, their patience. She was done hiding, and there was no better place to start than the present. If nothing else, the blow-up with Owen had convinced her that anonymity was creating more problems for her than it was solving.

Plus, she needed them. Desperately. She'd spent the last twenty-four hours marinating in her own sadness and it was time to get her shit together. And this was the best way to even the playing field.

One by one, the screens turned from black to grey, her friend's faces materializing on them. Like she had said, Reiko had a giant cup of coffee covering half her monitor and her hair was up in a messy bun, but she was smiling. Maddy's blonde hair was frizzed out to the sides and she was squirming excitedly in her seat, while Kara was just grinning broadly at her, eyes shining. All three squealed with happiness when her picture unfroze.

"I knew you'd be hot!" Maddy yelled over the rest of the noise.

Tears rose to her eyes. "I'm sorry I was so weird," she said, half laughing, half crying. "And for the record . . . my name is Victoria."

"Victoria!" said Kara. "That's lovely. And Maddy's right, you're very pretty."

"So what spurred this on?" Reiko asked.

"Some shit went down with, uh, well . . . I guess I have to start at the beginning," she said.

It took longer than she thought it would, given that they all knew about both Luke and Owen, but it was hard for her to admit it all, and even more so to do it sort-of-in-person. She felt raw and open, but her friends just listened sympathetically.

She took a deep, shuddering breath as she neared the end of

the story. "So basically, he thought I knew, and the other night we hooked up and he was under the impression everything was all clear between us but it wasn't, and now I feel . . . gross."

"Like he took advantage of you?" Reiko asked.

"No, more like . . . the playing field was uneven. And it makes me feel vulnerable."

"Ah. Yeah, that feeling sucks," Maddy chimed in.

"How do you get over it?"

"You don't. You find someone who makes it okay to feel that way." Reiko flicked her gaze over towards one of her boyfriend's boxes, and Victoria's heart curled in on itself. "If Luke-Owen doesn't make you feel safe like that, he's not worth it, no matter how much fun we found him on Twitter."

Victoria blinked back sudden tears. "I don't know. Maybe he is, maybe he isn't. But it's all so sudden, and I just—I don't know. It hurts."

Her screen erupted in a chorus of *oh honeys* and Reiko seemed to be leaning forward like she wanted to hug her. "Then let it hurt," Kara said. "Embrace that, for as long as you need. We'll be here for you."

"Even though I wasn't honest?"

Maddy made a face. "You were, though. You told us everything except your name, and we knew it wasn't your name."

"But I feel weird. Like I lied to you."

"Even if that's how you feel, we still love you," Reiko said. "Right, ladies?"

"Right," they chorused.

"I'm sorry I was such a weirdo about my name and face," Victoria said through tears. "You guys still love me? Really?"

The unanimous and fierce *of course* was enough to make her smile tremulously but genuinely for the first time all day.

Chapter Twenty-five

It was astonishing how comforting it was to watch her mother make dinner, even in her own apartment. Victoria sat on the kitchen stool with her arms folded against the counter while Kimmy pulled the hot dogs out of the microwave with a critical eye. "I think these are done, yeah?" she asked, holding them out.

"They just need to be hot, you know," Victoria teased. "There's basically no cooking involved with those."

Kimmy rolled her eyes. "Did you want me to cook for you or did you want to be a brat?"

"Sorry, Mom." Victoria grinned.

Kimmy stirred the pot on the stove and sighed. "I really didn't feed you enough vegetables when you were little, did I?"

"You did your best. It's not like I was malnourished."

Kimmy poured the noodles into the strainer and then expertly transferred them back to the pot. "You going to tell me about the boy who broke your heart, or do I just have to pretend that's not happening?"

Victoria rested her chin on her folded forearms. "Can we pretend it's not happening?"

"If you want. But talking might help, unless you've already talked it all out with your girlfriends."

"Just call them friends, Mom. Calling platonic friends 'girlfriends' makes it harder for women in relationships with women to correctly identify their partners."

"Okay then, your friends. Do they sufficiently have your back?"

"They do."

"Is it a situation that requires murder, or just mild maiming?"

"Probably just maiming?" She was furious with Owen, but there was an odd tinge to her sadness, because even though she'd said goodbye to Luke—she thought—long before this, somehow it felt like losing them both again. She watched Kimmy chop up the hot dogs and toss them into the macaroni and cheese. Disgusting, yes, but also delicious. She remembered telling Luke about her favorite comfort food, and now she knew exactly the way he'd look while laughing about it. Owen's eyes tended to sparkle when he was teasing her, and she missed that about him. "Don't get me wrong, I'm pissed as hell at him. But . . . I don't know."

"Could you forgive him for it?"

"Maybe? With sufficient groveling, I guess, but I may have given him the impression I never wanted to see him again, so I don't think that would happen anyway. But really, I don't want to talk about it."

"Honey, we should—"

"Mom, please."

"Okay then. How's work?"

"Ugh," Victoria said. They tucked into their dinner, sitting side by side on the stools. "Ever since I got thrown off the case, things have been, I dunno, rough."

"Your boss riding you about it?"

"More like I'm clearly not the favorite," she admitted. Her ego could handle that blow, but without being the star litigator of the department she was questioning why she was doing it. The only thing going for it was the money, and that seemed like less and less of a reason these days.

"There must be another job out there for you," Kimmy pressed. "With a resumé like yours you should be able to find something."

Victoria shrugged. "Anywhere else would be a lateral move. I'd still be working for a big corporation, and it's not like any other companies are much better, you know?"

"Then what about something else entirely?"

"Not with my loans," Victoria said, and Kimmy winced. "It's fine, Mom, really. I'm an adult and this is the choice I've made, even if Reproductive Justice would be—Never mind."

"There's a job at Reproductive Justice?"

"It doesn't matter."

"Of course it does," Kimmy argued. "They offered you a job? You love them!"

"The pay cut would be too much."

"How much?"

"Too much."

"Don't pretend like you don't have a spreadsheet of all your income and expenses. You've had one of those since you were a kid," Kimmy chided. "Exactly how much are we talking?"

"Thirty percent."

"You could still live on that."

"Not with what I have earmarked for savings."

Kimmy set down her fork. "You mean the money you send me."

"I told you I would—"

"Then I have a confession to make," Kimmy interrupted. She pushed back from the stool and retrieved her phone from her purse. She tapped at it for a few moments and set it down in front of Victoria expectantly.

Victoria frowned. "What's with the two savings accounts?"

"One's yours. One's mine. Well, it's in my name, but that top one? That's every penny you've ever sent me."

"But that's for you! For the house."

"No, it's for you. I told you when you started sending me money that I didn't need it, but I knew you needed to feel like you were taking care of me. So I saved it for you, and I started my own savings account."

The two numbers were a fair distance apart, but closer than she thought they would be. "How did you save all this?"

"When I've got a steady job, I can budget. It's not like you taught yourself how to make those spreadsheets, you know." Victoria knew her mother's earlier years had been eaten up by motherhood. Babies were expensive, and when you didn't have reliable day care or a job that provided health insurance, they were even more expensive. Government assistance helped, but it only went so far. To paraphrase Eminem, you can't buy diapers with food stamps. The only way to survive was to figure out exactly how to spend every penny.

"And you don't have a kid to take care of anymore," Victoria said quietly, and Kimmy shook her head.

"Don't you do that. Don't you think for one second you were a burden."

"But I was. That's just a fact."

"No. I never once thought of you that way."

"Not even—"

"Never. And I was never going to let you deprive yourself

because you wanted to take care of me. So I started reading budgeting blogs and I've been doing a lot of research on FHA loans and I think I can buy that house on my own in the next few years anyway."

"But if you used the money from me, you'd have it sooner. You could get a good mortgage and set up a 401k with—"

"I have one. I told you, I've been working on this for a while. I'm not rich, but I need to do this on my own. I won't stand in the way of your dream."

"But—"

"If you took the job with RJ, what would you cut? Aside from the money to me, of course."

"It'd be hard to save as much. I'd probably have to cut back on that, probably significantly."

"Would this money help? If you had it, would you take the job?"

Victoria blinked. She hadn't seriously considered the gig, and it was entirely possible they had found someone else already. But with a bigger padding in her savings, she probably could take a lower paying job without stressing quite so much. So long as she could still pay rent and her loans she could do okay, and the savings would provide a buffer for any unexpected expenses that popped up. She might even be able to pay off one or two of the higher interest loans and lower her monthly payments. Her stress levels would be lower, just from the sheer fact of knowing that she wasn't making the lives of people like her mom even worse.

"It's probably not even available anymore."

"That's not what I asked. Would you take it?"

"I can't, Mom," she said quietly. Her heart was pounding, because she hadn't let herself even consider this possibility, not really. She had responsibilities to her mom, and the pressure of not-going-back-to-being-poor was so integral to her identity she didn't know how to think of herself without it.

"You could. And I think you should."

"I can't—"

Kimmy fixed her with a stern look. "I'm your mother. And if I say you can, you can."

Owen arrived at the lake house at the same time as the pizza. He took the stack of steaming cardboard from the driver and slipped her an extra couple of bucks, just in case his dad was stingy on the tip, and then knocked on the front door with his elbow. Ashley pulled the door open and the girls immediately swarmed him, although less from enthusiasm for him and more because of the presence of pizza.

Charles was in the kitchen, pulling down plates. Normally, Owen only accepted Ashley's invitations to come over for dinner when he knew his father was out of town, but this time she had persisted and he had relented, because, well, he didn't have a lot else going on in his life. Losing Victoria hadn't gotten any easier and he had taken to moping about his house, refusing any invites from his friends to meet them for drinks and spending most of his time watching *Parks and Rec* for the fifteenth time on Netflix. At least dinner with his father would be interesting, even if that meant a fight.

But his dad just glanced at him and frowned thoughtfully. "Everything okay there?" he said.

"Yep." Owen set down the pizza boxes and boosted Olivia up onto a stool so she could pick her slice.

Charles and Ashley exchanged a look. "You sure about that?" Ashley said, and he shrugged.

They let it go for the time being but after dinner, the girls started a clearly familiar game that was half hide-and-seek, half tag, and ran shrieking around the spacious downstairs while Ashley opened a second beer for all the adults. "You've been in a mood since we got back," she needled. "What gives?"

Charles smiled at his wife. "She's right, son. You're not yourself. Did something happen?"

Owen shrugged. "I screwed up," he admitted. Opening up with his father in the room was surely a sign he'd hit rock bottom.

"With a woman?" Charles asked.

"Yeah."

There was a crash from the den and Ashley stood up. "I should go make sure there aren't any broken bones," she announced with little pretense at subtlety, even though the girls were giggling loudly.

"Have you tried apologizing?" Charles said as soon as Ashley was out of sight.

"No, that never occurred to me," Owen said sullenly.

But his father was undeterred. "Sometimes you need to wait before apologizing," he suggested. "Sometimes, you deserve the anger. Wait it out, then try again."

"Speaking from experience?"

"Of course," he said, and Owen was once more surprised by his father's honesty. "I never apologized with your mother, or rather I always apologized too early. I was just looking to avoid fights, not actually take ownership of my actions. Same with Judith."

"When did you learn to talk like this?"

"Since Ashley insisted on pre-marital counseling."

"She's too good for you, you know," Owen said, sipping his beer.

"Trust me, I'm well aware of that," Charles said. "How long ago was the fight?"

"A little over a month. While you were gone."

"And have you talked to her since?"

"She said not to."

"You screwed up that bad, huh?"

Owen snorted and Charles chuckled, the tension between them releasing suddenly. "Yes. Monumentally."

"Then you need to apologize monumentally. The apology should be proportional to the mistake."

"So you're saying I should hire a sky writer."

Charles winced theatrically. "Wow, you really messed up, didn't you?"

"Like I said: monumentally."

"Well, is that something she would appreciate? Because it has to be about her, not you."

"Who the hell is this therapist you went to?"

"A very expensive one," Charles deadpanned. "But worth every penny. This woman, though, is she someone who would want some public groveling? Or would she prefer it in private?"

A memory of the day they spent watching rom coms resurfaced. Victoria was lounging with her feet in his lap, pointing at her television. *"That right there, that's the good shit," she announced as Billy Crystal sprinted into a New Year's Eve party to declare his love for Meg Ryan in a long, rambling speech. "It's my favorite part of these movies."*

"The part where he lists her flaws?"

She rolled her eyes at him. "The grand gesture. The big grovel. The dramatic speech. Maybe it makes me a basic bitch, but I love it. Like when Heath Ledger sings in the stadium in 10 Things? *Or Freddie Prinze Jr. goes to graduation naked? It doesn't get better than that."*

Owen polished off his beer. "You know, I think she might want it public. And big."

"Then get to work, son," Charles said, patting his shoulder.

Chapter Twenty-six

The waiting was killing her. Kimmy had stayed late into the night, helping her proof her resumé and going over her budget for the fifteenth time to be sure that what Reproductive Justice was offering was livable before she emailed to say she'd love to interview with them. But now three days had passed with no word from the hiring manager and her nerves were wrecked.

It wasn't that long of a wait, really. She knew that intellectually, but telling that to her racing heart every time a new email pinged into her inbox was something else entirely.

@Noraephronwasagenius
I'm dying, guys.

@Keanuisadreamboat
No word on the job yet?

@Neverthelesskararesisted
How long has it been?

@Noraephronwasagenius
Only three days. I need to find my chill, but I just . . . can't.
Distract me?

@MadisonHughes95
Have you figured out what you're gonna do about Luke?

@Keanuisadreamboat
MADDY.
THAT IS NOT WHAT SHE MEANT AND YOU KNOW IT.

@MadisonHughes95
🤷‍♀️🤷‍♀️

@Noraephronwasagenius
What is there to do?
We're done. Both versions of us.

@MadisonHughes95
But are you, though?
Because last time you brought him up you were saying you missed him
And then said you wouldn't talk about it, yes, but like . . . girl
Here's your distraction

@Noraephronwasagenius
Maddy, I would hate you if I didn't love you so much.
Which is, uh, maybe how I feel about him?

@Keanuisadreamboat
WAIT WHAT
You love him?

@Noraephronwasagenius
And hate him.
That part is still true too.
and it feels too soon to say I REALLY love him, but I might????
He fucking lied, guys. And I want to get over it, and I need to know he's SORRY first, but also: feelings.
And really sorry, not just post-coital, oh fuck I got caught lying sorry.
Idk if he IS and the only way to find out is to ask.
But like, I have some pride here. And if he's not, that'll really suck, plus I'm still really pissed at him so basically I have ALL THE FEELINGS AT ONCE.
Congrats Maddy, you distracted me but I also might murder you.

@MadisonHughes95
So long as you kill me before my next chapter is due I won't even fight you

@Neverthelesskararesisted
But if he reached out and genuinely apologized, you'd consider it?

@Noraephronwasagenius
More or less, yeah.

I'm still not sure how I'd react, but I don't feel like we have closure.

He might apologize and I'd realize it's just too much and I can't forgive him, which is why I can't reach out and talk to him. That doesn't seem fair either, you know?

Victoria chewed on her thumbnail. Maddy had sufficiently distracted her, but her stomach still felt like a beehive. Out of habit she clicked refresh on her email and her heart lurched out of her chest. Pa Vang appeared in the "from" field, and with shaking hands she clicked it open.

Dear Victoria,

Thank you for attaching your resumé and expressing your interest in the position. The hiring committee would like to bring you in for an interview next week. We have openings on Monday afternoon and Thursday morning. Please let me know at your earliest convenience what works for you.

Best,
Pa Vang

Human Resources Director
Reproductive Justice
(612) 555-4982 extension 233
761 University Ave
Saint Paul, MN

Victoria leapt off her couch and shrieked. *I have an interview!!!!* she texted to Kimmy, and relayed the message to the group chat. The excited gifs rolled in and she picked up her phone to tell

Owen. She stopped, but the fact stared her straight in the face: she wanted to talk to him, even when she was furious with him.

So that was one answer, at least.

Owen Pohl
I need some help

Andy Lee
Yeah dude we know.

Mark Olsen
Yeah that's not new information

Owen Pohl
Fuck you both
But for real, I need help. Of the romantic kind

Mark Olsen
MY MOMENT HAS COME
DO YOU KNOW HOW LONG I HAVE WAITED FOR THIS MOMENT
K-Ci & JoJo have NOTHING on me

Owen Pohl
Andy come get ya boi in line

Andy Lee
No.

Owen Pohl
Jfc okay
I have to apologize to Victoria, and I think it's gotta be big

Mark Olsen
Already looking up hot air balloons

Owen Pohl
I was actually thinking karaoke

Andy Lee
One problem with that.
I've heard you sing.
I'd rather play golf with every partner in my firm every Saturday for the rest of my life than hear that again.
And you know how I feel about white dudes who play golf.

Owen Pohl
Yeah I'm aware
You're not exactly quiet about your feelings on that front
But that's sorta the point. Humiliate myself a little, grovel a lot, hope she forgives me

Mark Olsen
So like Heath in *10 Things*

Owen Pohl
Exactly

Andy Lee
You realize you're nowhere near as hot as him, right?

Owen Pohl
Are you gonna help or not

Andy Lee
Undecided.

Mark Olsen
Of course we will and if you screw this up for me Andy I'll fucking kill you

Andy Lee
Wait how is this about you?

Mark Olsen
BECAUSE I AM THE ROMANTIC HERE
What do you need help with?

Owen Pohl
Well, she and her mom have this karaoke thing that they do and I thought I could go there
But I don't know where it is

Mark Olsen
So ask her mom
Because honestly, you're gonna have to win the mom over sooner or later so you might as well start with that
Priyanka's mom loves me, btw

Andy Lee
And we're very happy for you but again, this is not about you.

Mark Olsen
It's a little about me

Andy Lee

I think I found her on Facebook. She looks too young but I definitely met this lady at graduation and Victoria is friends with her.

Cassie says it's for sure Victoria's mom.

Owen Pohl

So I just what, send her mom a Facebook message and ask if I can crash their karaoke thing?

Mark Olsen

In a nutshell, yes

But the mom usually knows when you fucked up, so be prepared to grovel to her first

Andy Lee

Can confirm, moms always know.

Owen Pohl

Then here goes nothing

Chapter Twenty-seven

Kimmy lurched from her chair to hug her the moment she walked in. "How did it go?"

Victoria tried to keep her face somber but failed. "I got it!" she squealed, and together they jumped and hugged in excitement. "I've got to put my notice in at Smorgasbord, but you're looking at RJ's new in-house counsel as of the start of next month."

"That deserves a drink," Kimmy crowed, and sauntered over to the bar. The regulars parted for her like the Red Sea and within minutes she was back at the table with Victoria's martini.

"To my baby, all grown up and protecting a woman's right to choose," Kimmy said, lifting her whiskey. They clinked glasses and Victoria settled back in her chair.

"How long until we're up?"

Kimmy's eyes darted towards the door and then back to Victoria. "Uh, a couple more people, I think," she said.

Victoria twisted in her seat but the door to the gravel parking lot was closed. "You waiting on someone?"

"Nope. Just thought I recognized someone," Kimmy replied breezily. "So tell me about the interview. I want all of the details."

But when Victoria started talking, she couldn't help but feel like her mom was only half listening. Kimmy kept flicking her gaze over Victoria's shoulder, but the second she caught her looking, Kimmy would be focused like a laser on her instead. Up on stage, one of the other regulars was growling his way through Johnny Cash's "Walk the Line."

"No seriously, Mom—who the hell are you looking for?"

"No one."

"Are you sure? Because it really feels like you're expecting someone to walk through that door."

Kimmy's jaw tightened almost imperceptibly and she touched Victoria's arm, keeping her from twisting around in her seat again. "Nope. But you were saying the HR person is someone you could see yourself being friends with?"

"I think so, yeah. She seemed super chill, at least."

"Mmmm," her mom said distractedly. The DJ took over from the latest performer with his usual patter about welcoming a newcomer to the stage, and Kimmy sat up a little straighter.

"Are we up already?" Victoria asked, confused.

"Hey, everyone," a familiar voice said over the mic. "You guys don't know me, but—hell, I'm here because I have some groveling to do. And before you throw tomatoes at me, just know that yes, I am aware of how terrible I am at what I'm about to do, but that's part of the groveling."

Slowly, Victoria turned her eyes to the stage. Owen was standing there, hair falling in pieces next to his jaw like he'd just shoved it back, which he tended to do when he was nervous.

Her heart fell into her stomach. He held her gaze solemnly and lifted the mic back to his lips. "To the person I'm here to apologize to: I'm sorry. I will detail the exact manner in which I'm sorry for my actions after this song, if you'll agree to talk to me. If you don't want to see me again, you can just stay in your seat. But god, I miss you and I'm just—I'm so fucking sorry." The crowd murmured quietly, and at least one man whistled.

Wave after wave of emotion crashed over her. Anticipation, nerves, a little anger, and a slow, inexorable melting that wrapped around her heart. He cleared his throat nervously. "You said once you always appreciated the grand gestures, so I hope you appreciate this, as horrible as it's going to be." The corner of his mouth quirked up into a half-smile, his eyes never leaving hers. "Okay, here goes nothing."

The music for "Can't Help Falling In Love" began and Owen let out a shuddering breath. It was the Elvis version, and suddenly she was back on the dance floor at Andy and Cassie's wedding, swaying in Owen's arms and wanting to tell him how she felt. He made it okay through the intro, mostly just swaying and smiling nervously. Within a couple of words of the first line, however, the crowd was laughing.

But Owen just grinned and kept going, even though it appeared he had no idea what the melody was, or really what "singing" was supposed to sound like. It wasn't even a particularly difficult melody to sing but even this was out of his abilities. He hit the first chorus and the crowd whooped, clapping as he struck a defiant pose and bravely slaughtered the notes.

She kept her face as neutral as possible and cast a sidelong glance at her mother. Kimmy was beaming, and the pieces fell into place. "You set this up?" Victoria whispered. It was hardly necessary to keep her voice down, since the din of Owen's screeching and the crowd's laughter was drowning out just about everything else.

"He did. He contacted me and asked if I thought it would be okay. Is it?"

Onstage, Owen reached the last verse and absolutely whiffed it. Victoria gave up and snorted. "Yeah, it's fine."

"You seemed open to reconciliation, so when he messaged me on Facebook, I agreed. Plus—I felt him out first. He seemed genuine, if his apology to me is anything to go by. I think if you're willing to listen to him, you'll like what he has to say."

Owen finished with a painful flourish and took a bow, but the moment he stood back up his eyes found hers again and her heart stopped. Here was her Moment—she could accept his apology, or she could shut the door on them completely. He looked positively scared in a way she rarely associated with him. He was so brave usually, so optimistic, that the fear in his eyes stood out.

Whatever tiny bit of reservation she had shattered. She stood up and the bar-goers turned to look at her, a few titters and cheers skittering through the crowd. She walked to the stage, keeping her face impassive. Owen lifted an eyebrow, still worried, and she took the microphone from his hands. "Hey there," she said drily, and the crowd chuckled. "How about this—I promise to listen to you apologize if you promise to never, ever make us listen to you sing again?"

"Make sure he's worth it, honey!" a woman yelled from the bar, and Victoria let a grin play on her lips.

"Well, I figure I'll let him grovel for a bit and then decide, how does that sound?" she said, and the crowd roared their approval. She watched Owen's shoulders loosen and tipped her head towards the door.

Applause followed them out.

* * *

Owen waited until the door closed behind them to look at her. His heart was still racing and his chest felt like it was surrounded by iron bands. He'd done his best to project an aura of bravado, but part of him had been petrified since the moment he decided to do it. Mark had even helped him practice, even though they both knew it was a lost cause. *Just, uh, make sure she knows you're aware how shitty you are at this*, had been Mark's parting advice. *So she doesn't think you're like . . . proud of your singing. That'd be bad, and delusional. But good luck, man.*

Suddenly, her lips were on his. "You're fucking terrible at that," she whispered against his mouth. "You can't ever sing in front of humans again."

Owen's arms snapped around her waist and he nearly lifted her from the gravel. Her hands were in his hair, her mouth hot and warm and welcoming, and his heart was singing. "Aren't I supposed to apologize now?" he mumbled when he came up for air.

"Later. Kiss first, apologize second," she ordered, and as always, he was helpless to resist. She tasted like vodka and he couldn't help but remember the first time they kissed, half-drunk and sniping at each other. At the time he'd thought it was a one-off thing, not something that would shake the foundations of his world. Her hair slipped through his fingers, soft and silky, and he nipped at her lower lip playfully. She had him pinned against the outdoor wall of the bar, and if he didn't lower the temperature between them soon he'd end up doing something they might regret, like fucking her right here while her mom waited inside.

Victoria seemed to have the same thought. She pried herself out of his grasp, lips pleasantly swollen, and crossed her arms against the spring chill. "Okay, now you can apologize," she declared.

Owen laughed and then did his best to pull a straight face. "For how much?"

"All of it," she said, with just a hint of warning in her voice. But her eyes were warm and her fingers flexed against her biceps, like she was itching to reach out for him.

"Okay, obviously, I should have just come into the coffee shop the night I realized you were Nora. I owed you the truth up-front, and I totally fucked it up. And I really shouldn't have gone on a date with you that night without telling you the truth, and I really, really, really should have insisted we have an actual conversation about things before we had sex again, instead of just like, hoping you'd magically found out and I didn't have to say anything."

Her hand twitched again. "Keep going."

"I should have told you the truth a hundred times, and I didn't. There's no excuse for that. And if you'll forgive me, I promise to always be honest with you, right away. Even if it makes me the bad guy. And if I get this one, I won't expect any second chances ever again."

She tipped her head in a familiar gesture, her hair spilling over her shoulder. "Then I promise to be less cagey. I could probably stand to be a little more open. I'm working on it, but—it's hard for me."

Owen reached out and was gratified when her hand found his. "Nora was very open with me," he said softly.

"Yeah, over the internet, under a fake name. It's a lot harder when it's face to face," she said, lacing their fingers together. Owen tugged her closer and traced her jawline. "And even harder when you do that and make me forget what I was saying," she muttered.

"We're both promising to be more honest," he prompted, lost in her soft grey eyes.

"Oh right, that," she said, and this time when their lips met there wasn't any urgency to it, just sweet, leisurely exploration. It felt right, kissing her like this, and the tension in his shoulders melted away. He'd screwed things up with her once—twice, actually—and he wasn't about to risk doing that again. Ever.

"My mom is inside though," she said eventually. "We should go back. We're celebrating."

"Did you get the job at Reproductive Justice?"

"I thought you weren't involved in that?" Victoria said as he pulled the door open.

"I've heard chatter that they were going to offer it to you. I assume they did, since they'd be idiots not to."

"I accepted their offer today." It took a moment for his eyes to adjust to the dim light of the bar, but in the center of the room he saw Kimmy waving at both of them excitedly. He snuck a kiss to Victoria's cheek and she snuggled into him, his arm automatically going around her back.

"Then that deserves a celebration."

Latest Tweets

Nora @Noraephronwasagenius
I hate all white men sometimes, you know?

Luke @Lukethebarnyardcat
I mean, same. But also you're my girlfriend so this feels oddly pointed?

Nora @Noraephronwasagenius
Did you. Did you just. Not all men me. In public. Right in front of my salad.

Luke @Lukethebarnyardcat
Does it matter if I was just flirt-joking with you?

Nora @Noraephronwasagenius
No.

Kara Hates Nazis @Neverthelesskararesisted
No

Reiko @Keanuisadreamboat
No

Maddy H @MadisonHughes95
No

Maddy H @MadisonHughes95
And I swear to god if you two don't start keeping your flirting in private I am gonna murder you both. I thought it would get BETTER when you got together but instead it got WORSE

Maddy H @MadisonHughes95
I am in hell

Epilogue

One Year Later

"Hey, have you seen my—"

"Right here," Owen said, handing over her phone. He was distracted this morning, and unusually nervous. "What time is court for you today?"

"Early afternoon. I've got some stuff to finish up at the office first. You?"

Owen nearly tripped over Luke and accepted a mug of coffee from Victoria. His kitchen was no less cluttered than it had once been, but Victoria had insisted that he at least start doing his damn dishes every night and the sink was blessedly empty. "We're scheduled first thing, which means I really need to get going." Luke meowed loudly from around their ankles. "And I already fed him this morning so don't let him convince you he's starving," he added.

Victoria bent over and scooped up Luke for a very unwilling cuddle. "Jedi Master Skywalker would never lie to me," she said, burying her face in Luke's fur before letting him jump down. If someone told her eighteen months ago she would one day be a cat person, she would have laughed in their face, but here she was, coddling a cat. "By the way, it would appear that Ashley's got a plan to set my mom up with someone after the gala this weekend. How worried do we need to be about that?"

"Only that it will probably work out, since Ashley tends to be very astute about these things," Owen said. Kimmy and Ashley had taken to each other like ducks to water the moment they met last summer, and Ashley was the one who suggested Kimmy front a band for the many charity galas the Pohls threw. It was good money—and a chance to be onstage in a fancy dress—and now Kimmy was getting booked regularly by wealthy white people from the suburbs. Kimmy had even talked the band into doing some covers of her favorite Garbage songs, which were surprisingly a huge hit with the country club crowd.

"That reminds me—can you pick up my dress from the dry cleaners on your way home?" Victoria said, rinsing out her coffee mug. She didn't officially live at Owen's house, but she might as well—and they had already had several conversations about ending her lease. And then there was that small box in the back of his dresser, the one he didn't realize she knew about.

They might be done keeping secrets from each other, but Victoria felt she could let this one go.

"Yeah, of course," he muttered.

She cupped Owen's face in her hands and kissed his cheek. "Your opening statement is solid. Don't let them get under your skin," she assured him, because he always got a little jittery before a trial started. She would never have guessed that, back when he was just a cocky jackass who annoyed the living shit out of her. Now she found it endearing. She'd known this about Luke, but knowing it about Owen made her even more protective of him. She couldn't say anything more specific to him—ethics kept her from spilling any information about Smorgasbord's strategy. But she was grateful she wasn't the one going up against Owen today, trying to defend the indefensible. She was much happier at RJ, fighting against unnecessary abortion regulations and generally helping people instead of helping a corporation hurt them.

For the first time in a long time, Victoria felt whole. Not just because of Owen, but because she felt settled. Fulfilled. Loved and accepted. Owen was a big part of that, but not all of it. She'd given up her secret identities but kept the people who made her feel safe, and as a result she was feeling steadier than she had in years. She'd even flown out with the rest of her group chat to celebrate Maddy's dissertation defense last week, and the love and support of those women had wrapped around her like a hug.

Owen nuzzled his face against her palm. "Sorry, just—this is the big one for me. If I win this, no matter if Smorgasbord appeals it all the way to the Supreme Court, it would force some real change."

"You've got this," she assured him. "Besides, you're the second-best lawyer I know."

He grinned. "Who's first?"

"Do you even have to ask? Be glad you came in second, because that's not easy."

"You're just saying that because I went down on you twice last night."

"Exactly," Victoria deadpanned. "But really, you've got this. You're the only one who's ever beaten me, remember?"

Owen leaned forward to kiss her, the strain around his eyes melting away, replaced by the grin she had come to love. "How could I forget?"

Acknowledgments

In the summer of 2018 I was dealing with a vicious bout of they-call-it-morning-but-that's-a-lie-it's-really-all-day sickness by lazing on the couch, scrolling through Twitter while watching *You've Got Mail.* I started thinking about how much our relationship with the internet has changed since that movie: it has gone from being a quirky set-up for a movie to an integral part of our lives, and no one would raise an eyebrow at a couple meeting online anymore. But so much of it still rings true, especially how honest Joe and Kathleen can be with each other thanks to the anonymity of the internet.

That got me thinking about my Pocket Friends—the people I talk to online day in, day out, many of whom I have never met in person but who still mean the world to me. It's an entire world of friendship that lives in my phone (and if women's clothes had functional pockets that's where my phone would be). Out of that *I Love You, I Hate You*, my love letter to internet friends, was born.

I have so, so many people to thank for getting this off the ground, but I should probably start with the person who did the heaviest lifting: Jess Dallow, otherwise known as the best agent I could ever imagine. You believed in this book—and me—so much, and I don't think it would even be half as good without your thoughtful input. There's no one I'd rather have my back on this, and no one else I would rather chat with about crime procedural TV, either. Same to Kate, Liz, Sophie, and everyone at Headline Eternal: you are all a dream to work with, and I am sincerely sorry that I will never, ever use the correct form of "lay" or "lie," not even accidentally. I swear, my mom and all my English teachers tried very hard to teach me the difference and the fault is all mine. Thank you for your dedicated, thoughtful work.

Linds and Swishy, thank you for supporting me when I was but a baby writer. Lindsey, you have read probably every single word I have ever written, and you have cheered me on the entire time. I don't know if I would have been brave enough to start writing if it wasn't for you. Swishy, I know you have a real name but I'm sorry I will never, ever use it. Thank you for letting me send you [redacted] way back in the days of [redacted.] Christina, if it weren't for us getting drunk and yelling about how fun it would be to write a romance novel all those years ago, I wouldn't be here today. Thank you for the inspiration, and thank you all for being such good friends. And to Kika, I wish you were here to read this.

Natalie, Meghan, and Porter, thank you for your feedback when this project was still in its infancy. You helped shape it into what it is today, and for that I owe you all a huge, huge debt. Thank you, Rachel, for answering all my inane questions and being my Publishing Fairy Godmother. Hännah and Britt, thank you for the love, laughter and friendship. And Hännah, thank you for asking me for a book that starts in the middle of a sex scene. Chapter one belongs to you (thank you and you're welcome.)

To Porter (again), Jeeno, and Tina: thank you for being my legal references, and I'm sorry that I sometimes ignored your advice to make things more dramatic. You have real law degrees while mine comes entirely from *Law and Order: SVU* and I bear sole responsibility for all of the (many, I'm sure) legal errors in here.

Toni and Alisha: I would not have made it through the hellscape that was 2020 without my Emotional Support Canadians and kdramas, so thank you for loaning me your Viki account (Alisha), letting me send you unsolicited snippets of my writing while I demand praise (Toni), and letting me scream in your DMs about Song Joong-Ki's charisma and Lee Min Ho's hair (both of you).

To the Fellowship of the Salt Hurgle: I don't even know where to start. For one thing, I just wrote "hurgle" in a place other people will see it, so that's a thing that happened. For another, the group chat wouldn't exist in this book without you. You all have made me into a better, kinder, smarter human in addition to being my Pocket Friends, and now I'm crying while writing this so I'm just going to say: thank you for everything. I love you all more than you'll ever know.

Mom, Dad, Tim, and Shirley, thank you for believing in me even though "romance novelist" is probably not what any of you thought I would be doing with my time. But I am who I am today because of you, and it was knowing I had a solid foundation to stand on that gave me the courage to write. Dad, thank you for saying "so the bad guy wins?" when we finished *You've Got Mail* the first time back in the mid-90s, because that has shaped how I look at stories ever since (and it's why in this, the big corporation definitely *doesn't* win.) I should also congratulate you on being the only person in the universe able to resist Tom Hanks's superhuman charms, because that is honestly impressive. Tdee Muay, thank you for your smiles, songs and giggles. Tdee Bee, you are the best thing that came out of 2020, hands down. Mommy and Papa, thank you for watching the kids whenever I had a deadline or just needed to write—they say it takes a village to raise kids, but it turns out it takes a village to write a book, too. Also to all of you: I'm sorry the sex in this is pretty graphic so let's just never, ever speak of that, deal?

And to my beloved husband, thank you for being a handsome lawyer who is everything a romance hero should be. I couldn't do any of this—the writing, the kids, the other job—without you. I'm sorry I couldn't work your joke about promissory estoppel into the final draft but trust me, if I had, it would have absolutely killed. You're the funniest, best person I know. There's no one else I'd rather be running towards.